Charlotte Boyett-Compo

Longing's Levant

ELLORA'S CAVE
ROMANTICA PUBLISHING

An Ellora's Cave Romantica Publication

www.ellorascave.com

WindWord: Longing Levant

ISBN #1419952153
ALL RIGHTS RESERVED.
Longing Levant Copyright© 2004 Charlotte Boyett-Comp
Edited by: Mary Moran
Cover art by: Syneca

Electronic book Publication: December, 2004
Trade paperback Publication: June, 2005

Excerpt from *Desire's Sirocco*
Copyright © Charlotte Boyett-Compo, 2004

Warning:

Also by Charlotte Boyett-Compo:

WindWorld: Rapture's Etesian
Desire's Sirocco
Ellora's Cavemen: Legendary Tails 1

Longing's Levant
WindWorld

Prologue

A muscle clenched and unclenched in his lean cheek as Lord Evann-Sin sat hunched over his tankard of beer. He stared into the amber depths of the liquid, ignoring the drunken laughter around him, the raucous music, the bawdy jokes being told by the gypsies sitting nearby, and the suffocating plumes from numerous foul-smelling pipes. Though he sat only a few feet away, he was barely aware of the heat of the tavern's roaring fire that warded off the chill of the high desert, but as preoccupied with the troubling dark thoughts that spun through his mind, he was as cognizant of his surrounds as any well-trained soldier.

No one seemed to be paying any attention to the dark-clad warrior who sat so still. The serviceable blade strapped to his broad back and the unmistakable aura of power, the undeniable essence of authority, set him apart from the other patrons of the tavern. His handsome face was creased with a savage scowl that kept those nearest him from looking his way more than once.

Seeming to shake the grim thoughts from his mind, the warrior lifted his tankard and took a long sip of the warm beer. He grimaced for the taste was bitter—bursting over his tongue with an unpleasantness that made him set the tankard aside. Wiping his mouth with the back of his hand, he pushed the tankard across the table then looked up, catching the eye of a tavern maid. He pointed to the tankard then turned his attention to the crackling fire.

He leaned back in the chair and stretched out his long legs. Folding his arms over his chest, he stared fixedly into the flames as though the conflagration was speaking to him.

The reluctant arrival of the tavern maid with a fresh tankard of beer failed to draw his notice and so intent was his concentration, so still was his posture, the woman made no mention of the coins he owed for the brew. She set the beer on the table then turned to go.

"Wait."

"Aye, milord?" the woman said scarcely above a whisper.

"Here," he said, digging into the pocket of his black leather breeches. He slapped two coins down on the sticky top of the table.

Bobbing a curtsy, the woman swept up the coins and backed away. She knew better than to turn her back on him or look directly into the eyes of a warrior they knew was a nobleman.

"What fare do you have for a traveler to eat, wench?" he asked, his words halting her in mid-step.

The tavern maid plucked at the folds of her skirt. "There is mutton stew, milord, and brown bread."

"Is it edible?" he asked.

"We are told it is the best in Nonica, Your Grace," she answered.

"Then bring me a trencher," Evann-Sin ordered.

"Right away, milord!" she answered, backing away.

Drawing in a tired breath, the warrior exhaled slowly and looked toward the tavern's door. The man he had come here to meet was over an hour late and that did not bode well for the Akkadian warrior's temperament. Punctuality was a virtue as far as Evann-Sin was concerned. An honorable man did not keep another waiting.

Sighing heavily once more, the warrior plowed a hand through the midnight thickness of his hair then lowered his head, giving in to the tiredness that was rapidly sapping his strength.

A loud commotion at the tavern's door caused Evann-Sin to look up. Hoping it was Rabin, he was as surprised as everyone else to see seven scarlet-robed women entering the common room, laughing and joking amongst themselves.

"Daughters of the Night!" he heard someone whisper.

"Hell Hags," a gypsy remarked and made the Sign of the Slain One.

Knowing little about the witches of Bandar other than what he had heard in outrageous tales, Evann-Sin was intrigued by their appearance there in Nonica. The women rarely ventured beyond the borders of their homeland and when they did, it was rumored they did so with vengeance on their minds and blood in their eyes. The yarns he'd heard of their warrioress' exploits had been too fanciful to be believed, but the swords they carried slung across their backs made him wonder if there might be some truth to the tales. The women looked capable of wielding those lethal blades and from the way they seemed to take command of the room, their posture gave evidence of the authority to which they were accustomed.

Unlike the now silent patrons who were meticulously avoiding looking at the newcomers, Evann-Sin openly watched them, curious to see what they were about. He was intrigued at the easiness with which they moved and more than a little curious about their nature.

The women were taller than average and as they took seats at the far end of the room they threw back the hoods of their robes to reveal waist-length hair in every shade from bright red to gray. They wore identical gold circlets around their long, flowing tresses, the circlets depicting quarter moons with a trio of silver stars riding on the lower curve. Boots of soft black kid showed beneath the ankle-length hem of the woolen robes and a cincture of braided gold silk circled their waists. The clink of bracelets as the women settled themselves at the table said these were not members of that part of the sect who had taken vows of poverty.

"Give us your most expensive wine, tavern keeper!" the tallest of the newcomers demanded, proving they were not poor. "We have a thirst not easily quenched."

"And desires not easily satiated!" another chuckled. "Who among you would like to be the first to soothe our desires?"

All the men in the tavern save one shot to their feet and scurried from the room amidst the noisy scraping of chairs and tables. The door was yanked open and the mass exodus of males stumbling out into the chill desert night set the women to laughing uproariously.

"Was it something we said?" the tallest woman guffawed.

"Or fear of performance?" another chuckled.

"Ah, peace and quiet at last," another said with a loud sigh. "No men to…" She stopped as one of her sisters pointed toward Evann-Sin.

The tallest woman arched a rust-colored eyebrow toward the warrior. "What ails you that you do no flee into the dark with your cowardly brethren?" she called out.

Evann-Sin stared at the woman without answering. She was tall but she was thick-bodied, overweight with a wide double chin and bloated face that said she embraced the habit of overeating. Her hair…perhaps once a bright color of auburn…was streaked heavily with gray and fell to her substantial waist in dull, bodiless orange strands.

"Perhaps he is hard of hearing?" one of the women suggested.

"Or mentally challenged," another chortled. "Only a fool would remain when we've made it clear we wish to be alone."

"He's so pretty, perhaps he is just a half-male and thinks he has a right to be here with us," another chortled and all but one of the women burst into laughter with her. "Think you he fancies himself part woman?"

"Leave him be," a woman sitting in profile to Evann-Sin spoke up. "He doesn't look the type to appreciate your humor, Sylviana."

The tall woman snorted. "I bet he would appreciate a good ride, though," she stated, and pushed back from the table.

"Sylviana, leave him be!" the woman warned again.

"By the Goddess, you are afraid of your own shadow, Tamara!" Sylviana scoffed. She headed toward Evann-Sin's table.

Evann-Sin realized the tall woman was uglier than he'd first thought, for the closer she got to him, the harsher were the planes of her wide face. He winced when she opened her mouth in what was no doubt meant to be a seductive smile, for he got a glimpse of rotting teeth like jagged tombstones behind her thin lips. So disgusted by what he saw, he said nothing as she put her thick hands on his table and leaned toward him.

"What do you say, warrior?" Sylviana challenged. "Would you like to find a room with me and pass the time locked in a feverish embrace?"

The thought of such an act brought bile to Evann-Sin's throat. As close as the woman was to him, he could not miss her overpowering, sour body odor, and wondered when was the last time she had bothered to wash her rancid flesh. Repelled by her leering stare, repulsed by her foul breath and appalled at her attempt at flirtation, he drew in his legs and sat up.

"Cat got your tongue, pretty boy?" she taunted him. She lowered her voice. "Would you like to ride me?" She licked her lips.

The suggestion sickened Evann-Sin. "I want nothing you have to offer," he said.

Sylviana's smile wavered. "How do you know unless you try it?" she asked.

"You really don't want me to answer that," he said.

The tall woman narrowed her eyes. "Aye, but I do. Give me your thoughts, warrior," she said then sneered. "That is if you are capable of having thought."

Evann-Sin smiled coldly. "All right, if you insist. I was thinking I'd rather hump a decaying corpse than take your reeking flesh to mine," he grated.

Shocked silence settled over the room as Sylviana straightened and stood glaring down at the warrior. Her lips drew back from her teeth and she hissed as though she were a pit viper preparing to strike. "Be careful what you say to me, warrior," she warned. "I am a ninth degree adept in the Order of the Celestial Descendency."

"I don't give a damn what you are," Evann-Sin growled. "I'm telling you to leave me the hell alone, woman. Go back to your table." His eyes narrowed. "Now while you still can."

One of the other women left the table and hurried over. She reached out to take Sylviana's arm, but the taller woman stepped back, shrugging away the contact. "Stay out of this, Tamara," Sylviana ordered. "This is between me and this reckless fool who obviously does not know with whom he is dealing here."

"He knows, Sylviana," Tamara disagreed, "but he has no fear of you, so leave him be."

Evann-Sin glanced up at the woman who had come to draw her companion back. He thought hers the voice of reason and was about to tell her so when he looked into her eyes and Evann-Sin's world tilted on its axis.

Those eyes were the color of amethysts and were framed in thick, spiky lashes that fanned her ivory cheeks when she blinked. Her face was a gentle oval with high, wide cheeks and lips the color of crushed cherries. Delicate ears, a slightly upturned nose and a strong chin added to the ethereal beauty that held him captive. He could not remember ever seeing a woman as beautiful as the one looking back at him.

"We want no trouble, milord," Tamara told him, and her voice held the unmistakable accent of the Highlands.

Stunned by the radiant beauty staring back at him, he could not seem to find his voice. Unaware his facial features had relaxed and a gentle smile came unbidden to his chiseled lips, it was all he could do to tear his gaze from her and look back into the ugly face of the tall woman who slammed her palms down savagely on the tabletop to gain his attention.

"I am the leader of our group, you stupid bastard! You will direct your attention to me, and not this sniveling coward of a girl!" Sylviana demanded.

A brutal glint turned Evann-Sin's amber eyes to molten gold. He glared at the woman who dared to insult him as well as issue him orders. Before he could gain control of his temper, he was on his feet, his strong hand wrapped brutally around Sylviana's arm just above her elbow.

Tamara Naibril stepped back defensively, but Sylviana's yelp of pain as the warrior's strong, unrelenting fingers bit into Sylviana's flesh made the young woman reach out a pleading hand. "Milord, please do not hurt her! She's been drinking all evening, and I fear she is drunk."

"She is a foul-mouthed whore," Evann-Sin grated, and increased the punishing pressure to Sylviana's arm.

On their feet and coming toward the warrior with drawn swords, Tamara stepped between her sisters and their target. "No," she said, halting her sisters in mid-stride. "This is between Sylviana and the warrior. Put your weapons away." When they hesitated at her order, Tamara shouted at them to do as they were told.

Reluctantly, the women sheathed their weapons but remained standing, hands on the hilts of their swords.

Sylviana was twisted sidewise against the fierce pain clamped around her arm. Though she struggled to free herself the strength of the warrior's fingers, his free hand on the dagger sheathed at his thigh, no doubt made her think better of attacking him.

"Release her, please," Tamara pleaded, and after one false start laid a gentle hand on the warrior's arm. "She has had too much to drink."

"Do you know who I am?" he snarled, turning his head to look down at Tamara.

"Someone of high importance in Nonica I am sure, milord," she replied in a soothing tone. "I beg you to release her and we will be on our way." She held his sharp gaze. "This I swear to you."

Evann-Sin cast the other women a hateful smirk. He swore beneath his breath then jerked his hand back from Sylviana, wiping his palm down his robe as though the contact had fouled him.

Staggering back, Sylviana pushed aside Tamara's offer of help. Massaging her rapidly bruising arm, she cradled it against her, her angry glower locked on Evann-Sin. "You will regret you ever laid hands to me, you sniveling beast," she threw at him.

"Sylviana, for the love of the Goddess!" Tamara hissed. "Leave him alone before he runs you through!"

"If she doesn't shut her mouth, I'll carve out her tongue!" Evann-Sin warned.

"Before or after I slice off your cock?" Sylviana screamed at him, and would have rushed him had Tamara not punched her. The tall woman went down like a felled tree to sprawl on the floor at Tamara's feet.

"For shame, Tamara!" one of the women gasped and rushed forward to make sure Sylviana was all right. "To hit a Sister because of a male is unforgivable!"

"She's not hurt, Sagira," Tamara sighed heavily with a roll of her eyes. "I'd rather knock her out than have her carried home to her burial. You and Luka pick her up and get her out of here before the warrior makes good on his threat."

The shortest of the women hurried to Sagira's aid and together they lifted the unconscious woman as though she weighed no more than a child. Slinging Sylviana over her shoulder, Sagira cast Evann-Sin a baleful glance then strode from the room, Luka in her wake.

"If I see that woman in Nonica again, I'll have her arrested," Evann-Sin snapped.

"We are passing through on the way to Ajaikabia, milord," Tamara said. "We will stay clear of Nonica, I promise you. You'll see no more of us here."

Evann-Sin stepped closer to the flame-haired beauty and reached out to cup her cheek. "You, I could see every day of my life and never grow tired of the sight," he said softly. He took her hand in his and lifted it to his mouth. Turning her wrist upward, he placed a gentle kiss on her warm flesh. "I am Riel Evann-Sin," he told her.

"The Lord High Commander of the Akkadian Forces. I am impressed," Tamara said, inclining her head as she withdrew her hand from Evann-Sin's grasp.

"No need to be," Evann-Sin told her. "It is merely a job."

"A very prestigious job, I hear." She smiled. "I am grateful you did not strangle Sylviana. She can be incorrigible, I fear."

"Does that foul approach actually work with other men?" he asked.

Tamara shrugged. "I wouldn't know. I've never had to use it."

He grinned. "I imagine not, wench."

She laughed. "Thank you again. I am sorry we caused you trouble. We'll be on our way now." She turned to go.

"Stay," he said impulsively. "It is getting late and the next tavern is over two hours ride from here. You will be starved by then."

Tamara shook her head. "Thank you, Lord Evann-Sin, but it is best we put distance between you and Sylviana."

"You think I fear that one?" Evann-Sinn questioned, his eyes narrowed.

"No, but why tempt the Fates?" she countered, pulling the hood of her scarlet robe over her hair. "Sylviana can be a mean drunk, as you saw this eve, and even though I am the co-leader on this leg of our trip, she can be a handful to control." She shrugged. "I care not to have to hit her again if it can be helped."

"I wish you would stay," he said. "If need be, I can ride out. The one I was to meet obviously won't show this eve."

Tamara shook her head. "It is best we be the ones to leave, milord." She glanced at the doorway. "My Sisters are waiting for me."

Disappointment settled on the Akkadian warrior's wide shoulders and made them sag. "Will I see you again?" he asked, staring into her sparkling amethyst eyes.

"Who knows, milord?" she questioned. "The Universe decides."

"I don't care to leave anything to chance. Sometimes we must take matters into our own hands," he mumbled.

Before she could turn away, he snaked out a hand and cupped her head, bringing her mouth to his. The kiss he bestowed on her lips was deep and hard, his tongue invading her mouth as his shaft yearned to invade her shapely body. He ravaged her lips with his own, his body pressed fiercely to hers in an embrace that shook them both. When he released her, she was trembling and he was breathing hard, his chest rising and falling as though he had run a race.

"You don't play fair," she accused, putting a shaky hand to her lips.

"When you get to know me better, you'll know I've never claimed otherwise," he responded in a husky voice.

Their gazes locked and in that brief span of time something vital passed between them. In the other, they recognized a kindred soul.

"Stay with me," he asked.

"I can not," she said.

"Although we belong together?"

"You don't know that," she said with a shake of her head.

"I know it as surely as I know the sun will rise tomorrow." He smiled. "Just as you know it."

Tamara moved back. "Please, milord. I have a duty to the Daughters of the Night. I am not free to…"

"In Akkadia, I am the law. I have the power to keep you here with me," he stated.

"Would you have me neglect my sworn duty to my coven?" she asked. "When I am free…" She stopped, pleading in her warm eyes.

He longed to drag her into his arms and carry her off with him. Such strong emotions as the ones flowing through him at that moment were as foreign to him as the dusky slant of her beautiful eyes. He had never known love, never thought to, but here it was creeping up on him. He was amazed at the feelings that overpowered him.

"Please try to understand," she said. "I have obligations, duties."

"Aye," he said with a sigh, having obligations and duties of his own that always overruled personal needs. "Until we meet again then," he whispered.

"Aye," she said, and began backing away as though she hated to lose sight of him.

He took a step toward her, but she held up her hand to stay his approach. After one final tremulous smile, she turned and hurried away.

Evann-Sin was of a mind to go after her, but there were more pressing matters at hand than the wayward ache of his lonely heart. Rabin's mysterious whereabouts had to be settled, and the grave problem that had brought the Akkadian warrior to Nonica was still very much in the forefront of his mind.

Even if the luscious beauty of a red-haired wench named Tamara would haunt him for the rest of his life.

Going back to his table, he slumped in his chair. He was bone-tired, hungry, ill at ease for a variety of reasons, and now heartsick that he had—he suspected—encountered the love of his life only to have her drift like sand through his fingers.

He ran his hands through his hair and pulled his elbows together in front of him in an attempt to work the kinks out of his shoulder muscles. He yawned, closed his eyes then smelled the rich aroma of gravy wafting under his nose. He opened his eyes to see the tavern maid standing beside his table.

"Are you r-ready for your meal now, m-milord?" she stuttered.

"Is it still hot?" he asked.

"Aye, milord," she answered, placing it before him.

"Well, then, at least I can ease one appetite," he said with a sigh.

Chapter One

In honor of his position in Akkadian society, Evann-Sin was the first to toss a handful of dirt into Rabin Jaspyre's grave. As he did, his attention strayed to Rabin's widow and twin teenage sons. He ground his teeth for her sons had to hold Momisha Jaspyre upright, her wails of grief filling the evening air, else it was feared she would fling herself into her husband's final resting place. The woman was beside herself with grief, unable to do more than shriek her agony to the heavens. The ululation of her cries was piercing, a strident noise that made the hair stir on Evann-Sin's arms. It was not the first time he had heard a Dabiyan woman's skirl of heartbreak filling the air but this time it unnerved him more than he would have imagined possible.

"He was her reason for living," an elderly woman whispered to the Lord High Commander. "She will follow him soon."

"I hope not," he muttered.

The old woman smiled sadly, her toothless mouth a gray hole around her words. "Such is the way with women, milord."

It was the custom of the Dabiya tribe to bury their females at first light, their males at the setting of the sun. The families of Rabin and Momisha stood silently, tearfully, in a circle around the perimeter of the grave, each with a handful of soil to toss into the gaping hole. One by one, they came forward to pay their last respects to their kinsman. When the last of them had flung his offering into the grave, the gravediggers advanced upon the final resting place of Rabin Jaspyre and began shoveling dirt into the hole.

Momisha Jaspyre unleashed a wavering scream then collapsed. The eldest of her twin sons swept the woman into his arms and carried her into the hut she had shared with her husband of twenty years. His brother followed closely behind, shutting the door on the mourners who were silently departing. Only two mourners would remain with the gravediggers—the Headsman and the Healer who would place one stone at the head of the grave and another at the foot.

Though Evann-Sin had promised her he would find the men who had murdered her husband, and make sure they were brought to Akkadian justice, there was little he could do for Momisha now. He would respect her privacy, her grief this night and come back later. Her pitiful condition tore at his heart, sending him to his horse with frustration dogging his footsteps.

Mounting the coal-black stallion that was as much a symbol of his office as the black robes he wore, the Akkadian warrior took one last look at his friend's grave.

A part of Evann-Sin mourned the passing of a man with whom he had spent many a hazardous hour. Another part rejoiced that Rabin was now beyond the worries and cares of ordinary men and no doubt sitting at the right hand of the Prophet, being fanned by luscious virgins and taking long sips of honeyed mead.

"Goodbye, my friend," the Lord High Commander whispered, surprised that his voice bore the unmistakable huskiness of grief. "May your rest go undisturbed."

Putting his heels to the steed, Evann-Sin slapped the trailing end of the reins lightly along the horse's flanks. He wanted to put as much distance between him and Rabin's burial site as he could. Having declined the offer of Rabin's brother to spend the night in Samarkan, the tribe's main compound, the warrior intended to make Nonica by morning light. There was work to do and at the top of the list was to find out who had taken Rabin's life.

As concentrated as his mind was on the matter at hand, Evann-Sin was too highly trained not to realize he was being followed when he left the burial site. Though whoever was trailing him was being cautious and staying well back to avoid notice, the warrior's instinct for survival had picked up on the danger and a nagging ache began between his shoulder blades. He refrained from turning around to take a look, for he didn't want his shadow to know he was aware of his presence. Rather than increasing his speed to outdistance the one behind him, Evann-Sin slowed the stallion to a slow trot.

The warrior continued on for several miles until he came to the place he sought. Ahead was a low mound of dunes that marked the beginning of the Quesa desert. Joshua trees bordered the vast sandscape between the Dabiya Province and Akkadia and a small oasis with graceful, lacy date palms ringed a small pond. It was to this picturesque respite that Evann-Sin guided his mount. If there was to be a confrontation, he wanted it to be on his own terms and at a place of his choosing.

Dismounting at the pond, the warrior led his horse to drink. Hunkering down beside the clear water, Evann-Sin cupped his hand and splashed some of the liquid on his face, rubbing his eyes to help relieve the tiredness. A slight breeze chilled the water on his flesh and helped to ease the weariness that seemed to be as much a part of him of late as his thirst for revenge. He hung his head as he squatted there, feeling the exhaustion creeping up on him. Had he not been conscious of being followed, he would have taken out his bedroll and curled up under the stars to sleep for an hour or two.

But the keen awareness of the situation made him watchful and as he stood, he looked around him — *a natural thing under any circumstances*, he thought — but saw no rider hanging back along the road from Samarkan nor did he hear furtive sounds of approach.

Mentally shaking off the nagging feeling that persisted with tightness between his shoulders, Evann-Sin unhooked his water bag from the stallion's saddle horn and uncorked it. As he brought the bag to his lips, something hard and unyielding slammed against the back of his head, and the gathering stars overhead fell with him to the ground.

* * * * *

There were six of them kneeling beside him—one at each limb, one at his head and another between his legs. A seventh stood gazing down at him with amusement. He struggled against the strong hands that held captive his wrists and ankles but it was useless. Naked, helpless and at their mercy, he viciously cursed them from beneath the rough cotton gag covering his mouth.

"Lie still, warrior," their leader—the one grinning down at him—commanded and he recognized her as the one Tamara had called Sylviana. "You aren't going anywhere."

"This one is a fighter," the one at his head observed.

"Aye," said another," but he will be conquered whether he likes it or not."

Laughter made the circuit of those gathered around the warrior.

Grunting with disgust, his face stained dark red with humiliation, Evann-Sin angrily shook his head from side-to-side, his sweat-dampened black curls glinting in the glow of a campfire.

"There is no denying your fate, warrior," the leader told him. "Protest all you will but the outcome will be the same."

"Here is the brew, Sylviana," an eighth intruder spoke, and Evann-Sin swung his head toward the voice. Fury turned his amber eyes to glacial chips and he howled beneath the constriction of the gag when he saw what was being offered.

"Ah, I believe he knows what that is," the leader quipped.

The one kneeling between his legs took the bottle from the newcomer and uncorked it. The sweet scent of gardenia filled the night air. In the shifting glow of the firelight, he watched as the contents of the cobalt-blue bottle were poured into waiting palms. There was a sucking sound as those palms were rubbed together to heat the oil. He flinched as they put their hands on him, smearing the slick oil on his flesh.

Every inch of his chest and abdomen was being coated with the warm lubricant. He wriggled beneath the feel of it, his nostrils flaring, his skin pebbling with goose bumps. As a hand smoothed over his side, along his rib cage, he tried to shift away from the contact but it was useless. Fingers were spreading over his belly and along his thighs, nails were grazing his shrinking testicles and he drew in an alarmed breath.

"Oil his shaft well," the leader instructed. "The less friction in the steel the better the weapon penetrates."

More laughter accompanied Evann-Sin's constricted shriek of outrage at that remark. He bucked under the restraint, dug his heels into the sand, his fingers clawing at the ground beneath them.

Intense rage filled his brain as a hot hand wrapped around his penis. Strong fingers slid up and down his flesh, manipulating his sleeping member until it roused from its slumber and lifted its head to see who had awakened it.

"His is a well-made sword," the one between his legs commented.

"Aye," the leader agreed. "And we will sheathe it well, don't you think?"

Grunting furiously behind the gag, Evann-Sin mentally ordered his rebellious soldier to stand down, but the chafing being generated by the strong fingers sliding down his length held more sway.

"Relax, warrior," the leader said, hunkering down beside him. "Allow yourself to enjoy your fate. You're not the first we've captured and you'll not be the last."

The strain of trying to make his shaft disregard the squeezing, gentle twisting motion sliding up and down it was beginning to take its toll on Evann-Sin. Sweat glistened on his forehead and upper lip, and ran in rivulets down his heaving chest.

"He is as hard as stone," the one holding his penis remarked.

"Give me the elixir, Sagira," the leader demanded.

"What is it we rub into him?" a young woman inquired.

"A very potent Akkadian elixir called guššurum, their word for 'to be very strong'. It is distilled from the brew of opium and thorn apples. It will keep his shaft as tempered as steel until we are through with him," one of the women chuckled.

"His kind have been raping women since the dawn of time," another put in. "It's time they find out what it feels like to be taken against your will!"

"Aye," Sylviana agreed. "Time and time again until his shaft is a bruised and bloodied stump before we slice it from his arrogant ass."

The loud screech that erupted from the warrior's throat was ignored as a second bottle was produced and handed to the one kneeling at his head.

"Tip his head back. Be careful he doesn't bite you when you remove the gag," the leader warned.

Anchoring the warrior's cheeks between firm palms, the one above the warrior lifted his head and tilted it back. The one on his left side reached under his neck to untie the gag then moved back quickly so there was no chance for Evann-Sin to snag his bared teeth in his captor's arm.

"You bitches will…" he began then snapped his jaw fiercely shut as the bottle was brought to his lips. His eyes glowed hell-hot as the woman on his left tried to pry his lips apart.

"Pinch closed his nose," the leader said. "He'll have to open those pretty lips sooner or later."

The women kneeling around Evann-Sin bided their time as the one on his left squeezed his nostrils together. They watched as his handsome face turned red then took on a slight bluish cast.

"He has a strong will," someone commented.

"Nay," the leader replied. "He's simply stubborn as are all men."

As the minutes ticked by and the loss of oxygen to his brain began to etch darkness around his vision, Evann-Sin knew he would be unable to keep his lips closed much longer. The moment his lips parted, the women warriors who had captured him would pour the contents of the bottle down his throat, and he would be lost because he knew damned well what was in the elixir he was being forced to drink. The thought of being unable to control either his weapon or his lust filled him with absolute fear.

"He's lost the steel in his sword," the one between his legs said with a sigh.

"It will return tenfold as soon as the elixir is administered, Hael," the leader assured her.

Feeling his consciousness slowly fading, his head throbbing with the pressure, it was only a matter of a few seconds more before Evann-Sin gave up and he gasped in the precious air. Not giving him the chance to clamp his jaws shut again, the bottle was thrust into his mouth and the contents poured in. He gagged as the sickly sweet liquid flowed in. An oily hand was slapped over his mouth to keep him from spitting it out. Sucking air through his nose, he felt as though he were drowning in the liquid he was holding in his mouth.

"We can wait longer than you, warrior," the leader chuckled, folding her arms over her shapely bosom.

No drop of liquid from the bottle had escaped Evann-Sin's mouth. Though he could taste the fluid, it had numbed his tongue so completely he could no longer feel that muscle. With every breath he drew in through his distended nostrils, the flavor of the liquid invaded his taste buds.

"Distract him," the leader suggested. "Give him something to occupy his mind."

Laughter punctuated her words, and Evann-Sin groaned as oily hands returned to his flaccid flesh. As two women plucked alternately at his nipples, pinching the sensitive nubs between wickedly sharp fingernails, another circled his belly button with an insistent thumb, dipping into the deep concavity to tickle him. The one whose firm fingers circled his penis began her ritual once more, twisting down firmly, tugging up tightly then circling the swollen head with the center of her greasy palm.

"Such remarkable restraint," a woman said.

"Not for much longer," the one holding his shaft replied. With one hand wrapped around him, her thumb and forefinger squeezing until the opening of his penis flared open, she used her other hand to slip a fingernail into the slit and scratch delicately.

Evann-Sin drew in a sharp breath through his nose and nearly choked on the liquid in his mouth. He groaned, his body shivering with a desire he was having trouble controlling. When her fingers slid under his scrotum, cupped, then squeezed lightly, her middle fingernail dragging along the sensitive ridges, he could no longer hold the liquid in his mouth and reluctantly swallowed it, closing his eyes in surrender.

"Now that wasn't so bad, was it, warrior?" the leader inquired.

He refused to open his eyes. Even when his mouth was free of the woman's hand, he would not look up at his captors. He would mutter no word. Humiliated as he was, shame filling his immortal soul, he kept his eyes closed until the moment the elixir invaded his system and changed his world forever.

"Here it comes," someone said with a knowing chuckle.

The first thing Evann-Sin noticed was the intense heat that rippled through his body from the scalp of his head to the pads of his toes. It felt as though he had opened an oven door and stepped inside. The strength of the warmth was such that he tried to gasp in an equalizing breath, trying to cool his flesh, but the heat increased until every pore of his skin oozed sweat.

Then the need began to build in his loins, flaring wide his eyes.

"Ah," the women sighed in unison when they saw their captive begin to squirm against the growing feeling in his shaft. They got to their feet and stared down at him as he arched his hips upward, groaning as need flooded his lower body.

Never had he known such powerful lust.

Never had he felt such a rigid erection as the one that now stood at attention between his thighs—throbbing, aching and oozing passion's nectar from its swollen tip.

Wiggling his hips in the sand, unconsciously straining his cock toward the woman kneeling between his legs, Evann-Sin began to pant.

"Who is to be first?" the leader inquired, looking around her.

"I drew the longest straw," Sagira said breathlessly. She waited until another woman gripped his right ankle before getting to her feet.

"Sheathe him well, then, Sagira," the leader said.

Evann-Sin's eyes narrowed dangerously as Sagira began removing her short tunic. She smiled wickedly at him as the tunic slid to her feet and she was revealed to him in her youthful voluptuousness.

"Like what you see, warrior?" she asked.

"Go to hell," Evann-Sin snarled, his numb tongue having trouble forming the words.

"I'd rather take *you* to the heavens, my handsome one," Sagira giggled then squatted over him, her wiry pelt poised at the surging head of his shaft.

Digging his hands into the sand, Evann-Sin turned his head away, his eyes squeezed tightly closed. He could do nothing about the raging passion in his body but neither would he strive to take pleasure from the rape that was about to take place.

Though he wished otherwise, Sagira was a beautiful woman with lush breasts and long tapered legs. She smelled of lilacs and when she leaned over him, her long hair tickled his bare chest as though a hundred eager fingers were caressing him. Her womanhood was hot and velvety smooth as it slid down the turgid length of him. The weight of her rump on his upper thighs, her pelvis on his lower belly spurred the hot passion coursing through him and he strained upward, wanting as much of his shaft to penetrate her body as possible.

"Ride the stallion, Sagira," a woman chanted and soon they were all saying the words in a hushed, reverent tone.

Despite the rampant lust that stiffened his member to hardened steel, the warrior did not release his seed when he felt the lazy ripples of release pulsing through Sagira. He looked up at her as she threw her head back and a deep, satisfying groan escaped her arched throat. When she lowered her head and looked down at him, he glared her.

"Now that wasn't so bad, was it, warrior?" Sagira purred. "You should be pleased that you sated me."

"Am I to be honored that you find rape enjoyable?" he asked with a snarl.

"I found it beyond enjoyable, warrior," Sagira said, removing her body from his. She stood, accepting her discarded tunic from one of the other women.

"Who is next?" the leader inquired.

"I am," the one called Hael replied. "Luka, Trista, Lanoi then Ijuni are after me."

"Don't forget me!" Oriel laughed. "I'm before Ijuni! What of you, Lanoi?"

"I am having my monthly," the woman holding his right wrist said wistfully. "Else I'd be on him, too."

"You shouldn't care about that," their leader chuckled. "Have his ass just the same!"

Evann-Sin's howl of rage echoed through the night air but the women paid no heed to his vicious, vulgar curses as the next woman knelt over him and impaled her hot flesh upon his staff.

Infuriated beyond reason, Evann-Sin glared at the women who raped him. In the undulating light of the campfire, he stared into eyes the color of summer skies and green fields and every shade in between. He watched small breasts, large breasts and conical breasts bobbing against tanned flesh and flesh as white as snow as the women rode him. He breathed in perfumed scents and musky odors that drove the wedge of passion deeper into his loins. He felt red hair and brown hair, blonde and black and silver hair fanning across his chest, tickling him. He tasted full lips and thin lips and lips that tasted of wine upon his own.

One after another, they took him, satiating their lust. Each in turn rode him hard, wriggling their luscious bodies atop the steel of his sword yet his erection held. The release he began to pray would erupt held off until he was whimpering with the pain of the friction of their bodies against his.

"Soon, warrior," they whispered and began the rotation again with Sagira squatting over him and impaling her musky flesh along his still-hard length.

"Please," he began to beg, the need for release turning him to a quivering mass of hopelessness.

"Soon," they told him. "Soon."

Long into the night, they used him for their pleasure. His shaft was sore, the tip as raw as ground meat, when, at last, they moved away and stood in a circle, their hands joined.

The first rays of the new morning sun would soon be cresting the trees. Already the false dawn was lurking on the horizon. The campfire had died down to smoldering embers and the desert air was cool as it played across Evann-Sin's naked flesh.

Tears were easing down his cheeks when the circle parted. He was whimpering with exhaustion, frustrated with need, helpless to the red-hot lust throbbing in his shaft. He turned his eyes to the movement on his left and watched a shadowy figure enter the circle.

Dressed in a sheath of shimmering gold cloth, the material hugging her body like a second skin, the newcomer came to stand over him. He was stunned by her physical beauty and in awe of the magnetic persona that reached out to grab his attention with velvety claws. Her hair was as black as midnight. The thick tresses reached her ankles, rippling gently in the pre-dawn breeze. She gracefully knelt beside him and ran a cool hand over his chest, threading her fingers through the thick hair that grew between his breasts.

"A prime specimen of maleness is this one, Sylviana. He will breed strong offspring. Come and take him now."

Mesmerized by the elegant beauty of the imposing woman kneeling beside him, Evann-Sin was barely aware of Sylviana positioning herself at the juncture of his thighs. So ensnared by this newcomer's beauty, he did not smell the rancid odor that pervaded Sylviana's overweight body nor the vile stench of her breath. His full attention was riveted on the seductive newcomer so that he barely glanced at Sylviana when she impaled herself upon his turgid staff.

"You are ours," the newcomer pronounced. There was a predatory smile on the seductive woman's face. When she leaned over him, lowered her mouth to his throat, he made no protest.

He drew in a surprised breath as her sharp teeth sank into his flesh, her lips pressed firmly to his jugular. The sting lasted but for a moment then peacefulness descended from the predawn sky as she began to feed on him. As he grew weaker, he closed his eyes.

She is killing you, Evann-Sin, his inner voice warned. *She is drawing the life's blood from your veins.*

He found he did not care. The lassitude that had claimed him had placed him far beyond the shackles that bound him to the earth and had carried him into a realm of starless nights and infinite space. He drifted in the ebony abyss, reveling to the cold winds blowing over him, and knew immeasurable serenity.

The newcomer removed her lips from his wound then circled the punctures with her tongue, laving the hurt. She stroked his cheek. "How do you feel, warrior?" she asked.

He was satiated as he had never been before and felt loose-boned and lost in a mind-numbing fog. So tired was he, so weak, he knew he would not have been able to raise his hands even had his wrists been free.

"Release your seed, warrior," the newcomer commanded. She stroked his cheek. "We want your get."

Passion burst upon the warrior like a dam escaping its banks. Hot semen surged from his steely weapon and spurted copiously, and long into the waiting receptacle perched upon him. He could feel the muscles of Sylviana's vagina pulsing around him as she reached her own strong climax and the sensation made him arch his head back and scream with the release.

"I will bear a son from this mating," Sylviana proclaimed as she ran her fingertips over Evann-Sin's lips. "Consider yourself lucky I do not castrate you as I long to do. Perhaps you'll live long enough to give my future son a sister or two to fuck!"

"The dawn comes, Highness," one of the women said.

The Queen of the Daughters of the Night winced and looked fearfully to the horizon. Upon seeing the first fingers of light clawing up the heavens, she hissed, "You fed me well, warrior. It is truly regrettable that I cannot finish what I started. You are only partly of the Blood." Placing her fingertips to her lips, she blew him a kiss then vanished as the first rays of the morning broke over the nearby dunes.

As morning spread over the desert, the women took to their mounts and departed, each to her own village or settlement. The Akkadian warrior was left where he lay—naked and spread eagle to the encroaching, blistering sun.

Sylviana, her hand on her belly, kept a secret smile on her fleshy face long after she slipped into bed. Lying awake, her thoughts on the handsome Akkadian whose seed was being carried within her body, she knew the child of their union would be magical. His blood tainted with the spores that had come from the queen's sharp fangs, the boy would be of the queen's ancient heritage. He would be *shedim*.

Chapter Two

Tamara awoke with a vicious headache that pounded through her temples with every beat of her heart. She found herself lying on a pallet of thick furs beneath a canvas tent. Sitting up gingerly, wincing, she looked about her. A small brazier on a tripod kept the desert cold at bay and beside her was a tin tray holding a bowl of fruit and a carafe of water. Hungry as she was, she ignored the peace offering and got up, swaying a little as she did. She stood still until the dizziness passed, then ducked under the tent's flap.

Though a fire blazed cheerily just beyond the tent, Tamara realized she was alone except for her horse. There was no sign of her fellow warrioresses or their mounts. Her horse had been unsaddled, hobbled for the night and left with a small amount of forage. Nearby, was a stream of water that trickled softly over rocks that gleamed in the moonlight.

Putting a hand to her bruised neck, she vaguely remembered the vicious hit that had rendered her unconscious.

"You are a dead woman, Sylviana," Tamara hissed through clenched teeth.

She knew where her sisters had gone.

And why.

Throwing aside the tent flap, she walked as fast to her horse as her pounding head would allow and searched for the saddle. Relieved when she found it, she bent down and retrieved the dagger and sword that lay beside it. Now, she had protection for she was alone in the vastness of the Quesa where thieves abounded. With a dagger and her own razor-sharp sword in hand, she felt more confident.

Back in the tent, she laid the weapons aside and took up the meager food that had been left for her. She was ravenous and made quick work of the repast. After draining the carafe of water, her headache subsided somewhat and she lay back on the furs, grateful for the small comforts her sisters had thought to leave her. Reaching for her black dagger, she pulled it to her chest and turned to her side, facing the tent's entrance. If danger presented itself, she would be ready with a hand that was well trained to the lethal blade.

Just as she closed her eyes, thinking to rest them a moment and no more, she sat bolt upright, her heart slamming against her ribs for her horse whinnied, alerted to something beyond the perimeter of the encampment. Knowing it could be a predator of either the two or four-legged variety, she eased her free hand toward her sword and brought it up. With the ease of many years of hard training, she got to her knees then slowly rose up to a crouch as the horses whinnied once more.

Not waiting for something or someone to attack, Tamara shoved aside the tent flap and rushed outside, ready to meet the threat. She blinked then squinted, a muscle in her jaw beginning to work.

"Did you finally wake from your beauty nap?" Sylviana sneered as she dismounted the big black brute of a horse upon which she was riding.

Seeing the woman she had vowed to kill, Tamara lifted her blade and would have plunged it into Sylviana's belly but a movement to her right stayed her hand. Sylviana's cronies were coming toward them, their hands on the swords at their hips. Casually, Tamara rested the steel of her blade on her shoulder. "It is not I that needs one," she replied.

Sylviana narrowed her eyes. "Are you inferring that I do?" she demanded.

"If the description fits," Tamara answered. She tapped the blade on her shoulder as the other women joined them.

"Be careful what you say to me, girl. I am the leader here," Sylviana snapped.

Tamara smiled but there was no warmth in the expression. Her eyes were as cold as the steel resting on her shoulder. "Then perhaps I should challenge you for the leadership, for I have no intention of being tarred with the same dirty brush you have been for your vile action."

Sagira looked uneasily from one woman to the other. "What action is it you mean?" she asked.

"Did you go after the Akkadian?" Tamara countered. Her stare was steady on Sylviana. "That is his mount you are riding, isn't it?"

A hateful sneer lifted one corner of Sylviana's mouth, revealing an eyetooth badly in need of pulling. "What if it is?" she asked with a snort. "It was my right for the insult he threw at me."

"Did you kill him?" Tamara asked softly.

Something in the way Tamara asked her question caused a ripple of unease to wiggle down Sylviana's spine. "Not I," she was quick to deny.

One finely shaped brow lifted. "But he has gone to the Underworld, has he not?" Tamara inquired.

"Our Lady came for him," Luka said.

Tamara nodded. "And was this before or after you raped him?"

Sagira bit her lip. "It was our right to take him, Tamara. Such is the way of the Daughters. This you know."

"What was he to you anyway?" Sylviana asked. She put her hands on her ample hips. "He was fair game to any woman who could capture him."

Tamara lowered her blade so that the lethal tip pointed straight at Sylviana. "I had claimed him as mine."

"How was she to know?" Luka asked. "You did not say as much to us."

"Well, that is certainly too bad," Sylviana sneered. "But it would not have changed anything. His life was forfeit the moment he dared to insult me."

"Just as your life is forfeit for daring to take what was mine," Tamara stated.

"Tamara, no!" Sagira said, stepping between the two women. "Fighting over a male is forbidden."

"And besides," Luka joined in, "Sylviana is with child."

"A child stolen from the loins of the man whose seed I would have been carrying had you left him the hell alone," Tamara said from between clenched teeth.

"I will not claim dispensation for being with child," Sylviana snapped. She drew her weapon. "Stand aside Sagira, and let me dispatch this sniveling bitch."

"You must not fight over a male," Sagira warned. "The Tribunal will…"

"We are fighting over the leadership of this troop," Tamara barked, and pushed Sagira out of the way. "That is allowed and even encouraged."

Sagira and Luka barely had time to scuttle back before Tamara and Sylviana clashed blades. The other three women of the troop who were watching from just outside the battle kept their distance.

The two warrioresses were evenly matched. Both were skilled with the heavy swords they wielded. Both had trained under the tutelage of expert battle mistresses. Though Sylviana was stronger than her opponent, she carried more body fat and was quicker to wind than Tamara. By the fifth collision of the blades, she was breathing heavily—by the tenth, she was panting and beginning to sweat profusely, her ripe body odor causing several of the women to cover their noses.

The sand beneath the feet of the women churned as they struck and parried, lunging at one another, jumping back to avoid the deadly thrust of the other. The music from the steel rang out over the desert air, punctuated by grunts and hisses escaping the throats of the combatants.

Sylviana caught a hit low on the blade of her weapon and the screech of steel meeting steel vibrated through her arm as Tamara came nose to nose with the older woman.

"You are jackal fare," Tamara promised, and with relative ease pushed against her sword to send Sylviana stumbling backward.

Sylviana nearly lost her footing in the loose sand but managed to right herself. With a bellow of rage, she came at Tamara, intent on bowling the younger woman over, sending her to the ground where she could skewer her with her blade.

But Tamara stepped aside, and it was Sylviana who stumbled past, once more nearly crashing to earth. Instead, she spun around, her lips drawn back from her rotting teeth.

"I will take your head, you worthless slut!" Sylviana screamed. She pulled her arm back, raising her blade to shoulder height then arced the weapon over her left shoulder.

"Sylviana! Lower your blade!" Lanoi cried out.

Tamara grinned. She knew Sylviana was beyond rational thinking and that expertise with the blade meant nothing once fury took over. Getting a firm grasp on the pommel of her own sword, she waited for the enraged warrioress to run at her, knowing Sylviana meant to swing the blade toward Tamara's neck in an attempt to lop off her head. Flexing her knees, she angled her weapon slightly.

Roaring with sheer ferocity, Sylviana rushed her opponent. She tried to stop as the tip of Tamara's sword pierced her belly but her forward momentum carried her to the weapon's hilt. She shuddered, feeling the agonizing burn of stomach acid spilling into her abdomen.

Luka turned away, as did Sagira. Both were Sylviana's friends—her only friends—and had no wish to see Sylviana's last moments. As they did, their gazes fell on a silent witness to the battle and they screamed, scrambling back over one another in an attempt to get away.

The three other women who had been watching the fight turned to see what had frightened their Sisters. They, too, screamed in terror and ran for their horses, Sagira and Luka close behind.

Sylviana's lips parted and blood bubbled out of her mouth. She sagged to her knees, grunting as the weapon buried in her gut sliced upward through her chest cavity. With her last breath, she looked up at Tamara but the younger woman was staring behind Sylviana, her face as pale as the dying woman knew her own to be. The last sound Sylviana ever heard was an Akkadian name spoken with a mixture of fear and relief. Turning her head, the last sight Sylviana ever saw was the Akkadian walking toward her. A squeal of protest wiggled from the dying woman's throat and she pitched forward, her eyes wide in horror, never to rise again.

Chapter Three

Tamara could not take her eyes from the Akkadian. He sat across from her and shivered, his hands held out to the blazing fire he had bid her stoke. Though she was sweltering inside the tent, his flesh was pebbled beneath a wicked sunburn.

"I cannot get warm," he said, and his voice sounded hollow, as though it came from beyond the grave. "I keep imagining myself naked and I cannot get warm."

Nothing had changed about his appearance save the redness of his flesh and, when he looked at her, a strange spark seemed to have settled in his amber eyes. He was as handsome as the night she had first met him, as strong-looking and as virile, but there was now a quality about him she could not put her finger on and it was this strangeness that troubled her.

"Their names were Tashobi and Jabali," he told her. "Had they not come along, I would have died. As it is, I felt as though I had, and I told them as much. My cock was as raw as fresh meat from what those bitches did to me but somehow or other Jabali healed me."

"He laid hands to your…"

"He healed me, wench," Evann-Sin snapped. "Let it go at that. The Magi were helpful in what they told me."

"What did they say?" she asked, thankful two nomads had ventured upon the Akkadian and untied him.

He shook his head. "That I should be glad your queen did not have a chance to drain me dry. I am only partly of the Blood, whatever that means."

Tamara shuddered. "Aye, that is a good thing."

"They also told me they were Magi," he said, "and could raise the dead so had I succumbed, they would have brought me back."

"They lied. No magic known to man can bring someone back from the Realm of the Dead," Tamara said.

"Jabali boasted that he could."

"How dare he make such a claim? When a Liln, a demoness of the abyss, draws the lifeblood from a man, that man is lost forever!"

"They told me there are creatures in this world more powerful than Liln, wench," Evann-Sin said. "I believed them."

"The sun has poisoned you, warrior," she said, and was somewhat relieved when her companion did not turn his alien eyes to her. "You must not entertain such troubling thoughts."

"I asked if they could bring my friend back," he said. He pulled the robe she had given him to help warm him tighter around his shoulders. "They promised me they would."

"Your friend?" she questioned.

"When those Hell Hags attacked, I was on my way back from Samarkan where I attended the funeral of a friend," he said and shivered, his teeth clicking together.

"I am glad they gave you clothing," she said to take his mind from his dead friend.

He nodded. "How they had the right size puzzles me for both were smaller than me. It was almost as though they went to my home and took what they thought I'd need."

"Will you return to Nonica, Evann-Sinn?" she asked.

He shrugged listlessly. "Where else would I go? That is my home."

"You need to be somewhere where you will be safe from my Sisters…"

He turned his head toward her, and those strange eyes glowed with a crimson spark that held her riveted, unable to look away.

"Think you I will allow myself to be violated like that again, wench?" he asked, and there was evil in his dry voice. "They will rue the day they dared lay hands to this warrior."

A tremor of fear rippled through Tamara. "You will go after them?"

The Akkadian laughed and the sound made the hair stand up on Tamara's arms. She watched him throw back his head and the strong column of his neck was revealed. "Go after them," Evann-Sinn repeated. "As surely as the sun rises will I go after them."

Tamara winced. "What will you do to the women who..." She stopped, seeing the crimson spark in his eyes flare.

"Who raped me," he finished. "Who took me against my will?"

"Aye," she whispered, mesmerized by the vengeance hiding in his gaze. "What revenge will you take upon them?"

He ignored her question. The robe she had given him was too short and his legs were bare from the knees down. He stood, tugging at the robe, growling with frustration that it did not cover him properly.

"I rather like looking at you almost nude," Tamara giggled.

Evann-Sin glanced around at her then arched one dark brow. He held out his hand. "Will you come to me?"

Something in the warrior's voice touched Tamara and she did not hesitate. She placed her hand in his, allowing him to draw her into his embrace. With her face pressed against the coarse fabric of his robe, she snuggled against him.

"We need to think here a moment, wench," he said softly. "My feelings for you have been strong since the first moment I looked into your eyes. In my heart of hearts, I have claimed you as my own."

Tamara smiled. "As I have claimed you."

He frowned then looked away from her. "Can you accept me as your lover now?"

"Nothing," she stressed, "has changed between us. Am I cringing in disgust here in your arms?"

He smiled gently. "But will you accept me?"

"With all my being," she pledged.

He circled her tightly within his strong arms, his firm body pressed closely to hers. "Then, let's divest ourselves of any impediments."

The Akkadian lowered his hand to the cincture at her waist and tugged at the cord. It untied easily so he pushed aside the ties, the ends falling to either side of Tamara's trembling body. Slowly he eased his palm beneath the opening of the robe, smiling softly at his lady's quick intake of breath as his bare hands touched the top of her undergarment.

"Have you known a man before now, my sweet one?" he asked as he reached out to pull her down with him to her pallet.

Tamara felt a tremor of anticipation ripple through her lower belly at his words. "I am not a virgin, warrior," she replied.

Evann-Sin sensed the apprehension in her answer and shrugged lightly. "It matters not except I would prefer to know how firmly and deeply my sword can thrust before I would cause you pain."

A little groan of excitement pushed from Tamara's throat. His gentle voice—low and mesmerizing—made the hair at the nape of her neck stir and the buds of her nipples harden. The coolness of his hand through the muslin of her undergarment as his fingers grazed the tops of her breasts filled her with growing need.

"So soft," he said with a satisfied sigh, trailing his fingers from the top of one orb to the other, stroking her, soothing her.

When his strong sword hand dipped beneath the edge of her undergarment, Tamara tensed. Se drew in a breath as he pushed the material down to bare her breast. The firmness of his palm cupping her, weighing her, lightly squeezing, created heavy moisture at the juncture of her thighs and she groaned again, caught up in the heady anticipation of what was to come.

Releasing her, laughing huskily at her protest at being denied his touch, he divested her of her robe, made quick work of the undergarment then came to his knees on the pallet, ridding himself of his own coarse robe.

Seeing the wide chest thickly pelted with dark curls, the pectorals that looked hard as rock, the ripples of honed muscles stretched across his abdomen, Tamara sighed deeply. This man was not only pleasing of face to look upon, his body was a marvel of manhood—taut and powerful, sleek and defined, as a warrior's body should be. His arms were sculpted with years of sword practice and—she had no doubt—weight training. His belly was flat, the navel sinking beneath a spiral of wiry curls that traveled downward to a commanding thrust from which she could not take her eyes.

"It has been awhile since my weapon has been sheathed in so lovely a scabbard," he said, drawing Tamara's gaze to his.

His words thrilled her and she reached for him, her arms aching to feel those broad shoulders, her body throbbing at the need to experience the weight of him atop her.

The Akkadian caught her hands, and pressed the palms together as though he bid her pray. He placed a feather-soft kiss on the fingertips then released his twin captives, stretching out to lie beside his lady, turning so his body touched hers from chest to toe.

"It has been awhile for me, as well," she told him.

Evann-Sin placed his lips to her ear and blew his breath lightly inside. Even as she quivered at the invasion, he used his tongue to lap at the sensitive inner surface, sending spirals of warm heat along the tender flesh. Another ripple of pleasure traveled through Tamara's tense body. "Turn over," he whispered.

She did not question his command nor hesitate. He moved back as she eased over to her stomach, her arms to either side of her head, gripping the pillow that held his scent.

"Spread your legs, my sweet."

Tamara opened her legs, reveling in the feel of him as he stretched out atop her. The demanding rigidity of his manhood pressed against the cleavage of her rump, sliding upward until it lay nestled along that fleshy valley.

"You smell of jasmine," he said huskily, and nipped at the sweep of her right shoulder, his teeth sending shivers throughout her lower body.

"Does that scent please you, warrior?" she asked breathlessly, for his tongue had replaced his teeth in traversing the plane of her shoulder.

"It does, though gardenia is my favorite scent," he answered, shifting his weight so he could plant tender kisses down her spine. His manhood dragged down her leg, leaving a slight wetness behind as he pushed lower in the bed.

"Jasmine is an aphrodisiac," she said, and sucked in a quick breath as he nipped at her side, clutching the indention of her waist between his teeth.

"It is working," he said, and there was amusement in his tone.

Nothing could have prepared Tamara for the invasion of his moist tongue between her cheeks. She tensed, clenching the muscles of her rump together, but she soon found that was no guarantee of protection from his questing mouth for he used his fingertips to spread the cleft.

"Ah," Tamara sighed, as his tongue darted against the puckered rim of her ass. She dug her fingers into the pillow—dragging it around her face for the sensation the Akkadian was causing demanded loud and fervent moans of supreme pleasure.

"You like that?" he asked with a chuckle.

"Um," was her reply. She was quivering, her stomach muscles clenching and unclenching as her lover replaced his tongue with the insistent tip of a cool finger. Her breath coming faster, shallower, expectant, she groaned as that finger delved inside her.

Not deeply, not enough to cause even a suggestion of pain, the probe was gentle and possessive as it wiggled slowly within her.

"Warrior, please," she whispered, lifting her rump.

Evann-Sin did not answer her need. He gently removed his finger to trail his fingertips over her goose pimpled flesh. Trailing his nails down her thigh to the very sensitive surface of her inner knee, he smiled at the grunt that came from his lady's throat.

Tamara was about to demand he do more than tease her with the promise of fulfillment when he whispered for her to turn over again.

Quick to do his bidding, she flipped over, her eyes going wide at the sight of his handsome face. He was staring down at her with a look that was all male, all conquering warrior. Possessiveness ran rampant through his amber eyes. As she turned, his hand had remained on her flesh so that now it rested coolly against her knee, caressing her.

"You are a beautiful woman," he said as he moved his hand up her thigh.

The sensation of his calloused palm trailing along her leg brought instant heat to Tamara's loins. She ached to have that hard hand clasped along her mound, those strong fingers thrusting deep within her moistness. She arched upward, the movement more a demand than a suggestion that he move his hand where she wished it to be.

"Patience, wench," Evann-Sin said.

With a moan of disappointment, she relaxed as much as she could as his hand made a serpentine path across her upper thighs, her sides, her abdomen and up to one breast. As he took the weight of that heavy orb into his hand, his thumb moved over the turgid nipple and Tamara growled low in her throat.

Working the engorged nub, running the pad of his thumb across the pebbly surface, the Akkadian lowered his lips to Tamara's neck and trailed kisses along the column, His heavily muscled thigh moved over her silken leg, capturing her as his knee slowly nudged her legs further apart. While his thumb drove her mindless with desire as it moved back and forth across her nipple, he moved his leg up and down hers, the wiry texture of his leg hair sending electric impulses along her nerve endings. When his index finger joined his thumb in tormenting her swollen flesh, plucking at it, his fingernails lightly scoring the inflamed point, Tamara could stand no more teasing and reached up to wrap her hand around his neck to pull his face to hers.

Claiming the warrior's mouth with hers, she thrust her tongue deep between his chiseled lips. Expecting warmth instead of the coolness that greeted her probing, she was taken aback for a moment but was soon lost in the heady feel of taking what she wanted. Invading him, conquering the warrior's sweet mouth, made her bold. As his hand lay flattened over the mound of her breast, caught between their bodies, she reached down for his manhood and circled him, gaining hold of the territory she wanted to possess.

Evann-Sin grew steel-hard beneath her firm grasp. His sword leapt in anticipation of its own thrusting, the tip oozing a plea to take full ownership of the female clutching it. Heavy passion spread quickly through his abdomen and a low, feral snarl started low in his chest and pushed its way upward as he freed his mouth from Tamara's ravaging and slid his body over his woman's.

Tamara drew her legs up and clamped them tightly around the Akkadian's slim hips, locking her ankles together as she felt the bulb of his penis pressing against her moist opening. She pulled him against her, needing the deep thrust hinted at by the size of his erection.

"Easy, wench," he cautioned, but he was fumbling between their bodies, positioning himself at her hot opening.

"I do not want it to be easy, warrior," she said through clenched teeth. "I would know your strength to the very core of me!"

Her words galvanized Evann-Sin and he took her at her word. He thrust himself into her hot center with a fierce grunt of possession so forceful, Tamara shrieked. "Damn, warrior!" she gasped.

"You said you didn't want it easy," Evann-Sin chuckled.

"Well, I didn't want you to shoot out through the top of my head, either!" she complained, but giggled to ruin the severe look on her lovely face.

"Poor little one," the warrior crooned. He held still within her for a few seconds then started to withdraw. "If you can't take…"

Tamara's legs tightened around his lean hips. "Oh, no, you don't," she said through clenched teeth. "You'd best start what you finish!"

Evann-Sin cocked his head to one side. "Like this?" he inquired, and began thrusting gently inside her, his large staff causing a delicious friction that captured the breath in Tamara's throat.

"Ah, perhaps with a bit more force?" she suggested, wiggling beneath him.

"Like this, then?" he asked, and put a bit more speed to his thrusts.

"More," Tamara whispered.

"Now?" he questioned as he added a slight circling motion with his cock.

"More," she repeated as she dug her fingers into his shoulders.

Evann-Sin drew in a long, heavy breath. "Well, if you insist," he said on the exhalation. Increasing both his speed and the depth of his thrusts, he heard a long, protracted groan escape his lady's throat. "Like that?" he asked.

"Ah," was all Tamara could reply, for the rhythm of her love's strokes had increased and the tip of him was pressing against a spot inside her that was causing more pleasure than she had ever experienced before.

Getting a better grip on Tamara's hips, Evann-Sin lifted her a bit higher and pushed himself deep within her.

"Yes!" Tamara shouted as she arched against him.

There was fierceness in the Akkadian's eyes as his speed increased. He slapped his body against hers, reveling in the sound of their flesh meeting. His penetration was as far as it would go and he worried that he might hurt her, but as her nails raked his back and he heard her growls of pleasure, he lowered his head to her shoulder and thrust one last time, and held himself still.

Tamara's orgasm began as a slight itch then increased to a roaring ripple that undulated through her lower body, bringing with it wave after wave after wave of intense pleasure. Her eyes went wide, her fingers dug into the warrior's hips and she released a scream of pure, physical release that left her trembling violently beneath her lover's hard body. Sapped of energy, she collapsed on the bed, her arms falling to her sides, her body as limp as she had ever known it to be.

The Akkadian, too, collapsed. His heavy body pressed along hers in such a way that Tamara found it entirely comforting. With an effort, she lifted her arms and encircled his waist, delighting in the light kisses he pressed against the side of her neck.

"You're damned good at that, warrior," she sighed. She lay exhausted in her lover's arms. A faint sheen of sweat dotted her upper lip.

"Glad to know you enjoyed it, wench," he chuckled.

* * * * *

The jackal caught the scent just as the sun was sinking below the horizon. It lifted its muzzle and sniffed the air, the hackles on its back stirring, its oversized ears twitching this way and that in search of movement. Though the scent was one of sustenance, the scavenger tucked its bushy tail between its spindly back legs and stood there undecided. There was something not quite right about the scent wafting its way across the desert sands. As his mate joined him, the jackal growled low in its throat, warning the female that unseen danger was close by.

With one more look toward the spot from which the strange scent originated, the male jackal shook its sandy-colored coat of wiry fur and turned with the female close at his side to lope back toward the den where the litter of pups awaited their evening meal.

Slithering across the ripples of cooling desert sand, the Saw-Scaled Viper stilled, lifting its triangular head, its forked tongue lashing out to sense the nearness of its prey. Swaying as though mesmerized by music only it could sense, the viper wavered in position for a moment longer then dropped back to the sand. As it moved, the rough scales made a harsh rasping sound across the sand. Whatever had caught its attention was obviously not something the snake wanted to encounter and it quickly disappeared beneath a rocky outcropping.

The yellow scorpion arched its lethal stinger and scuttled away, looking for a place to hide from the danger it sensed. The falcon and vulture, eagle and buzzard spied the danger as they rode the currents and flew quickly away, screeching a warning as they went.

As the sun set and darkness settled like a heavy mantle on the sands of the Quesa desert, a hand thrust its way from the grave to claw at the evening air. Another hand shot up and sand cascaded from a naked chest as harsh, rasping air was dragged into lungs that had lain dormant. A bellow of rage broke the stillness of the night as a body pushed away from the ground.

Growling sounds punctuated the movement of feet being pulled from the sand.

From its hiding place behind a date palm, a sand cat watched in terror as the being righted itself, coming erect with another roar of fury. It watched as the being trudged woodenly to the nearby stream and bent over the slow-moving water, staring at the moonlit surface for a long moment before raising its balled fists to the heavens and shaking them. Unable to stop itself, the sand cat mewled pitifully, catching the attention of the thing that had risen from the sand. A little stream of urine ran down the little animal's leg as the being turned scarlet eyes toward it and bared long, wicked fangs. For a moment, sand cat and entity looked at one another then the entity turned away and began plodding purposefully across the desert, its bare shoulders hunched against the chill, its powerful legs digging deep furrows in the sand.

* * * * *

There was a light scratching on the tent flap and Tamara came awake, flinging over on the pallet to reach for her weapon.

"Be easy, wench," Evann-Sin said. "I suspect it is my friend from Samarkan."

Tamara looked around at him, her eyes wide. "Your *dead* friend?" she whispered.

Evann-Sin grinned and called out, "Is that you, Rabin?"

"Aye," came the gruff reply from the other side of the door.

"Are you presentable?" the Akkadian inquired.

"How would I know? I can't see myself!" the gruff voice complained.

"Stay here," Evann-Sin told her. "I'll see if Rabin looks any the worse for his time underground."

"You don't really think that is your friend," Tamara gasped.

"I know it is," the Akkadian snorted.

Tamara winced at the thought, but remained where she stood as the Akkadian stomped over to the flap and flung it open. She was relieved when she heard him announce to his friend that he was as ugly as ever and not the oozing pulp he should have been. She watched a very handsome Dabiyan stride nonchalantly into the tent.

"You look none the worse for being nearly sucked dry as a husk, either," Rabin snapped. He looked at Tamara, bowed his head in greeting then turned to his friend. "How the hell am I to see to shave?"

"I suspect nothing will grow on you from now on," Evann-Sin replied.

"That can't be true," Rabin grumbled. "I've seen corpses with hair down to their hips and fingernails a good six inches long."

"But have you seen corpses with beards?" his friend inquired.

Rabin frowned, thought about that for a moment then smiled. "Nay, I have not!"

"And think of it, Rabin. There will be no need for water or food!" the Akkadian exclaimed.

"And I suppose no more long, satisfying pisses or healthy dumps," Rabin sighed deeply.

Both men looked at one another and grinned, saying at the same time, "No boogers to pick and flick!"

Tamara winced. She wondered why the two of them would think of such a gross thing at the same time, but knew she probably wouldn't want to be enlightened. A vague thought of some disgusting contest passed over her mind and she swept it away as the men clapped each other on the back and laughed.

"I am glad you are here, my friend," Evann-Sin said, sobering. "Together we will find those who did this to you and seek our vengeance and renewal there."

"The Magi said what I do with the ones who murdered me is up to me," Rabin acknowledged. "I can either take their lives as they took mine or make them wish they had never been born!"

"Vengeance is sweeter the longer it lasts," Evann-Sin stated. "I've no desire to take the lives of those who waylaid me, but I have a great desire to make them regret having done it."

"As do I," Rabin agreed. "That I fell victim to women who…"

"Women?" Evann-Sin and Tamara questioned at the same time.

Rabin nodded. "Hell Hags," he said.

Tamara's face drained of color and she put a hand to her mouth. Slowly she turned her gaze to the Akkadian. "Sylviana spoke of him. It was done before I joined them on the road to Nonica."

"Aye," Rabin said. "I was dead long before we were to meet, Riel."

"Why did they kill you?" the Akkadian demanded. "What had you done?"

"Crossed their vile path," Rabin snorted. "Apparently they were…hungry."

"They raped you, as well?" Tamara asked, ignoring the Akkadian's hiss.

Rabin blinked and turned to Evann-Sin, cocking a brow at the disgusted look on the warrior's face. "They raped you?" he asked then hooted. "By the Prophet but that is rich!"

"I'm honored you find it amusing, you worthless mealy worm," Evann-Sin snapped. He waved away his friend's laughter.

"More amusing than…" Rabin began then coughed to hide his merriment for the look on his friend's face was not conducive to continuing the teasing.

"They didn't rape you, then," Evann-Sin wanted clarification.

"No," Rabin said with a shake of his head. "They killed me to keep me from telling what I know."

Evann-Sin blinked. "They are part of the alliance?" he gasped.

"Hell," Rabin snorted. "As far as I can tell, it was their idea."

"What alliance?" Tamara asked. She looked from one warrior to the other.

"A Prophet-be-damned alliance," Evann-Sin said, gritting his teeth. "An alliance I aim to squelch."

"Before or after we take our revenge on the Hell Hags?" Rabin inquired.

"If those bitches are part of the plot, we need to see to them first. Pull the root and the weed will die," Evann-Sin replied.

"I've never killed a woman," Rabin sighed, "and I'm not of a mind to start, but I intend to see them punished for what they did to me."

"They will be," Evann-Sin assured him.

"What of the other one?" Rabin asked. "What do we do about him?"

Evann-Sin frowned. "What *other* one?"

Chapter Four

Kaibyn Zafeyr turned his eyes from the glare of the blazing sun. Already his mouth was dry and his flesh hot. He could feel the searing heat beating down on his head and knew this would be an agonizing way to atone for his sins.

"You should fear the Wrath of Alel," the captain of the palace guard sneered. "He has judged you and found you guilty!"

Where was his protection? Kaibyn thought hopelessly. Where were those who were sworn to protect him? Had they abandoned him? Did they, too, seek his death? What had he done to offend them?

"Lay him down," the captain ordered.

The brutal hands of the Osteran slaves that held him tightened on Kaibyn's arms and the heavy weight of the iron chains pulled painfully on his torn and bleeding wrists. The dark men dragged him down to the blistering sand and as his bare back touched the hotness, he cried out.

"You will know pain far greater than this, you Rysalian demon," the captain smirked.

Kaibyn had no powers in the light of day, and he was helpless to prevent the Osterans from unchaining his wrists, pulling his arms wide apart, then anchoring them with heavy hemp to the iron stakes which had been driven into the hot desert sand. As his legs were spread apart and his ankles bound to another set of stakes, he felt the first moments of blind panic.

The captain of the guard hunkered down beside him and snaked out a ruthless hand to yank Kaibyn's face toward him.

"My woman swears you did not touch her. If you had, I would have gutted you," the captain hissed from between tightly clenched teeth. His fingers dug cruelly into Kaibyn's chin. "How many women did you corrupt before you were found out, demon?"

Kaibyn stared steadily into the captain's glaring eyes, but did not answer. His life was forfeit anyway and he would protect his ladies for as long as he could.

The captain's lips thinned into a long, nasty line and he nodded, as though he could read Kaibyn's thoughts. "You will scream," he prophesied. He glanced up at the noonday sun, then back down at Kaibyn. He relaxed his fingers to slide them up Kaibyn's cheek to pat him almost tenderly. "Before the Eye of Alel turns your skin as black as the darkest Osteran, you will talk. This, I promise you."

Grinning hatefully, the captain stood up, put his fists on his hips and stared down at the bound man. "But will you scream before the scorpions find you, I wonder?" He cocked his head to one side. "Before the blinding pain their venom spreads through your worthless body?"

Kaibyn had never been so hot. The sun's rays were like invisible fire scorching his flesh, and all the moisture in his mouth had fled. Not a hint of the life-sustaining wind that had borne him to this mad world stirred to ease his discomfort.

"Perhaps a serpent will seek you out," the captain chuckled. He nudged Kaibyn's bare thigh with the toe of his sandal. "A strike here." He touched the linen that covered his prisoner's hip. "A strike there. I am told the viper's poison will not kill you. Is that true?"

"The sun will kill him, Meketre," a bored voice put in. "Leave him to do its work. I am sweltering here."

The captain turned and bowed politely to the High Priest who sat beneath the relative comfort of the canopy of his litter. "As you will, lord," Meketre replied.

Kaibyn winced as the captain drew back his heavily muscled leg and delivered a particularly savage kick to Kaibyn's side. "When the jackals come down from the mountains," Kaibyn heard the captain saying. "They will tear the flesh from your bones and devour your organs. There will be nothing left of you to enter the Underworld."

"His kind are not allowed in the Underworld," the High Priest reminded Meketre. "He has no ka."

Meketre shivered. A man without ka was truly a demon. With one last look at the bound man, the captain of the guard turned away, the memory of the sweating face and blistering flesh etched into his mind.

Kaibyn strained to hear the last jingle of harness, the last huff of a horse's nostrils, the fading laughter of the captain of the guards as they left him to die. He strained at his bonds, but knew he had no strength with which to free himself. The light of day was his rival, and the glaring red ball above him, his most vicious enemy. His existence would end beneath the sun's eager glare.

Steaming minutes passed into baking hours then heated to a suffocating intensity that made it hard for him to draw breath into his seared lungs. He could feel the skin over his lips cracking and darted out a dry tongue to touch the bleeding corners. All he could see was a white-hot blur before his eyes, but he knew soon the sun would blind him and he would be in at least one form of his precious darkness once more.

Sudden sharpness pierced the calf of his left leg and he yelped with surprise, wondering what manner of predator had attacked. Although there was no animal, insect or reptile in the land that could take his life, during the daylight hours, he could experience their bites and venom just as a human man could, he could feel the pain just as any man would and be agonized by it.

Another sting at his waist brought an involuntary jerk of his body and he felt something scampering over his naked belly and onto the linen breechclout covering his hips. When another sting kissed the top of his left thigh, he opened his mouth and bellowed with rage, pulling frantically against the hemp that cut into his wrists and ankles. As a venturing scorpion crawled up his shoulder and stuck its venomous tail in his throat, he screamed in pain.

Zara and Dakhla looked at one another as the screams filled the hot desert air. The two women had risked much to come after their lover, but neither would turn back. Both would risk even more for Kaibyn, but they had to wait until the sun set before they could rescue him.

"I can not bear the sound of his agony," Zara whispered and as another piteous scream ripped through the air, she buried her face against Dakhla's shoulder.

"There is nothing we can do," Dakhla replied. She put her arms around her sister and held her.

There were four other women with the two sisters. All of them were sobbing quietly as the screams came. Each was clenching her fists, nails digging into bloody palms, head bowed beneath the weight of her guilt.

"He can not last much longer," one of the older women said.

Dakhla looked over at her mother-in-law and nodded her agreement. Her gaze shifted to the sun that was now low in the sky. It would be an hour, maybe two, before this horrible day was ended.

"How could she have betrayed him?" the youngest woman there asked. She put up a trembling hand to wipe at the tears coursing down her smooth cheek.

The Lady Auklet shrugged. "To save herself from her mate," she answered. "He is insane, we all know that."

"Hush!" Dakhla insisted. "You speak of our king!"

Auklet gave an unladylike snort. "And because he is king he can not be mad?" She flung out a dismissive hand. "Ugly, insane and mean as a pit viper! This is his doing, not the queen's."

"She betrayed Kaibyn to her husband," the second youngest woman stressed. "It is no other's fault save her own."

"Yes, Meritaten, and for your mother's sin, we all must suffer," Zara agreed.

"Not as much as Kaibyn does," Dakhla reminded her sister.

"Her days are numbered," Auklet grated. She looked to the beautiful doe-eyed girl sitting beside her. "I would not be your mother for all her beauty and grace."

Meritaten nodded. She understood well that her mother had fallen from the good graces of her mentally defective husband. The young girl shuddered, closing her eyes to the quiet of the late afternoon. There was no doubt in her mind that the king wanted her as a replacement for his out of favor queen. This scandal involving the Rysalian would be all the impetus the insane fool needed to force Meritaten to wife.

"Why must it be so quiet?" Teti asked.

The other women raised their heads for the terrible screaming had stopped. In unison, their eyes went to the horizon where the sun was balanced on a single ray. As they held their combined breaths, the russet orb sank behind the shimmering western sands.

"Now!" Dakhla spat.

The women scrambled to their feet and raced to their horses whose reins were being held by their sole male companion.

"We must hurry, Omahru," Auklet ordered. She put her foot into the waiting hand of her Osteran slave and the hulking giant lifted her into the saddle.

Omahru did not answer his mistress for it was physically impossible for the dark man to do so. The Lady Auklet's husband, the High Priest, had cut out Omahru's tongue when the slave was only a boy of three.

"Without a tongue, he can not repeat what he hears in this household," the High Priest had declared.

At age ten, the dark man had been castrated to ensure the wellbeing of the lady and her daughters.

Dakhla swung herself into her saddle and pulled cruelly on the reins to turn the beast toward the desert. Digging her heels into the stallion's sides, she whipped him into a run, oblivious to the other women following closely on her heels.

Their earlier ride out of the city of Marrupa had been nerve-racking for the women feared their husbands would see them and stop them. But, with the Goddess' help, the six women had been able to flee the watchful eyes of their guards and individually make their way to a curve in the stream that ran just beyond the city gates. The journey to the place of Kaibyn's execution took them across the stream and into the cooling desert—a distance that normally took fifteen minutes to travel was accomplished in less than ten. By the time they reached the Killing Ground, their mounts were lathered and the chill night air was settling in.

"There!" Meritaten cried out, pointing. "There he is!"

As the riders neared the spread-eagled body, a jackal standing over Kaibyn howled his anger at their intrusion and raced away, darting damning looks over his shoulders as he ran.

"Did it hurt him?" the youngest woman cried out.

Dakhla spared the girl a spiteful look before answering. "Nothing can hurt him, now, Teti."

Omahru was the first to reach Kaibyn and he vaulted from his mount, his naked feet digging into the hot sand as he ran. He stopped, squatted down and reached out to touch the unmoving chest of the bound man.

"Well?" Auklet demanded as she shifted uncomfortably in her saddle. "Is he...?" She stopped as the dark man held up a restraining hand.

Dakhla could feel her heart thudding in her chest as she waited. Beside her, her sister and the other women were gripping their mount's reins as tightly as they had once held Kaibyn's body to their own.

With his hand still on Kaibyn's chest, Omahru turned and looked at his lady. He shook his head slowly.

"No!" Teti sobbed and she let go of her horse's reins to bury her face in her hands. Without the firm command of its rider, the mare sidestepped away from the man on the ground and flung its head in fear.

"Teti!" Dahkla hissed. "Control yourself and your mount! You knew he would not be alive!"

"Omahru," Auklet said firmly, drawing her servant's attention to her. "You know what to do. We dare not be gone long; we will be missed, but we will return when the moon has risen high."

The Osteran nodded. He went to his knees beside the dead man, took out his knife, slid the blade under the hemp and began to saw at the bond that held Kaibyn's wrist.

Dahkla took one last look at Kaibyn's still body. She looked at her mother-in-law and knew the High Priest's days were numbered, as well. Turning her head, she caught Teti's glazed eyes and wondered if the girl would have the courage to end her husband's life. If not, Dahkla mentally shrugged there were others who would gladly spill the captain of the guard's blood.

The Osteran barely took note of the women as they rode away. He was too busy cutting through the ropes binding the Rysalian's ankles. When he was finished, he re-sheathed his dagger and cursed the fates that had brought him to this wicked land. Stooping over to run his calloused hands under the dead man's knees and back, the dark man lifted his burden and stood, cradling Kaibyn's body against his wide chest. The dark man carried the still one to his horse and draped him over the saddle, mounted behind Kaibyn's limp body, then turned his horse toward the necropolis beyond the village.

* * * * *

When the moon was high overhead, the sound of approaching footsteps down the carved granite steps of the burial chamber brought Omahru slowly to his feet. He had been sitting by the body, keeping watch as he had been told to do, fearful of being so near the Rysalian demon, but determined to do his mistress' bidding. He relaxed only when he recognized his mistress and her daughter-in-law.

Auklet studied his black face in the moonlight and smiled. "Were you afraid, Omahru?"

The Osteran firmly shook his head in denial and sniffed, displaying his disdain for such a question.

"We don't have much time," Dahkla stressed. "The sleeping potion I gave my husband will not last long."

"I have no such worry," Auklet snorted and the younger woman looked quizzically at her.

"Why not?" Dahkla asked.

Auklet's grin was brutal. "I am a widow, now," she replied.

Dahkla shook her head in mock sadness. "My condolences, lady."

"Thank you," Auklet said. "I shall grieve appropriately at a later date." She grinned. "If I decide to grieve at all."

Dahkla reached up to untie a satchel from the saddle of her horse. She carried it over to the place where Omahru had laid Kaibyn's body and opened it.

"You know the ritual words, do you not?" Auklet asked her daughter-in-law.

"I know what I need to know to see this done," the younger woman answered without looking up at Auklet.

"He is the most beautiful male I have ever seen," Auklet sighed as she lowered herself gracefully beside the dead man. She reached out a gentle hand and caressed his cold cheek. "So very, very beautiful."

"And he will remain so," Dahkla stated.

For over two hours, the women worked their embalming magic on Kaibyn. Omahru helped them to wrap the corpse and then picked up the linen-encased body and laid it gently in the simple cedar coffin where the Rysalian would spend his next eternity.

"Sleep, my beautiful one," Auklet sobbed.

Dahkla looked at the tightly wrapped body lying in front of her. Her guilt was a cruel master and it rode her mercilessly. She dared not tell Auklet what she knew. The old woman would interfere as surely as the Nile flowed with teeming life. Nothing would be gained and, considering the possible consequences, all would be lost should Auklet and the others ever find out.

"You should return to the palace, lady," Dahkla said, looking up at the older woman. "I can finish here."

"But you will need Omahru to help you close the lid of the coffin," Auklet protested. She motioned her slave to do just that.

"No," Dahkla insisted, putting out a hand to stop the Osteran. "That is no hard chore."

"But you might get lost down here," Auklet said, flinging an arm around the tomb in which they stood. "At least let Omahru stay to show you the way out, to re-seal the entry of the burial chamber."

"I know the passageways, lady," Dahkla replied. "I can re-seal the hidden entry with no trouble."

"But, Dahkla…" Auklet began to protest, but the younger woman held up a hand.

"As his First, I, alone, must be the one to see him into the Dark World. I need to be alone with him for a moment, to bid him goodbye."

Auklet hesitated, chewing on her lip. While it was true her daughter-in-law had been Kaibyn's primary partner, there were others who had loved him. Others who had thought of the Rysalian as the ancient love-god instead of the demon he was.

"I can well understand your feelings of responsibility, but you should not be out here alone," Auklet reminded the younger woman. "At least let Omahru stay until you have buried our beloved one."

Dahkla shook her head. "What must be done must be done by my hand and my hand alone. What must be done now must not be witnessed by none other than the First."

Auklet opened her mouth to protest once more, but Omahru gently placed his large hand around his mistress' upper arm, gaining her immediate attention. When the older woman looked up into the midnight-black orbs of her slave, she could see his agreement with Dahkla. After a long moment of staring at the Rysalian, Auklet sighed heavily.

"All right, but I am not pleased," she stated.

"I will not be long," Dahkla promised.

Auklet sighed again then allowed her slave to lead her to the steps. She looked around her and there was a hitch in her voice as she spoke. "He will rest in such a lonely place."

"We will know where he is," Dahkla answered. "No one would look for him here."

The oil lamp that Omahru held flickered with the wash of an unseen wind, casting Dahkla's face and her mother-in-law's keen eye into deep shadow. And it was a good thing that happened for the old harpy would have seen the terrible guilt in Dahkla's face and all would have been lost.

"They must never find his body," Auklet insisted as she turned away.

"They will not," Dahkla swore.

A final sigh of hopelessness came from the Lady Auklet as she moved out of sight up the serpentine steps.

Dahkla hung her head.

"Forgive me, my beloved," she whispered, placing her hand lightly on Kaibyn's bound chest. Instantly, she jerked her hand back with a gasp and began to tremble violently.

Beneath the stillness of that wide chest, there was once more a faint flutter of life, growing stronger with each shift of dark wind flowing over the demon's body from the opened doorway. Had he been left to the night, to the high-riding moon and sweet desert winds, he would have risen on his own and come back to them. Nothing could have stopped him. That was the way of his kind for Kaibyn Zafeyr was a Nightwind, an ancient demon brought up from the muck of the Abyss to serve the Ones who had called him. A lonely woman's tears, her desperation had brought him forth and it would be to her and her kin—for generations to come—to whom he would be bound by a blood oath neither could ever break. Had she allowed him free reign he would have grown harder and harder to control.

And that could not be allowed to happen.

A soft intake of breath came from the tightly bound head of the mummy and Dahkla panicked.

"No," she hissed. "I will not permit it!"

Quickly, she grasped the lid of the coffin and slammed it shut, cutting off the increasing rhythm of breaths coming from the mummy.

"Shut out the Light, still the Wind," she muttered the incantation as she sealed the lid of the coffin with special oil.

There was movement inside the coffin—a shifting and a faint cry, but Dahkla ignored it. She whispered her chant and smeared oil all around the edges of the cedar coffin.

Dahkla, she heard and flung her hands up to cover her ears. *Dahkla, do not do this!*

Lifting her own lantern from the ledge on which it sat, she held it high and hurried to the steps.

Dahkla, please!

Dahkla knew the voice was in her head, but it began to fade as she wound her way up out of the burial tomb. When she had re-sealed the doorway into the hidden chamber, she rushed outside, tripped and fell to the sand, scraping her knees.

Please, do not leave me here, she heard one final whimper of great sadness invade her mind.

"Be still, demon!" she hissed, swiping angrily at the tears which cascaded down her pale cheeks. "I will not listen to your deceitful voice again!"

Scrambling to her feet, the young woman ran for her horse, stumbling twice in her haste to flee this place of betrayal and going down to her knees in the sand.

Dahkla! You will regret this!

She reached her horse and pulled herself up into the saddle. Like the mad woman she had become, she spurred her horse and raced back to Marrupa.

Even later, as she lay beside her hated husband in the safety of the king's palace, she could hear the feeble cry of her name that was fading with the coming of dawn.

Dahkla turned her face into her pillow and wept hysterically. When her husband woke and pulled her into his arms, she shuddered against him.

"What is it, sister?" he asked, smoothing the hair back from her damp forehead. "What troubles you so? A nightmare?"

How could she tell her husband that she had buried a man alive this night? How to tell him that she was one of the women the Rysalian demon had seduced? That it had been she who had enticed him to pleasure her and her alone? That the demon had felt the loneliness of the others and had given of himself to them, thus garnering Dakhla's jealousy and revenge? Or that it had been she, not the queen, who had betrayed him to the king's men?

She could not, Dahkla reminded herself. To do so would surely bring about her ruin.

"It was just a nightmare," Ahkmed declared and patted his wife clumsily on her back. "A nightmare that is over now."

Perhaps, Dahkla told herself. As long as Kaibyn's body lay deep in his borrowed burial chamber and was never discovered by his Bloodkin.

Chapter Five

Jabali armed the sweat from his brow, squinted against the heat of the noonday sun and wondered if the day could get any hotter. He sighed as he took a water skin Tashobi extended toward him. "You are a fine assistant, 'Shobi," he said. "You anticipate what I need before I need it."

Tashobi inclined his head. "It is my privilege to serve you, Master." He looked about them. "There are many graves here. Do you know into which one they have hidden Lord Kaibyn?"

"There," Jabali said, nudging his dripping chin toward an entranceway a few yards to their right. "He is aware. If you listen closely, you will hear his anger."

Closing his eyes, the apprentice allowed his mind to venture into the necropolis until the faint words of he whom they sought could be heard cursing the women who had betrayed him.

"He is, indeed, very angry," Tashobi commented.

"And rightfully so," Jabali said.

"As angry as the Akkadian was."

"True, but where one will demand the lives of his enemies, the other will want them to live to regret their foul deed," Jabali replied, handing the water skin to the younger man. "Yet, we need them both for what must be done."

Knowing it would do him no good to question the mysterious statement, Tashobi slung the water skin over the pommel of his saddle. "Should I wait here, Master?"

"Aye," Jabali said tiredly. "I will free him from his burial place and bring him into the light."

A ripple of fear went through Tashobi. "Will he be frightening to look upon?"

The young man's teacher chuckled. "No, lad. He will be just as he appeared in life."

Tashobi shrugged away his unease. He watched his Master walk slowly, painfully toward the entrance to the necropolis. He knew the old man would need a massage before turning in that night for the bones of a man in his tenth decade often pained him.

"Keep close watch," Jabali said over his shoulder as he climbed the steps to Kaibyn's burial chamber. "We want no Kebullians to impede our mission."

Tashobi watched as his mentor stopped at the entrance of the necropolis to light a fat candle he had pulled from his satchel.

There was only a slight difference in temperatures as Jabali descended the steps into the burial chamber where Kaibyn lay…now quiet though his spirit was seething still with fury. The mage once more wiped the sweat from his forehead with the sleeve of his robe, finding it hard to breathe in the stifling heat. His joints ached as he walked and he longed for the warm waters of the bathing pool at the temple in Shalda.

There will be time for that when you free me!

Jabali winced, holding his candle higher to view the room around him. "Patience, Lord Kaibyn," he said. "Patience."

There was a muted growl that reverberated through the Mage's head but no more shouted words.

The coffin containing Kaibyn's body sat off to itself in the burial chamber, partially hidden behind other cheap coffins that held the remains of former servants. The lid was slick with the special oil the Lady Dakhla had spread on the rim and lock to prevent him from freeing himself.

Setting down his satchel, placing the candle on a ledge of rock, Jabali opened the satchel and removed a fleece cloth. He used the soft material to wipe away the oil. When there was hardly any residue left of the magic potion, he lifted the coffin's lid, staggering as a strong wind blasted out of the box, extinguishing the candle.

"What took you so long, Mage?" Lord Kaibyn roared, his loud words echoing off the walls of the burial chamber.

Jabali closed the coffin after one look at the empty shrouds lying within its confines. Before he answered the demon lurking behind him, he bent over...grunting with the effort...and removed a vial of the same kind of oil the Lady Dakhla had used to seal Kaibyn in.

"There were others who needed our help, Lord Kaibyn," Jabali explained as he smeared the oil on the coffin's rim.

"And who is more important that I?"

The Mage dared not tell the demon that a simple Dabiyan warrior had been raised from death first. "Lord Riel Evann-Sin of Nonika, Your Grace," he replied instead. "We found him lashed to the..."

"An Akkadian barbarian?" Kaibyn exploded, the fury of his shock making the walls of the necropolis tremble. "You think that jackal more important than I?"

Gathering his courage, Jabali turned to face the demon. He lifted his head, allowing him to take in the face of the tall form in front of him. "No, Your Grace. He is not more important than you, but our freeing him had to be accomplished in order for him to help you."

Kaibyn narrowed his eyes, the color of a winter sky. "Help me in what way, Mage?" Though the words were not as forceful or loud, they sounded like a warning to Jabali.

"There is great evil afoot, milord," Jabali said, "and the Council of Elders dispatched me to come to your aid as well as one other whose life was terminated before the Gatherer sanctioned it."

The Rysalian demon folded his arms and glared at the Mage. "What other foul fiend?"

Hearing Lord Kaibyn call another being a fiend might well have made Jabali laugh under safer circumstances, but while standing in the presence of an angry demon was not the time for levity.

"You are the strategist behind the coalition the Council bid me form. Lord Evann-Sin is the brawn—his sword hand will set things to right. The third arm of the Triad will be the eyes and ears."

"What is this third lord's name?" Kaibyn demanded. "Do I know him?"

Jabali swallowed hard before answering. "I think not, milord. He is but a simple peasant but one who will aid the project well."

"A peasant?" Kaibyn sniffed. "What brand of peasant?"

"Rabin Jaspyre is a Dabiyan, milord," Jabali said softly.

"A darkling?" Kaibyn gasped, and his image pulsed, shifted and sparked with myriad harsh lights that caused Jabali to throw up a hand to ward off the painful intrusion of the brightness. "I have no love for darklings! It was darklings that left me to die in the desert!"

"He is but a spy, milord," Jabali said, trying to soothe the irate demon shimmering before him. "Would you lower yourself to such a task?"

Kaibyn's ghost rippled for a moment then subsided though the wavering image increased in size. "What is this coalition of which you speak? What is the purpose of such a thing?"

Relieved the demon had accepted begrudgingly the existence of the third member of the coalition, Jabali breathed a sigh of relief. Once again, he armed the sweat from his brow. "To rid our world of a dangerous alliance that has come about within the last three days," he replied. "An alliance...left unchecked...that could well destroy the world as we know it."

"Between whom?"

Jabali wished he could sit down for his aged bones were plaguing him. He was overly hot and his heart was racing, his head pounding. Being well into the eighth year past his 100th birthday, he was beginning to feel the arms of the Gatherer closing around him. It would not be many more months before he was laid to rest in a necropolis similar to the one in which he stood.

"You can rest when you have given me a reason for not pulling the head from your puny body," Kaibyn sneered. "Tell me who this alliance is!"

"The King of Kebul, he who ordered you put to death, and Lilit, Queen of the Daughters of the Night," Jabali answered.

For a moment, the faraway sound of bats winging about the interior of the necropolis was all Jabali heard. Though the tomb in which he stood was as bright as day with the image of Kaibyn Zafeyr hulking in front of the Mage, there was a gathering darkness beyond that was harsher than a moonless night.

Kaibyn sidled closer to the Mage. "How do you come to know of an alliance between those vile offspring of their mother's diseased wombs?"

"It was the Dabiyan who discovered the connection, milord, and he was on his way to tell Lord Evann-Sin when he was ruthlessly murdered."

"The Dabiyan was a servant of the Akkadian jackal?"

"An operative, I believe the word to be," Jabali corrected. "He was Lord Evann-Sin's eyes and ears in the desert."

Something wicked moved over the demon's face. "And was his friend," he said with a jeer.

Jabali reminded himself to be more careful of his thoughts for the demon had plucked the connection between Evann-Sin and Rabin from his overly tired mind. He nodded. "Aye, Your Grace, they were friends," he said, daring not lie to the demon. "They still are."

Kaibyn grimaced but made no comment. Instead, he turned toward the stairs and with a great rush of wind fled the confines of the hot burial chamber.

Jabali closed his eyes for a moment, grateful that the demon had fled the heat. He gathered his satchel and candle and wearily climbed the steps to the outside, grateful for the residual light of the demon's passing that lit the stairs. Once in the brutal glare of the desert sun, the Mage walked as fast as he could to his assistant.

"Did you see him exit the necropolis?" Jabali asked.

Tashobi shook his head. "I saw nothing, Master." He hastened to supply the older man with the dwindling water skin. "I felt his passing, though. It knocked me down."

Jabali swigged the tepid water, easing the parching of his throat. He poured some of the precious fluid into his palm then swiped it over his face.

"Will he return?" Tashobi inquired.

"When he has accomplished two things—secondly, he will punish the woman who left him in this place," Jabali replied. "I doubt that will take long, for he is intrigued by news of the alliance."

"Did he say as much, Master?"

Jabali shook his head. "He did not need to. I saw the fury in his eyes the moment I mentioned who the villains in this are."

"And his first task, Master?"

"He will seek out Evann-Sin."

Chapter Six

"I've not heard of this Zafeyr," Evann-Sin mumbled. He glanced at Rabin. "What about you?"

"What I know is this—there are two men by that name in the Inner Kingdom. Both are deadly and both are demons in their own right. One is confined to the island at Akasha, unable to flee for he cannot travel over running water. The other runs free. It is rumored there is a demon in Kebul and I believe that is Kaibyn Zafeyr," Rabin replied.

"Until today, I would not have thought such beings existed, but I'm talking to a dead man so what do I know?" Evann-Sin sighed.

"I've always believed in demons," Rabin said. He grinned. "Have you seen the women of Kebul?"

"Not the prettiest of females," Evann-Sin remarked.

"Aye, but I would venture to say the hairiest, by far," Tamara giggled.

"Thus the need for the black robes that cover them head to toe," Rabin put in. "And a demon to warm their beds on cold desert nights when their menfolk can't bring themselves to touch those hairy bodies."

"Why would we need a demon, though?" Evann-Sin asked. "I…"

"When you need to deal with women, you bring in an expert."

The disembodied voice was smug, filled with amusement. Evann-Sin, Rabin and Tamara looked up as a body materialized there in the tent with them. To the men, the entity that took form was nothing out of the ordinary, but to Tamara he was the handsomest man she had ever seen. Her lips parted and she stared at him as though she were starving.

"You are Zafeyr," Evann-Sin snapped, very aware of his woman's reaction to the newcomer.

Kaibyn ignored the question, turning his full attention to Tamara. His eyes widened. "The Mage did not tell me I would have a beautiful lady with whom to work."

Tamara blushed, lowering her eyes to the compliment. When she glanced at Evann-Sin, she saw a muscle working in his cheek, his gaze unfriendly as he regarded the demon.

"The only thing you will be doing with my woman is showing your respect," Evann-Sin grated.

Still ignoring the men, Kaibyn walked to Tamara and took her hand, and brought it to his lips. With his eyes locked on hers, he placed a gentle kiss in her palm. "Milady," he whispered, "I have all the respect in the world for one as lovely as you."

The fierce growl that erupted from the Akkadian's throat made Rabin step back quickly. He'd heard that sound of fury before, and it did not bode well for whoever caused it. He winced as the demon was shoved across the tent to land in a heap on the pallet Evann-Sin and Tamara had shared.

"Don't you *ever* touch my woman again, demon!" Evann-Sin roared, going to stand over Kaibyn. He stood there—rigid as stone—with his hands clenching and unclenching at his sides. Eyes flashing dangerously, teeth clenched, he looked every inch the lethal warrior he had been trained to be.

Tamara rushed to her lover's side and took his sword arm, clutching it to her as fiercely as any woman had ever tried to stay her man's anger. "He meant nothing, warrior," she was quick to say. "He knows I belong to you!"

Kaibyn lay on the pallet, glaring up at the Akkadian. His own hands were balled into fists, his eyes narrowed into slits. With his lips skinned back from his teeth, he no longer looked as handsome as Tamara first thought, and she realized what was said and done now would either make it possible for these two men to work together or would forever have them at each other's throat.

"Riel," she said softly, drawing her lover's surprised eyes to hers. "I am yours and will be 'til the day I draw my last breath on this earth. If there is an afterlife, I will continue to love you 'til time is no more." She squeezed his arm. "Do you doubt that?"

The Akkadian shook his head. "Nay, but…"

"Then know that nothing and—" she turned her gaze to the demon, "—no man will ever come between us. I am yours for as long as you want me."

For a long, charged moment, the warrior and the demon glared at one another then slowly their body postures relaxed. Tamara's words had diffused the rage coursing through the men and put the matter into a perspective both could tolerate.

"Now behave like the gentlemen I know you are, and let's get on with what needs to be done," Tamara advised. She released Evann-Sin's arm and stepped back, casting a rolling eyes look at Rabin that made that warrior smile.

Despite his dislike and distrust for the demon, Evann-Sin extended his hand. "As long as you know how things stand."

After a momentary pause, Kaibyn reached out and grabbed the Akkadian's hand and levered himself to his feet. As he stood there, his wrist in Evann-Sin's grip, his own fingers wrapped around the warrior's strong wrist, their gazes fused, he made a silent vow to take the Akkadian's woman away from him.

When the two men let go of each other's wrists without further male posturing, Tamara breathed a sigh of relief. "So where do we start?" she asked.

"First, we get out of this tent," Rabin said. "I may not be sweating but I do not care for such close quarters."

"For a darkling," Kaibyn remarked, "you have no vile stench."

Rabin blinked.

Tamara groaned, thinking now there would be a problem between these two men, but Evann-Sin threw back his head and laughed.

"And that is a definite improvement," the warrior chuckled.

Rabin lifted his arms and sniffed his armpits. "Are you sure the scent is gone, Riel?" he asked, his forehead creased.

"Aye, I'm sure. I hadn't noticed until Zafeyr commented on it, but your sour smell is no longer there." Evann-Sin looked down at Tamara. "The man has always reeked so badly his wife could not share a bed with him."

"What of me?" Kaibyn inquired. "Do you suppose my natural body odor has fled?" He frowned. "That would not be a good thing because I have been told the ladies find it alluring."

Evann-Sin walked over to Kaibyn. He frowned. "You have a musky odor." He turned to Tamara. "Come smell him, lady, and see what you think."

Tamara shook her head. "No, I can smell him from here and it is an unpleasant scent."

"What?" Kaibyn gasped. He did as Rabin had then slowly lowered his arm. "I stink!"

"Could it be that whatever you were in life, you are the opposite in un-life?" Evan-Sinn asked.

Horror shifted over Kaibyn's face and he backed away, one hand up as though to forestall any further bad news. "Nay, for I had ladies flocking around me constantly." He shook his head. "I liked it that way. To know that I no longer will be able to have their affections is a fate far worse than this un-death!"

"Perhaps the gods have something loftier in mind for you, milord," Tamara said softly. "Something infinitely more important."

"Like finding the women who harmed us," Evan-Sinn suggested.

Kaibyn narrowed his eyes. "Aye, now that I will gladly make my un-life's work!"

"I believe you have no worry about enticing women, milord," Tamara said. "I find you most alluring, if a bit unripe." She put a hand to her nose but her eyes were twinkling.

A pained look spread over Kaibyn's face. "But what can I do about that, wench?" he asked, trying once more to sniff at any offending odor under his armpits. He could detect no difference.

Evann-Sin put his arm around his woman. "You find him handsome, Tamara," he stated. "Not alluring."

Tamara rested her head on her lover's shoulder. "That was what I meant," she mumbled.

Still annoyed that he possessed a smell a beautiful woman found offensive, Kaibyn shook his head. "What can I do?" he repeated.

"Myrrh?" Rabin suggested.

"Cinnamon," Tamara said with a knowing look. "Cinnamon will cover the muskiness."

The demon winced at her description of his smell. "Have you this spice?" he asked.

"Nay, but it is easily procured," she replied.

"I hope it works better for him than it ever did for Rabin," Evann-Sin muttered.

Tamara shushed her lover for she feared another confrontation between the two warriors. She took a seat at the fire and held her hands to the heat. She smiled as Rabin came to sit down beside her.

"Were they Hell Hags who murdered you?" Evann-Sin asked, as he seated himself on the other side of Tamara.

"Nay," Kaibyn replied. "They were Kebullian, but I have heard of such bitches."

Lifting her chin, Tamara speared him with a haughty look. "Not all the Daughters of the Night are bitches, milord."

"True," Evann-Sin agreed. "One is a veritable goddess." He took his lady's hand and kissed it.

"That she is," Kaibyn said seductively, pretending not to see Evann-Sin's glower.

"The ones who killed you were not part of the alliance, then?" Rabin asked quickly.

"The King of Nebul ordered my execution but it was Dakhla who tried to deny me my return to the world of the living. I do not believe the other women knew what she had planned for me," Kaibyn said through clenched teeth. "Jealous bitch that she is, I can see now my taking pity on her friends made her wish revenge."

"By taking pity, I presume you mean seducing them," Evann-Sin scoffed.

Kaibyn nodded slowly. "Aye and I have no quarrel with them. My Lady Auklet took the High Priest's life, and for that I will reward her. It is Dakhla, King Oded and Meketre, the Captain of the Guard, who will soon know my vengeance. As for why she betrayed me? Dakhla has dreams of being Queen of Kebul. It was she who informed the king, not the Queen Lilabet. That one would never have betrayed me."

"Did the Magi tell you why this alliance was formed?" Evann-Sin asked.

"All I was told was that the alliance could destroy the world as we know it," Kaibyn answered.

"King Oded wants to live forever," Rabin pronounced, and the others turned to him.

"Oded is as crazy as a loon!" Kaibyn snorted.

"Aye, but our queen could make him One with the Blood," Tamara reminded them softly.

"What exactly does that mean?" Evann-Sin asked her.

"A vampire," Kaibyn replied. "Aren't all Hell Hags?"

Tamara wrapped her arms around and leaned closer to the warmth of the fire. "I am only partly of the Blood, for I chose not to become an eleventh degree adept."

"That bitch, Sylviana, said she was ninth degree. What are you?" Evann-Sin asked.

"Tenth now that I have taken Sylviana's evil life for what she did to you," Tamara told her lover. "I can go no higher unless I agree to become One with the Blood."

"A drinker of blood," Kaibyn put in.

Tamara agreed. "Such was not my desire. I have had my blood taken by our queen—as we all must—but I have never drank of hers." She shuddered. "The thought of living forever never appealed to me."

Evann-Sin put his arms around her and pulled her close to him. "The thought of that wicked thing sticking her fangs into you makes me ill."

"So Oded wants to live forever," Kaibyn stated, annoyed with the sight of the lovely Tamara in the warrior's embrace. "What is it Lilit wants?"

"His protection?" Rabin questioned.

"She doesn't need it," Tamara said. "She is more powerful than any human king will ever be or hope to be as One with the Blood, for she was supernaturally born."

"There has to be a reason she is willing to share her authority with a retarded prick like Oded," Kaibyn spat.

"But will she be sharing her authority?" Evann-Sin asked.

"What do you mean, Riel?" Rabin asked.

"Who will be Oded's queen?" Evann-Sin countered.

"That bitch Dahkla if she has her way, but you can take her out of the equation," Kaibyn sneered. "That I will never allow! And I will protect my Lilabet. Oded will not put her aside to wed Lilabet's daughter Meritaten either, though he's been conniving toward that end!"

"My king will need to know this is in the making," Evann-Sin said. "Our Tribunal believes Oded has too much power as it is."

Kaibyn lifted his head. "You and the darkling have been watching him, eh?"

"The darkling has," Rabin snapped. He threw the demon an angry look. "Riel is the warrior to whom I report what I find."

"What is a Rysalian doing as Lord High Commander of the Akkadian Forces anyway?" Kaibyn asked. "Don't Akkadians hate Rysalians even worse than they hate Kebullians?"

Evann-Sin's arms tensed around Tamara. "I am half-Rysalian and half-Akkadian. My mother is from Nonika and that is my home."

Kaibyn blinked. "Your father is Akkadian?" When Evann-Sin did not answer, the demon slowly smiled. "The King of Akkadia is your sire?"

Feeling her lover's body go rigid, Tamara turned so she could look into his face. "You are a prince?" she whispered. He looked down at her but remained silent.

"King Numair, the Panther, is your sire!" Kaibyn exclaimed, and slapped his knee with the flat of his hand. "Aye, but that is rich!"

"Is it true?" Tamara asked but still her lover did not speak.

"His parentage is not something he likes to talk about," Rabin injected. "Leave him be, lady."

"Aye, but *why* doesn't he want to talk about it?" Kaibyn chuckled.

Evann-Sin let go of Tamara and bounded to his feet. He cast the demon a warning look then stalked out of the tent. Tamara would have followed him, but Rabin pleaded with her not to do so.

"He's a powerful man," Tamara said, looking from Rabin to the demon. "He is a man much respected in all lands. Why would Riel not be proud of his sire?"

Kaibyn settled back on the cot and folded his arms. "Aye, darkling. Why would he not be proud to admit he is the son of the almighty Numair?"

A muscle ground in Rabin's dark cheek. "Riel Evann-Sin is as mighty a warrior as King Numair is a powerful man. He has no reason to ride the coattails of the Panther."

"That may be true, but something tells me the son denies the father," Kaibyn cooed.

"That isn't it!" Rabin snapped. "It is the father who denies the son!" Realizing he had been tricked into making that statement, the Dabiyan warrior doubled his fists and would have flung himself upon the demon if Kaibyn had not fled the tent in a rush of cold wind.

"Coward!" Rabin yelled.

Evann-Sin turned at the angry shout. He found himself almost toe to toe with Kaibyn Zafeyr.

"It is as I thought," the demon said. "Your father does not claim you."

"Did you even have one or were you the drizzle off some hyena's prick?" Evann-Sin challenged.

Instead of provoking Kaibyn Zafeyr, the question seemed to amuse him. "I might well have been for I never knew who my sire was."

"What a shame," Evann-Sin snorted, and pushed past the other man.

"The Magi want us to work together, to be a coalition against the alliance, but if you are going to be prickly over something as insignificant as whose cock made you, this isn't going to work, boy," Kaibyn told him.

Evann-Sin narrowed his eyes. "It is not an insignificant thing that the Panther sired me, but I have no desire to discuss it now or ever again. Is that understood?"

Kaibyn shrugged. "Whatever you say, warrior."

"Nor do I wish to have it discussed outside my hearing. Do you understand that as well?"

"Aye," the demon sighed. "You take the fun out of it, don't you?"

"It isn't a humorous matter!" Evann-Sin snapped.

"So," Kaibyn said, turning away. He drew the word out in a long sigh. "What do we do first?" He looked back at the warrior. "After I punish Dakhla."

"Can you lay that vengeance aside until we have done what we need to do?"

The demon thought about it for a moment, and then grinned nastily. "Aye, I suppose I can. Perhaps time will give me more vicious ideas with which to discipline that treacherous bitch."

"I have a few disciplines I would like to set in motion, myself, so I will not try to discourage you from exercising yours, but I believe the greater good is more important than the revenge we seek against a few deserving women."

Kaibyn grinned. "Say the word, and I will take delight in helping you teach your women a lesson they will never forget."

"If they live that long," Evann-Sin mumbled.

"You would slay them?"

"Nay, but my woman might."

At the mention of Tamara, Kaibyn felt another pang of jealousy ripple through him but pushed it aside. Such emotions were new to him and he found he did not like being envious of any human male.

"So, Oded wants to live forever," the demon stated. He hunkered down on the sand and used his finger to draw a haphazard design as he thought.

"And an alliance with Lilit will accomplish that, but what is it they plan?"

"According to the Magi whatever they are scheming will change the world as we know it."

Evann-Sin folded his arms over his chest and stared out across the undulating sand. "How is it we know the world?" he asked.

"Depending on where we live and how, that is different for each of us," Rabin said as he joined them.

"Perhaps it is not the world then, but the quality of life we should be considering," Evann-Sin mused.

"Well, my life was spent seeing to the needs of lovely women," Kaibyn replied. "My un-death will be spent much the same way, I'm thinking."

"Our hearts beat, our blood flows, we breathe and eat and procreate," Evann-Sin said.

"Well, we did," Rabin corrected. "Now, I find I'm not hungry at all. How about you?"

Evann-Sin shook his head. "There are jobs for which certain people are suited. There are gifted ones and those with talents."

Kaibyn lifted his head then slowly turned his eyes to Evann-Sin.

"What?" the warrior inquired, instinctively knowing the demon had hit upon the answer.

"Slave or freeman," Kaibyn said quietly. "King or peasant, woman, man or child. They each have something in common."

"That being?"

"They think," Kaibyn stated, coming to his feet. He dusted his hands together. "Even a man in chains is free to have thoughts of one day being liberated. A freeman may envision one day owning more of his world and sets out to make that happen."

"But if they have no thoughts, no dreams or opinions or feelings..." Rabin whispered.

"And instead have but one purpose in life, and that is to see to the needs of that bastard Oded and the Hell Hags?" Evann-Sin queried.

"No one with whom to wage war," Kaibyn continued. "No voices of dissention or denial. Nothing but a world of mindless, soulless workers making Oded's life a virtual paradise."

"But how would they accomplish it?" Rabin asked.

"By setting the Daughters of the Night upon Oded's warriors and turning those men into thralls," Tamara said softly, and the men turned to her as she came toward them.

"Thralls who would in turn make other thralls until there are no free thoughts and no free men left," Rabin said.

"And once that has happened, our queen will turn on her former ally and relieve him of his freedom, as well," Tamara told them. "She will make him One with the Blood to serve her."

"Or drain him dry as a husk and be done with it," Kaibyn snorted.

"I can see that happening, too. She enjoys tormenting men more than being pleasured by them," Tamara agreed.

Evann-Sin nodded. "So it is the Hell Hag and not the Kebullian madman who is behind this?"

"I believe so," his lady replied. "For now, she needs Oded's help in bringing the tribes of this world under her command. There are too many for the Daughters of the Night to take on. But once he has served his purpose, his usefulness at an end, she will discard him."

"And the entire world will be nothing more than fodder for those Hell Hag leeches!" Rabin grumbled.

"How do you propose we stop this from happening, wench?" Evann-Sin inquired.

"Who cares if Oded is sucked up into that bitch's maw?" Kaibyn chuckled.

"How do we save the world from being enslaved?" Evann-Sin clarified.

"Aye," Rabin said. "I have family and friends I have no desire to see crippled by the yoke that bitch plans for them!"

"We could assassinate Oded," Kaibyn said on a long sigh. "I will gladly take that assignment."

"There are men far worse than Oded," Evann-Sin said. "The Panther, in his way, is far more wicked. If Oded is eliminated, would Lilit not go after another powerful man with whom to ally?" He grimaced. "Would she not go after the Panther?"

"I may be wrong, but I believe the plan has been in motion for some time. She's already chosen her plan of attack," Tamara said. "We were not the only scouting party sent out from Bandar. I know of at least five other teams of Daughters who have been gathering information for our queen."

"That was why you were at the inn?" Evann-Sin asked.

"We were supposed to be on pilgrimage, but in every village where we stopped, one of our group took note of how many people lived there, and what sort of protection, if any, they had. When we returned to Bandar, Sylviana reported the findings to our tribunal scribes." She shrugged. "I thought it an odd assignment but our queen has ever been concerned with how many uninitiated there are."

"Keeping her finger on the enemies' pulse, eh?" Rabin asked.

"To drain it dry when the time comes," Evann-Sin said and shivered. "What, if anything, does the woman fear, Tamara?"

"She's a blood-drinker so she fears being staked out in the broiling sun and left to die," Kaibyn said between clenched teeth. "I know that feeling well!"

"The rays of the sun can kill her?" Evann-Sin inquired.

"She will turn to ash at the first touch of sunlight," Tamara replied.

"That is why the bitches warned her," Evann-Sin grated. "I suppose I should be thankful she did not have the chance to drain my blood."

Tamara shivered. "Being her thrall would have been a fate worse than un-death, warrior."

"We've talked around this long enough," Kaibyn said. "How do we stop Lilit, wench? I have business of my own to tend to."

"First, we need to know how many—if any—of Oded's men have been turned," Tamara replied. "Those who have been will need to be laid to rest for they are but walking dead."

"I am the eyes and ears of our little group," Rabin remarked. "I can handle that part of it. I can go to Kebul and..." As Tamara frowned heavily, the dark man asked what concerned her.

"Did you hear the name of the Daughter who took your life?" Tamara asked.

"Does the name 'Reva' ring true with you, lady?" Rabin countered. At Tamara's nod, he cocked one shoulder. "That was the one."

"How many were with her?"

"Three, four," Rabin answered. He patted his chest as though counting the stab wounds that had slain him. "Three plus the killing blow."

"Then it was Sagira, Oriel and Luka with Reva," Tamara said. "Sylviana, Lanoi and Trista were with me before we met up near the inn. None of those women have ascended to the Blood yet so none of them will be aware of your presence, Rabin. Only those Daughters who are One with the Blood could detect you, and they never leave Bandar."

"And this matters because?" Kaibyn encouraged.

"We must find out just how many teams of my sisters are about and where they are scouting," Tamara replied. "And if any warriors have been turned beyond those at the Kebullian court." She laid a hand on Rabin's shoulder. "Your first task should be to seek out my sisters and report where they have been and where they are going next."

"They won't see me, eh?" Rabin asked.

"No."

"Then why can you?"

Tamara blinked. Her lips parted and she looked to Evann-Sin for the answer.

"I don't know, wench," her lover told her. A frown settled on his handsome face.

"She shouldn't be able to see me, either," Kaibyn mumbled. "I, too, am Undead."

Shaken by her knowledge, Tamara staggered back into the tent, her face blanched white. She started as Evann-Sin entered behind her and flinched as he took her into his arms.

"What is it, beloved?" he asked, his voice tight with concern.

"By all rights I should not be able to see them," she said. "How is it that I do?"

He could feel her trembling against him and lowered his head to place a gentle kiss on her brow. "Perhaps the Magi have a hand in this." When his lady looked up at him, he put a finger under her chin. "I imagine they knew we would need your help."

"Only the Undead can see the Undead," she whispered, her voice breaking as tears threatened to spill from her stricken eyes.

"Then how is it I see them, too?" he asked gently.

Tamara sucked in her breath. "You do, don't you?" At his slow nod, a tremulous smile hovered upon her lips. "And you are not Undead."

"As close to it as I ever want to be, though," he said.

She eased out of his embrace. "I was fearful my life had been taken while I was unconscious," she admitted.

"You are very much alive, wench," Evann-Sin assured her. "I can feel the hot blood throbbing through your veins."

The tent flap slapped aside and Kaibyn entered. "Riders are headed this way," the demon stated. "The darkling has gone to investigate."

"My guess is her Sisters are coming back for her," Evann-Sin suggested. He grinned. "Now they've screwed up their courage."

"You rising out of the night as you did scared them, that's for sure," Tamara agreed. "It took them until now to realize you were no specter."

"Best make ourselves scarce, warrior," Kaibyn said.

"And where do you propose I...?" Evann-Sin started to ask but Kaibyn reached out, took his hand and the two of them vanished in the blink of an eye, leaving Tamara stunned.

Charlotte Boyett-Compo

Chapter Seven

Evann-Sin was disoriented as he fell to the ground. The world was spinning about him and he was violently sick to his stomach. Twisting to his side, he gagged though there was no substance in his belly of which to be relieved. Lying there—straining—he grabbed handfuls of desert sand in an effort to anchor himself to the earth.

"You'll get over it," Kaibyn smirked.

"Wha...what did you do?" Evann-Sin managed to ask.

"I have always had the ability to travel time and space at will once night falls," Kaibyn stated. "Now, I find I can move even faster than I suspect human eyes can follow." He grinned hatefully. "Faster than a human male can comfortably accompany me, apparently."

Brain reeling, completely off-center, Evann-Sin eased himself to a supine position and closed his eyes to still the rampant nausea. His fists still clutched handfuls of sand. He lay there panting, willing his vertigo to leave. "Where are we?" he whispered.

"Just outside the gates of the Akkadian palace," Kaibyn replied. "Your men will see to you."

Evann-Sin opened his eyes. "What?" he croaked. That was fifty miles from where he had been but a moment earlier.

"You take it easy and I'll see to the wench."

Before the warrior could react, there was a harsh rush of wind and he was alone, the shouts of the guards running toward him all but drowning out the laughter floating back from the demon's departure.

Throwing up an arm to shield his eyes from the bright glare of torchlight thrust toward him, Evann-Sin felt hands on him, inspecting him for wounds. Ignoring the worried questions of the Chief Guard, the warrior was helped to his feet. He grunted as his knees gave way beneath him and two guards grabbed him under the armpits to keep him from pitching forward. His legs dragging uselessly behind him, he was unceremoniously carried toward the palace gates.

"Run for the Healer," the Chief Guard ordered. "The Commander has been attacked!"

"Where is Aswad? Where is his horse?" someone shouted. "Has the beast been slain?"

"It looks that way. This is terrible news!" the Chief Guard said.

Evann-Sin did not attempt to correct the Chief Guard. He knew his men would be looking for the culprits who had dumped him outside the palace, but they were more concerned for his stallion than they were for him for the horse had come from the personal stable of the king.

"Even though I, personally, come from the loins of that damned king," Evann-Sin mumbled.

"What is he saying?" a guard asked.

"He is talking out of his head with the pain," the Chief Guard replied.

Pain? Evann-Sin thought. No, it wasn't pain he was feeling but an anger that was growing with every sick breath he took. As his head hung down on his chest and the world was still cantered off to one side, shifting in strange jerky motions, he realized he was sweating profusely and was still so sick to his stomach he had to swallow to keep from gagging. But it was the anger right down to the toes of his dusty boots that kept him from passing out.

He's with my woman! he thought and bile crowded his gullet.

"Lay him down gently!" the Chief Guard hissed and Evann-Sin became aware he was being placed on his own bed. Someone was tugging at his boots while another was bent over him, tugging aside his robe.

"Was he stabbed?"

"Where is his mount?"

"Will he live? Should we call a priest?"

"Who would dare lay hands to the King's High Commander?"

The questions were flying fast and furiously over his head as the warrior tried to focus on first one face and then another as they moved across his line of vision.

"The king!"

Immediate silence sucked all sound from the room and the next face that sailed into Evann-Sin's sight was that of King Numair, one thick black brow cocked as he studied the man he had never acknowledged as his son.

"How seriously is he hurt?" the king asked quietly.

There was a shuffling sound as another face loomed in Evann-Sin's sight. It was the Healer.

"I have not examined him yet, Your Grace, but I see no blood," the Healer replied.

"As soon as you know his status, I want to know!"

The Healer bowed out of Evann-Sin's line of vision with a quick agreement to do as he was told.

Bending further over the prone warrior, the king lowered his voice. "Get well quickly, boy. We have work to do."

There was a light pressure on Evann-Sin's sword arm, a firm but reassuring grip that passed as quickly as it had been applied.

Staring up at the face that retreated from him then disappeared, Evann-Sin released a breath he had not realized he held. Not once in his entire life had the Panther spoken any words directed at him. On previous occasions, commands, suggestions or reprimands concerning him had gone to men standing nearby but never had they been aimed at the warrior.

"Strip him so I may see the extent of his injuries." The Healer's command brought the warrior's mind back to the there and then and he mumbled he was not hurt.

"Keep your dirty hands off me, you pervert!" Evann-Sin snarled, trying to push the Healer's hands away.

"He keeps babbling," a guard stated. "I have yet to understand one word of what he is trying to say."

"I am unhurt," Evann-Sin repeated but his voice was weak and sounded garbled to his own ears. Rather than try again, he gave himself up to the cool wash of air that flowed over his naked body as his clothing was removed then closed his eyes as professional hands prodded here and there.

"There are no wounds but he is very ill," the Healer pronounced.

"Poisoned?" someone asked.

"Of course not," Evann-Sin mumbled.

"That may account for his condition." Snapping his fingers, the Healer ordered a purgative to evacuate his bowels.

"No!" Evann-Sin hissed, trying to get up but his head began a wild spinning that caused his eyes to cross. He felt hands on his shoulders, pushing him down.

"Bring a measure of tincture of chalk," the Healer added. "We must purge his system."

The thought of chalk being poured down his throat brought back the nausea and Evann-Sin twisted violently to the side, gagging.

"Poison," the Healer stated succinctly.

* * * * *

Tamara jumped as a heavy hand fell on her shoulder. She dared not glance around even though she knew — by the musky scent—whose fingers were kneading her shoulder in far too intimate contact.

"So where did he go?" Sagira demanded. "His horse is still here." She pointed to the black beast tied beside Tamara's own bay gelding.

"Tell her he is crazed and is no doubt wandering the desert searching for them," Kaibyn said softly.

Even though she knew her sister could not see the demon, Tamara winced, fearful they could hear his low voice, but the six women facing her did not appear to have heard him speak.

"Why are you so skittish, Tamara?" Luka queried, her eyes narrowed. "You jump at every sound."

"You saw him," Tamara said between clenched teeth. She shrugged off the heavy hand on her shoulder and put distance between her and the demon. "Is that not reason to be edgy?"

The Daughters of the Night exchanged glances. They had already searched the tent, not finding their quarry. The fact that his very costly steed remained troubled them. No warrior would leave behind such a valuable mount.

"Did you talk to him?" Oriel asked.

Tamara shook her head. "He is not in his right mind. The evil you did to him obviously stole his senses."

"But what a way to lose one's mind, eh, wench?" Kaibyn chuckled. "I can think of worse things than being fucked into insanity!"

Ignoring the demon, Tamara told the women the warrior had wandered off into the desert, not even recognizing her.

"Where he will die," Luka pronounced. She looked out across the dark landscape. "Mayhap we should go after him to make sure."

"Mayhap you should leave him the hell alone and let him die in peace!" Tamara snarled. She took a step toward Luka. "Haven't you done enough to the poor man?"

"Easy, now!" Sagira, who had pronounced herself in charge, cautioned. "We do not need to fight over a man, Sisters."

"Especially not an Akkadian," Lanoi commented. "They are of no importance to our plan."

Tamara turned toward the tall woman. "And what plan is that?"

"To have dominion over…" Reva began, but Sagira cut her off.

"When we return to Bandar, you'll learn all about what is planned," Sagira stated. "As a tenth degree adept, you will be made privy to all our queen's tactics."

"Ah, well, she wouldn't have risen to that degree if she had not murdered Sylviana," Luka murmured.

"They fought fair and square, Luka," Sagira admonished her half-sister. "Tamara proved herself a better woman than your friend."

Luka cast Tamara a hateful glance but said nothing more.

"That one is your enemy, wench," Kaibyn warned. "Best keep a close watch on her."

"I will," Tamara said beneath her breath.

"You will what?" Sagira inquired, her forehead crinkled.

"I will wait to hear what plan our queen has engineered," Tamara responded. She steeled herself not to react as the demon strolled casually over to the women and began eying them up and down.

"This one is a bit hefty in the hips but then there's more flesh to pinch," he said and reached out to do just that to Reva's broad ass.

"Ow!" Reva screeched, putting a hand to her plump butt. "Something bit me!"

Tamara bit her lips to keep from laughing. She covered her mouth with her hand.

Lanoi jumped, grabbing her arm where a vicious pain had suddenly twisted her flesh. "That hurt!"

Oriel rubbed vigorously at her face, swatting away an invisible touch that had lightly slapped against her cheek. "Stop it!" she ordered.

Luka's head jerked back as though someone had yanked brutally on her long hair. She fell backwards, landing on her rear end.

"I'd snatch her baldheaded for you, wench, but I'll save that pleasure for you," Kaibyn quipped.

"What is this?" Sagira asked in a fearful voice, her head swiveling side-to-side as she looked for the unseen assailant that was suddenly plaguing her Sisters.

"Demons," Trista spoke up for the first time. "There are demons about!"

"Mount up!" Tamara suggested. "Let us be away from this accursed place!" She headed for her horse, casting Kaibyn an amused look as she went.

Every woman save Tamara was being assaulted by unseen beings moving amongst them. Too busy with trying to get away from the physical attack, the women barely noticed Tamara mounting her horse.

"I'll take this brute with me," Tamara called out. Already Kaibyn was seated on Evann-Sin's huge black destrier. "I claim him as my right since Sylviana slew my would-have-been lover!"

The Daughters of the Night rushed to their own mounts, leaving behind the invisible terrors that had bruised their flesh. As they galloped away—fast on the heels of Tamara's racing steed—they glanced back at the tent where demons had come out of nowhere to torment them.

"That was my tent," Oriel complained as she lashed the flanks of her mount.

"You want it," Luka told her. "You go back for it!"

Sagira whipped her own horse until the beast was running alongside Tamara's. "You were untouched!" she accused.

Tamara turned her head as the wind tore at her hair. "Mayhap it was the Akkadian come back to get even," she shouted. "He was the son of the Panther, you know."

All the color drained from Sagira's face. She could do no more than stare at Tamara, so stunned at such news she allowed her mount to fall behind Tamara's.

"I don't think that piece of information set well with the bitch," Kaibyn remarked.

"Good," Tamara said in a normal tone of voice, knowing the demon would hear despite the thundering of their horses' hooves and the rush of the wind coming at them. She glanced at Luka and Oriel as they raced by, their heels drumming into the flanks of their mounts in order to put distance between themselves and the place where hidden powers had attacked them.

One by one, the other horses passed Tamara's until she was a hundred yards or so behind her Sisters.

"Are you spurring on their mounts, demon?" Tamara asked, amusement rife in her voice.

"Let them outdistance us, wench," Kaibyn advised and reached over to grab the reins of Tamara's horse.

Annoyed that the demon would take such a liberty, Tamara was about to admonish him but in the next instant, they were no longer galloping over the desert sands and were sitting astride their mounts at an oasis she did not recognize.

Blinking to rid her head of the strange spinning feeling that made her a bit nauseous, she reeled in the saddle only to feel the demon's hand steadying her.

"Easy, wench," he said and in the next instant, she was lying cradled in his arms as he lifted her down from her horse.

Though at first glance the oasis was barren of all but a few sweeping date palms, glistening water from a wide pond, and soft-looking sands, a large multicolored tent suddenly appeared.

Unable to speak for the nausea that welled in her throat, Tamara felt herself being carried into the tent and was immediately assailed with the sweet scent of gardenia and a pleasant warmth leeching from a fire in a glowing brazier. As she was laid down on a soft, plump mattress she knew must be stuffed with goose down, she stared into Kaibyn Zafeyr's dark eyes.

"The feeling will pass, Sweeting," Kaibyn said gently.

Knowing she had been transported in much the same way Evann-Sin had, Tamara wondered if her lover had felt the same disorientation.

"Aye," Kaibyn said, reading her thoughts. "You will get used to it."

"Will he?" she couldn't help but ask.

Kaibyn shrugged as he stretched out besides her, turning to lie on his side and look at her. "If he doesn't get too prickish with me, he will."

Tamara swallowed, closing her eyes. The strange feeling was passing. Even though she was alarmed at what the demon had done, she could see the advantages of such immediate travel.

"Where did you take him?" she asked, putting a hand to her forehead.

"Just outside the gates of the Akkadian palace," Kaibyn replied as he took her hand. "I waited until his men found him. He's being taken care of, wench."

Firmly, Tamara removed her hand from his grip. "I belong to Riel Evann-Sin, demon."

"Kaibyn," the demon said on a long sigh. "My name is Kaibyn."

She opened her eyes and looked over at him. "Kaibyn," she repeated but when his eyes lit, she put steel into her voice. "I belong to him."

Kaibyn's forehead puckered for a moment as he looked deeply into her amethyst gaze. When he found what he searched for, he sighed again. "You can't stop a man from trying, Sweeting."

"There is a woman for you somewhere," she said. "But it isn't me."

Kaibyn shrugged. "Things change."

Tamara wanted *things* straight between them so against her better judgment she sat up. The dizziness was not as bad as at first but the nausea still lurked in her throat. She swallowed, willing it to pass.

"We've time to discuss this," Kaibyn reminded her.

"Nay," she insisted. "We will discuss it now."

Kaibyn listened as she told him how she felt about the Akkadian warrior. There was a pleasant, respectful look upon his handsome face and he nodded in all the appropriate places, murmuring his agreement to her assertions that she would never love another man save Riel Evann-Sin. He assured her he would behave, would not attempt to seduce her, while actively plotting how he could take her away from the warrior.

"Do you understand?" she asked.

"I do," he said, putting a hand to his chest. "And I swear I will do nothing that will ever cause you the first moment's hurt, Sweeting."

"Then bring Evann-Sin back to me," she said then added, "Now."

"At this moment, he is being taken care of by his father's Healer," Kaibyn informed her. "If I should journey there and grab him up, he will have one helluva time explaining it."

Tamara knew that was true. As much as she wanted to be with her lover, he was many miles away. Despite the demon's assurances he would leave her alone, she didn't trust him.

"Then where is Rabin?"

The mentioning of the darkling put a harsh frown on the demon's face. "Where he was when the Hell Hags came back to your encampment," he replied. "He circled behind them and was waiting not far away when they left. He is following them at a safe distance. They can't see him but they can see a riderless horse following them." He chuckled. "They no doubt think it hell-sent."

"Go fetch Rabin, then," Tamara ordered. "There are things that need to be done."

Kaibyn groaned. "You don't want to be alone with me. Is that it?"

"Aye," she answered truthfully.

One moment he was lying beside her, the next he was seated across the tent, probing at the fire with a poker. He didn't look at her but kept his attention on the flames in the brazier. "He's outside," he said.

Rabin entered the tent at that moment, staggering just a little as he sat down on a thick cushion. He cast the demon an angry look. "Don't do that again," he warned.

Kaibyn clucked his tongue. "You men are such babies." He cocked an eyebrow at the dark man. "Are you going to allow me to do what you can't?"

Narrowing his eyes dangerously, Rabin squatted before the fire. "I find my hearing has vastly improved, wench," he told Tamara and ignoring the demon's challenge. "I heard one of the Hell Hags say Kebul is firmly entrenched. Do you think that means Kebul and its inhabitants are now under Lilit's spell?"

Kaibyn looked up from the fire. "If Kebul is entrenched, does that mean Dakhla and her bitches are now blood-drinkers?"

Tamara nodded slowly, disturbed by Rabin's news. "I believe so, Lord Kaibyn."

The demon grinned. "Well, now. That is good to hear."

"Why?" Tamara questioned.

"I wasn't planning on killing Dakhla, but rather making her suffer for what she did to me. But if she is no longer human, we will need to kill her. Correct?"

"To put her soul to rest, aye," Tamara agreed.

"And one way to kill a vampire is to stake it out in the sun," Kaibyn reminded them.

"Just as you were staked, eh?" Rabin asked.

"Tit for tat," Kaibyn replied with a chuckle then his eyes clouded. "Will that also mean my beloved Lilabet is now one of those things?"

"If she's been turned," Tamara replied. "And if the court is firmly entrenched as Rabin has reported, no one will be left that is entirely human."

"None?"

"It is highly doubtful, Kaibyn," Tamara answered. "I would think…"

One moment the demon was sitting beside the fire, the next a rush of wind blew across Tamara's cheeks and Kaibyn was gone.

"Rude bastard," Rabin remarked. His forehead crinkled. "Do you think I could learn to…?"

Tamara's mouth dropped open as Rabin disappeared before her eyes.

Chapter Eight

Queen Lilabet was hunkered down as close to the wall as she could press her pregnant body. Her hands were clapped over her mouth to stifle the scream that threatened to escape at any moment. Beside her, her last surviving Lady-in-Waiting was trembling so violently, the queen could hear the woman's teeth clicking together. The two were squatting over a small pool of their own urine—released when a hulking warrior had shuffled aimlessly by their position, his neck gaping open from multiple bite wounds.

The dark corridor was silent now, the last of the screams and skirls of metal as soldiers fought to save their own lives stilled as the day neared its birthing and the ghastly inhabitants of Kebul slithered into whatever hidey-holes they could find to escape the rays of the sun. Here, beneath the palace, Lilabet knew they would not be safe for the darkness was their enemy.

When the sounds of the attack came, palace guards had come to barricade the doors to the seraglio. As it became apparent the palace would fall, word was passed to Fareeq, the Head Eunuch, to get the women to safety. The queen and her women fled the seraglio, following close behind the Head Eunuch as he led them—some forty-five strong—through the curving stone corridors of the palace and into the vast underground cavern that would see them safely outside and to the docks. Hopefully there would be a ship waiting to take them to Akkadia.

But the invaders had been waiting in the cavern and the women were attacked, scattering to the four winds as glassy-eyed warriors attacked like scavenging beasts. The queen and two of her ladies-in-waiting had stumbled through an open door and into the corridor where they now hid. Where the second woman had disappeared to was anyone's guess.

Easing her hand from her mouth, Lilabet reached out a shaky hand to touch the woman beside her. Without a word, both women got quietly to their feet, the lady-in-waiting helping her queen to stand. Silently, they eased down the corridor, careful not to make a sound.

It was damp and dank in the corridor and the horrid stench of spilled blood wafted over them. The floor was slick beneath their sandals, sticky between their toes as they waded ankle-deep through the congealing fluid. Broken bodies littered the pathway and the women stepped gingerly over the obstacles, knowing well that come the night, the dead would begin to stir.

A startled moan came from the woman at her side, and Lilabet looked to where she was pointing. Beneath the sputtering light of a dying torch, the sight was a grisly one.

Dead eyes wide, mouth open in a silent scream, Lady Dakhla was sprawled like a broken doll, her neck twisted, the flesh hanging in tatters where fangs had ripped eagerly into her throat. Lying near her was Lilabet's daughter, Meritaten.

Meritaten had fared no better than her best friend Dakhla. Her gown had been ripped down to her waist and her breasts were bloody with puncture wounds.

The queen would have knelt beside her child, but her lady-in-waiting grabbed her arm and tried to pull her forward, away from the horrific find. When Lilabet resisted, her companion hissed beneath her breath and laid a firm hand on the protruding mound of the queen's belly. The reminder of her unborn child stiffened Lilabet's resolve and she nodded curtly.

Though she was loath to leave her daughter without one last touch, Lilabet understood the urgency of quitting the corridor and making their way into the bright sunlight. The door to the outside was still fifty feet away and that end of the corridor was devoid of light save the thin sliver of illumination that marked the portal's header.

Stumbling over a corpse, Lilabet would have fallen had not her lady-in-waiting reached out to steady her. Something squishy—spongy and slick—coated the bottom of the queen's sandal and she had to force herself not to retch. In her mind's eye, she envisioned a human organ clinging to her foot and her bile grew hot and cloying in her throat.

From behind the women, a harsh rush of hot air buffeted their retreat and each turned, expecting a cadaver to loom up out of the darkness, but when Lilabet recognized her lover, Kaibyn Zafeyr, she could not stop the shriek of hopelessness that overcame her.

"Nay, Lady!" Kaibyn told her, holding his hand out in entreaty. "I am not one of them!"

Relieved that the man she had come to love so desperately—and rely upon so thoroughly—was untainted by the blood-drinkers, the queen threw herself into his arms.

"Oh, Kiabyn!" she cried, clinging to him. "Take us from this evil place!"

"Hold to me," he said, soothing her back with his strong hand. "I will place you beyond danger."

"Karmaria!" Lilabet cried out, reaching a hand toward her Lady-in-Waiting.

"Milady, what are you doing?" the lady-in-waiting cried, stepping back. "Why do you call the demon?"

Kaibyn snagged the other woman's arm and in the blink of an eye, the three supernaturally fled the dark corridor, spinning like dervishes into the Void between space and time.

* * * * *

Evann-Sin was as weak as a newborn, unable to stop the Healer from pouring vile concoctions down his throat and pumping them into his helpless body. By the time the man was finished with him and had declared he would live, the warrior was madder and sicker than he could ever remember being in his thirty-odd years. Clinging to the edge of the mattress as the

Healer's helper braced him so he could take a sip of cool water, Evann-Sin thought of every conceivable agony he could visit upon the demon and then some.

"Who attacked you, boy?"

Hearing his father's gruff voice—the commanding tones of the Akkadian King—Evann-Sin looked past the Healer's helper. Standing at the door to the room with his bodyguards flanking him, the Panther was an imposing sight. His dark eyes were sharp, his lips pursed in anger and his hands clenched into fists at his side.

"Who dared harm you?" King Numair demanded.

"I am unharmed, Majesty," Evann-Sin stated. "Lest I was until your Healer took it upon himself to torture me."

The Panther advanced into the room. "Where is your horse?"

Sighing heavily, for he knew the beast's safety was of more import than his own, Evann-Sin assured his king the mount was in good hands.

"And in whose hands is the steed?"

"My lady's," Evann-Sin said and realized he had said the wrong thing for his king's eyes narrowed and a muscle jumped in the older man's lean jaw.

"What lady is that, Riel?" the king queried. "I was not aware you had a mate."

Pushing himself up in the bed with the intention of getting out of it, Evann-Sin realized his head was still spinning, his stomach queasy, and he stilled, swallowing against the bitter bile that loped up his throat at the movement.

"What is the woman's name, boy?" the Panther asked. "How did you come to know her?"

"Tamara Nabril," Evann-Sin managed to say. "We met in Nonica."

"Nabril? That is not an Akkadian name," his king snapped. "From where does this female come?"

Knowing he dared not lie, Evann-Sin mumbled that the woman he had chosen as his own was from Bandar.

King Numair's eyes widened and his lips parted. Among those who were witness to the scene between father and son, one bodyguard would swear on his life he saw the thick white mane of hair on the king's head stand straight up like an angry porcupine's quills.

"A Hell Hag?" the Panther asked in a whisper that hinted at his shock.

Evann-Sin flinched but he raised his chin and met his king's unwavering stare. "Some would call her such but she is the woman I love and she engaged in battle the woman who harmed me and took her life."

The king blinked. With his mouth still hanging open, he cocked his head to one side as though he doubted what he had heard. Lifting a hand to his head, he slapped the palm against his right ear three times then asked the warrior to repeat what he had just said.

Acutely conscious of the other four men in the room, Evann-Sin related what had happened at the inn in Nonica then told his king of Rabin's funeral. He was somewhat surprised to see a passing glint of grief in the Panther's dark eyes.

"I liked the dark man," was all King Numair said then nodded for Evann-Sin to continue.

"I realized I was being followed after I left the funeral," the warrior said, very uneasy about telling the whole of it. "I was drinking water at an oasis when I was hit from behind and rendered unconscious."

The Panther held up a hand. "You did not sense danger, boy?" he wanted clarified.

"I sensed it, Your Majesty, but it came before I could stop it."

Staring intently at his son, King Numair folded his arms over a thick, barrel-like chest. "Go on."

"I woke to find myself tied spread-eagled to the ground," Evann-Sin said, looking away from that intense gaze.

"It was the Hell Hags who attacked you," the king stated.

"Aye, Your Majesty," Evann-Sin mumbled.

"They raped you."

Evann-Sin winced. "Aye," he answered almost inaudibly.

Silence settled on the room. The king's two bodyguards stood staring down at the floor and the Healer's helper was looking at the coverlet over the warrior's feet. As the stillness lingered on, Evann-Sin raised his head and looked up into the steady eyes of his king. Expecting to see disgust, shame or fury flashing from the Panther's heavily lined face he was surprised to see the shimmer of tears.

"And this woman," he heard the king say. "This Tamara? She was not among those who abused you."

"Nay, Majesty," Evann-Sin replied.

"She fought for your honor?"

Nodding because he could not speak past the lump that was lodged in his throat, Evann-Sin waited for the infamous temper of the Panther to explode.

"Hand-to-hand?" the king asked.

"Aye, Your Majesty."

"I've heard the Hell Hags are almost as good at warfare as the Amazeens," King Numair stated.

"I did not see the battle but I saw the aftermath," Evann-Sin said. "Tamara was very angry."

"No doubt," the king said. "They took what she considered hers."

Forging his gaze with his king's, Evann-Sin acknowledged that he was hers and she was his.

"So how did you get here?" the Panther asked. "Minus your steed and as sick as a dog who has lunched on rancid meat?"

The mental picture made Evann-Sin's mouth water and he squeezed his eyes shut to keep the nausea at bay. Digging his fingers into the sheet, he told his king of meeting the Magi—of encountering Kaibyn Zafeyr and the resurrection of Rabin Jaspyre.

"He's alive?" the king asked, his eyes wide.

"He's Undead," Evann-Sin clarified. "Zafeyr is a demon and it was…"

Once more the Panther slapped his ear with his palm. He shook his head to clear it then told his son to repeat what he had just said.

"He is a demon," Evann-Sin stated. "It was he who transported me here, but I have no idea how he accomplished the feat. When I found out, I…"

"First you are raped by a band of Hell Hags then you are fought over by two women warriors. Your best friend dies but though the dark man is dead, yet he is not dead," the king said. "You meet a demon who brought you here by supernatural means, conveyed to the palace on the wings of this demon and you leave your horse with a woman you barely know!" He squinted. "Does that about cover it, Riel?"

"You left out the Magi," Evann-Sin said quietly. "And I didn't leave Aswad. I was jerked up by that demon and delivered here so no doubt he can attempt to seduce my woman."

Throwing his hands into the air, the king looked to the heavens. "Have you any notion how priceless that steed is to me, boy?"

"I know he's more priceless than my life is to you," Evann-Sin replied, hurt apparent in his voice. As soon as the words left his lips, he wished he could snatch them back.

The Panther slowly lowered his head. His dark brown gaze went unerringly to his son's pale face and held. For the space of a full minute, nothing was said—the room was as devoid of sound as a grave. No one moved. Then King Numair told the other men to leave the room.

Uneasy at leaving their king unprotected, the bodyguards hesitated though the Healer's helper made quick work of departing. They looked at one another—concern puckering their foreheads—until they were ordered out in a tone that brooked no denial. Hurrying to do their king's bidding, they bumped into one another as they attempted to get out the door at the same time.

"And close the door behind you!" the king ordered.

When the portal was pulled shut and silence once more reigned, King Numair broke eye contact with his son and looked around him. Spying a chair, he went to it, grabbed the back and swung it around to stand beside Evann-Sin's bed. He straddled the seat and sat—his knees braced apart, and leaned forward with his forearms on his thighs.

"I don't know where you got the notion your life is of little value to me, Riel, but let me disabuse you of that impression," the Panther stated. His deep voice was devoid of inflection though his face was set and his eyes hard.

"Your Majesty, I…" Evann-Sin began but his father held up a hand.

"For once," the king grated. "For *once* will you call me Papa?"

Shocked at the request, Evann-Sin could only stare at the man sitting at his bedside. It was hard enough for him to recline there on the bed with his king's head lower than his own but to have such an appeal thrown at him was staggering.

"I have acknowledged you as my son," King Numair stated. "Many times over have I acknowledged you to my men."

"Yet never to me," the warrior interrupted.

As though he had not heard Evann-Sin, the king continued. "I have spoken often of how proud I am of you, and all that you have accomplished."

"Yet never once said as much to me."

The Panther drew in a long breath then exhaled slowly as though he were trying to calm his infamously raging temper with the release of his breath.

"How many fights did you have as a boy, Riel?" he countered. "How many bruises visited upon you for being the son of a king?"

"More than I care to remember," Evann-Sin admitted.

"And how many more cuts and bruises do you think you would have had if I had shown my affection for you?"

King Numair had two legitimate sons and three legitimate daughters by his marriage to Queen Hessa of Inaya. The oldest of the boys was thirteen and the youngest nine. The daughters were born first and the youngest had married just the year before at the age of nineteen. The two older daughters had given the Panther seven grandchildren between them.

"I was but a boy, myself, when you came along," the Panther said. "Not much older than Haytham is now." He snorted. "What does a fourteen-year-old boy know about being a father?"

"You knew enough to get my mother with child," Evann-Sin accused.

"Ah, Anbar," the king said wistfully, and his smile was sad. "Your mother was the gentlest of creatures and as beautiful as her name was sweet."

"I wouldn't know," the warrior said.

Memories of the woman-child he had loved so dearly came back to haunt King Numair. He had been there when she had brought Evann-Sin into the world, and had held her as her life's blood drained away, the Healers unable to save her.

"She would have been just as proud of you as I am."

Watching a single tear slide slowly down the king's face mesmerized Evann-Sin. He stared at the crystal drop until it disappeared into a deep crease on the older man's cheek.

"The kingdom will go to Shafiq when I leave this world and we both know the boy will need your counsel at every turn. He is so tenderhearted he would make all the wrong decisions or none at all," the king said. He shrugged. "Haytham would make a better ruler but being second-born the chances are slim he will ever hold the scepter."

Silence reigned once more then the Panther seemed to shake himself mentally. He released a heavy breath, slapped his knees with his palms and fused his gaze with Evann-Sin's.

"You are my son and I have never denied that. If it were possible to make you my heir, I would do so but that will never happen. As for caring more for a mere animal than I do for you that is so much shit piled on a stone. I don't know who told you such an evil thing but it is not true."

Holding his father's stare, Evann-Sin felt his heart thundering in his chest. Such an admission was something he had never dreamed of hearing. He had grown up thinking the man before him refused to acknowledge him. The chip had grown to a boulder on his shoulder and had become harder to bear over the years. Now, he could feel it sliding away and the relieving of the pressure felt good.

"That's not to say I am blasé about the welfare and safety of your steed, Riel," the king growled, shaking a finger at his son. "Are you sure he is safe with this Tamara?"

A smile tugged at Evann-Sin's lips. "As safe as I would be, Your..."

"Papa," the king corrected, his head cocked to one side in admonishment.

"Majesty, I can not," the warrior whispered. "I..."

"You are not proud to be my son?" the Panther demanded.

Evann-Sin's eyes widened. "I am honored to be your son!"

"Honored but not proud?"

"Honored and proud!"

"Then do as I ask and call me Papa."

Evann-Sin squirmed in the bed. Such a request was more command than appeal. It would be hard to break a thirty-five-year-old habit and it did not feel right to the warrior. He could not make himself say the word for it felt disrespectful, almost treasonous to him. His cheeks were stained crimson.

"Oh, all right," King Numair sighed. "I'll not make you say it but perhaps one day you will want to."

Once more silence settled over the room. The two men glanced at one another but neither knew what else to say. At last, it was Evann-Sin who spoke.

"There is evil afoot in Kebul," he said.

"There is always evil afoot in Kebul," the king snorted. "Oded is an ass."

"An ass who is in concert with Queen Lilit of Bandar."

The wrinkles in King Numair's forehead grew deeper as he frowned sharply. "What are those two up to together?"

"Making slaves of the rest of us," Evann-Sin replied. "And I mean to keep them from succeeding."

* * * * *

Queen Lilabet closed her eyes as quickly as she opened them for the room was spinning around her violently. She was lying upon a thick mattress with only a thin shift between her and the light coverlet covering her. Her hand was being tightly held in Kaibyn's but nevertheless, she felt as though should he let go, she would go flying out the window.

"Where am I?" she asked.

"We are at the inn in Nonika," Kaibyn answered. "I fetched the others while you slept."

Putting a hand to her head, the queen could not remember anything past the nightmarish trip down the corridor at Kebul.

"Where is Karmaria?"

"Holding fast to the headboard of her cot in the next room. Tamara is seeing to her."

Risking a glance at her lover, Lilabet opened her eyes though the room still spun crazily around her. "Who is Tamara?"

"She is the Akkadian's woman," Kaibyn answered through clenched teeth.

"You said others," Lilabet muttered.

"There is a darkling here, as well, but he is of no consequence. He is merely a servant to the Akkadian. Do not concern yourself with him."

The queen tried to push herself up but the vertigo was too great. She slumped back on the bed with an unladylike grunt. "By the Prophet, Kaibyn, you smell," she told him. "What have you gotten into?"

A pained look passed over the demon's handsome face, and he lifted his arm to sniff at his armpit. He could smell nothing different about his person. He had to make haste to find cologne of some kind to mask the stench.

"Lie quietly, Lady, and I will see to that situation," Kaibyn replied with a grimace.

"As though I could do anything save lie quietly," Lilabet muttered. She felt the wind of the demon's passing but did not open her eyes.

Kaibyn came to rest in a grotto. Quickly, he shed his clothing and plunged through the placid depths of the grotto's milky-white waters. He swam underwater for a spell then surfaced to wade over to the shallows and stand waist-deep while he used his hands to scrub vigorously at his flesh. Though he could tell no difference in his body odor when he waded out of the water, he suspected there might not be a change in his aroma. With another blink of his golden eyes, he landed in a bakery and went in search of cinnamon oil. Crinkling his nose, he splashed a copious amount of the liquid over his bare chest and arms, under his arms and over the rippled ridges of his belly and into the thick curls at the juncture of his thighs. Taking the rest of the oil with him, he flew back to the grotto, got dressed then hastened to rejoin the queen.

Lilabet turned her head as her lover materialized in the room. She inhaled the overpowering scent of cinnamon and sighed. "Much better, Kai. Much, much better."

The demon went to her bed and sat down beside her. "No more stench?" he inquired, his forehead puckered.

"No," she answered. "You have a most pleasant smell, my love."

Before the lady could protest, Kaibyn shed his clothes and climbed in bed beside her, reaching out to take her into his arms. Her supple body gave instant rise to a portion of his anatomy and he hoped she would acquiesce to soothing him.

"My husband, I fear, is dead, Kai," Lilabet whispered, snuggling close to her lover and reaching her hand down to lay her palm against his thigh.

"I am loath to tell you, Lady, but I fear Undead is more like it," he told her.

Despite the jerky sensations of the room canting about her, the queen opened her eyes, tilted her head back and looked at Kaibyn. "What mean you *Undead*?"

Kaibyn put his hand on her head and stroked her hair. "You have heard tales of the witches of Bandar?"

"The Hell Hags?" Lilabet asked with a shiver. "Aye. What of them?"

"Their queen, Lilit, formed a pact with your husband and now the entire of Kebul is under thrall to the witches," he explained. "I would think King Oded is as much under Lilit's power as are the common folk."

"For what purpose, Kai?" she asked.

"To turn the world into Lilit's slave pen, milady."

Lilabet's eyes widened. "It is that far-reached, this plan of hers?"

"It will be unless I can stop her," Kaibyn said. "Well, with some help from the coalition I have formed."

"Oh, Kaibyn. This greatly distresses me," the queen said. "What will I do? Where will I go? Who will take care of me? I have a child growing inside me to consider."

Kaibyn increased his hold on the lady and dipped his head so he could press a light kiss on her cheek. "You have nothing to worry, my love," he said. "Your safety is of the most import to me, and I would give my life to keep you safe." He laid his hand on her belly. "I will protect the child, as well."

"Dahkla is dead," she said. "You were blood-sworn to her."

Kaibyn knew what was coming and also knew it would be best if he broached the subject, making himself the leader of the situation. "I will swear to you — in blood if you require it — that I will be your protector for now and until the end of your days. If you doubt me…"

"I would have you all to myself this time, Kaibyn," she said, staring into his eyes. "I do not want to ever share you again."

Though he sighed inwardly, Kaibyn agreed. He wanted Tamara but for the time being she was out of his reach. Such — he thought — would not always be the case and Lilabet was in the sixth decade of her life and might not live that many more years.

From out of nowhere, an intricately carved dagger appeared, its double-edged blade thick with ancient runic lettering. The black jade handle was encrusted with blood-red rubies. Kaibyn removed his arm from beneath Lilabet's head and sat up. Without a word, he drew the sharp edge of the blade across the flesh of his left forearm. He took Lilabet's left palm in his hand and held it under his arm.

"I pledge in my own blood," he said, allowing a few drops to drip into her palm. "I will be yours until the end of your days."

"Keeping only unto me," the queen wanted clarified.

Kaibyn winced. "Keeping only unto you until the end of your days."

"Forsaking all others."

"Aye," he sighed. "Forsaking all others until the end of your days."

Seemingly satisfied with the blood oath, Lilabet used her bloody hand to reach up for her lover's head. She brought his mouth down to hers to seal their bargain.

Vanquishing the ceremonial dagger in his grip, Kaibyn put his energy into the kiss. He slipped his tongue between the queen's lips and probed deeply. He claimed her breast, kneading the fullness beneath the thin shift. The pad of his thumb flicked over the swollen nipple and worked it to a hard little nub then scraped the tender flesh with his thumbnail.

Lilabet groaned as her lover bit her lower lip lightly. His hot tongue slid over her upper lip before delving quickly into her mouth then away.

"Kaibyn!" she protested, but before she could bid him continue kissing her, his mouth dragged down her neck and that wicked tongue of his stabbed at the hollow of her throat. She threaded her fingers through his thick hair and held his mouth to her neck, reveling in the feel of his tongue's wet heat.

Kaibyn was an expert in the seduction of women. He knew every nuance of lovemaking and spent hours on foreplay that would elevate a female from total disinterest in the sexual act to complete, unbridled abandon. His mouth, his hands, the mighty tool between his legs had been trained to give ultimate pleasure. He wielded that power like any artist and set about to bring Lilabet to the heights of uncontrollable pleasure.

The queen did not protest when her shift was ripped from her aching body. Already a thin sheen of moisture clung to her flesh and her love nest was slick. She hated how her distended belly must look and crossed her arms over it.

"Nay, Sweeting," Kaibyn whispered. "Every inch of you is as lovely as a spring morn." He lowered his head and placed a light kiss on the protrusion of her navel, circling it with his tongue.

The demon had made love to many pregnant women over the years, and he had taken superb care to see they were thoroughly satiated when he was through. His hands would be infinitely gentle, his mouth hotly effective. Through no fault of his would he ever leave a lady wanting.

Sliding his hand down Lilabet's quivering thigh, he rested the palm gently against the core of her. He smiled, capturing her eyes with his and he tenderly rubbed the dampness.

"I crave you, Kaibyn," the queen said in a husky voice.

"And I will not leave you in need, milady."

He pulled his hand upward until the tip of his middle finger touched the pearl of her love mound. Lightly he stroked the dewy pebble with long upward pulls that went from the base of her opening to the hood, easing back that tiny wrinkle of flesh in order to heighten the sensation.

Lilabet reached above her and took hold of the brass swirls of the headboard. She bit her lip, closing her eyes to the exquisite feelings flooding her lower belly. She squirmed on the bed and at his nudging, opened her thighs a little more.

"So lovely," he said as he moved lower on the bed until his cheek was pressed against the curve of her hip. "Such an exciting aroma coming from your sex."

The queen felt a tremor go through her and her womb tightened at his words. She could feel her vagina oozing love juice and wished her lover would taste her.

Intercepting the thought, Kaibyn dipped his finger gently into her slit and swirled it ever so softly inside her, smiling as Lilabet arched her hips upward. Looking up at her, once more holding her gaze, he removed his finger and placed it in his mouth, sucking the slick fluid from his flesh. He drew on the digit then took it from his mouth and held it under his nose. He inhaled deeply.

"So sweet," he told her. "So sweet and so delicious."

Lilabet groaned and writhed.

"Let me pleasure you, milady," the demon whispered.

He cupped her sex once more then slid his middle finger inside her. His lips, he placed upon her clit and delicately suckled the little nub. Flicking his tongue across the swollen root, he moved his middle finger in and out of her slit very slowly.

"Ah, Kaibyn!" Lilabet sighed. "You are a handsome devil, you are, but one who knows how to soothe a lady's needs."

Kaibyn looked up. "You see me, don't you, milady?"

"Of course, I see you, Kai," the queen said and wiggled, wanting his ministrations to continue. "Unfortunately, I am beginning to smell you again, as well." She wrinkled her nose.

"Just as Tamara sees both Rabin and me," he muttered.

"Why wouldn't I see you, beloved?" his lady asked. She pushed his head down to her nether region and arched her pelvic upward to accommodate his wicked mouth.

Forcing a portion of his mind to the task at hand, the demon's thoughts were racing. How was it, he wondered, that Lilabet could see him yet he was sure the silly Karmaria had not? The lady-in-waiting had shrieked bloody murder when he had dropped her in the room next door, staring wildly about her, terrified of what she apparently could not see. As the woman stumbled about the room in a blind panic, he had been forced to bring Tamara to her to quiet the stupid chit.

"Stop doing that!" Tamara had hissed, her lovely face a rather strange shade of green as she tried to acclimatize herself to the rapid transportation across time and space. "Rabin! Where is Rabin?"

Thus the darkling, too, had been brought to Nonica.

The muscles of Lilabet's vagina rippled around Kaibyn's finger and he held it still inside her as she climaxed. Her clit was a hard little pebble against his tongue as he laved it one last time, grimacing a bit as the queen's fingers pulled at his hair.

It was a known fact that Lilabet loved to talk after consummating the act and Kaibyn had no desire to do so. He slid up in the bed and put his hand over her eyes.

"Sleep, milady," he commanded and when he removed his hand, the queen had sunk deep into the arms of sleep—where she would remain until he bid her wake. He bent over and placed a light kiss on her cheek then scooted out of the bed.

Tamara glanced up as the door to Karmaria's room opened and she frowned. "Don't you ever knock?"

"Who came in?" Karmaria asked, her head swiveling from side to side. "I don't see anyone."

"If she can't see me, she can't hear me, either," Kaibyn grunted.

"What is that vile odor?" Karmaria asked, fanning the air.

"It's good that she can't. You nearly scared this poor girl to an early grave when you flew her to this place."

"W-who are you talking to?" the lady-in-waiting asked. Her eyes were wide, her face as white as chalk. "I d-don't see anyone!"

Striding quickly to the bed, Kaibyn placed a hand over Karmaria's face, wincing as her scream was cut off in mid-vibrato.

"Sleep, bitch!" he hissed. "You have an annoying voice!"

The lady-in-waiting slumped against the pillow, sound asleep.

"Well, she might not see or hear you but she can obviously feel your touch and smell you," Tamara said.

"All women can feel my touch, wench." Kaibyn bragged, ignoring her other comment.

Tamara rolled her eyes. "Is the queen asleep, too?"

"I thought it best until I can get this settled."

"Get what settled?"

Kaibyn put his hands on his hips and stared at her. "How is it Lilabet can see me?"

Tamara frowned. "How would I know?"

"Is she turned that she can see me?"

"Does she appear turned?"

Kaibyn shook his head. "Nay and there are no marks on her that I could see. I don't believe the vampires got to her." He nodded at the sleeping lady-in-waiting. "Did you find marks on that one?"

"She hasn't been touched. That was the first thing I checked once I got over my dizziness. Thank the Prophetess it didn't take too long this time."

"The more often you travel in that fashion, the easier it will become until you will no longer feel the dizziness," Kaibyn told her.

Tamara narrowed her eyes. "I have no intention of traveling like that again, Kaibyn!"

Kaibyn waved a dismissive hand. "That is of no import right now. My concern is with Lilabet being able to see me."

"What was it Riel said about Tamara being able to see us?" Rabin asked.

Tamara and Kaibyn turned to find the dark man leaning nonchalantly against the doorjamb.

"He said he could see you, too," Tamara answered.

"He also said he thought the Magi had a hand is this," Kaibyn added. "I think he might be right because I think we will need Lilabet's help if we are to put things to rights in Kebul."

"And wherever else my sisters have ventured," Tamara put in. She turned her gaze to Rabin. "Are you concerned about this ability for some to see us, Rabin?"

Rabin ducked his head. "Do you think my lady will be able to see me?" When his companion's did not answer, he lifted his head.

Tamara went to the dark man and laid a hand on his arm. "Your lady-wife believes you dead, Rabin."

"I am." Rabin sighed deeply. "And shall remain so."

"So?" Kaibyn asked.

"Perhaps he should go to her and see whether she can see him or not," Kaibyn suggested.

"What if she can't?" Rabin asked quietly.

"What if she can?" Kaibyn countered. "How will it affect her? You must think of that."

Rabin flinched. "Aye, I have thought of that but I love my woman. I miss her."

"Loneliness is a terrible thing," Kaibyn commented, rolling his eyes.

"Spoken by a being who knows nothing of such things," Rabin snapped.

Kaibyn raised his chin. "Oh, but I know more about it than you will ever know, darkling. Try spending time in the darkness of the Abyss then make such a comment!"

Tamara moved between the two men to defuse any possible trouble. "Perhaps you should go to your lady, Rabin. At least it would ease your mind."

"Or make the situation worse, but what do I know?" Kaibyn said.

Without another word, the demon and Rabin disappeared, and Tamara let out a shriek of frustration. Such goings and comings were disconcerting. She stomped her foot, her hands balled into fists at her side.

"Stop doing that!" she shouted.

* * * * *

Rabin's head was swimming but he managed not to stagger. The last thing he wanted to do was reach out for the demon's aid who stood perfectly still, legs braced wide apart, his head slightly lowered, eyes squeezed tightly shut.

"What is her name?" Kaibyn asked as he looked about the village.

"I do not like traveling in that manner," Rabin mumbled. "I beg you do not do that to me again without first asking."

"You are Dabiyan, are you not?" the demon asked, ignoring the dark man's request.

"Aye," Rabin whispered and took a tentative step. His head reeled and he froze, swallowing the nausea that threatened to erupt.

"You bury your women at first light, don't you?"

Rabin's eyes opened of their own accord and he looked out over a gathering standing beside an open grave. The light of morning was but a few ticks of the clock away and as he watched, the rush door to his hut opened and his sons came out ahead of four men carrying a securely wrapped bundle resting on a long flat board.

"No," Rabin groaned. He would have stepped forward despite the roiling of his belly and the jerky motion of his vision, but the demon put out a restraining hand.

"She is lost to you, darkling," Kaibyn said. "Unless we can find the Magi."

"Momisha," Rabin whimpered. Tears were cascading down his cheeks.

"In order to rise, she must first go under the dirt," Kaibyn told the dark man. "While she is resting, let us go find those Magi and see what can be done."

Rabin had no chance to reply to the demon's suggestion before he found himself once more hurling through space, the desert dunes and mountains speeding by beneath his dangling feet. Once more he closed his eyes, and when he felt himself once more on solid ground, forced one eye open.

"Mage!" Kaibyn shouted, letting go of Rabin's arm. He strode through the dark corridors of the place where they had materialized, peeking into every room. "Magi!"

Master Jabali grunted as the door to his room was flung open. He put up an arm to shield his eyes from the glare of the torch that burned beside the entry. He smelt the demon before he actually heard him stomp into the room.

"The darkling wants his woman resurrected."

Jabali nodded. "And he shall have his wish, Lord Kaibyn, but could it not have waited until these old bones were ready to wake?"

"Do we have such time, Mage?" Kaibyn groused.

The Master's assistant, Tashobi, appeared at the door for his room was across from Jabali's. He grimaced at the musky odor clinging to the demon but said nothing as he skirted their visitor and went to help Jabali out of bed.

"I am infirm, Lord Kaibyn," Jabali said as he took hold of Tashobi's arm and levered himself to his feet. "Such is the burden of the last decade of one's life."

Kaibyn grunted but made no comment. He stood there with his arms folded over his chest as the younger man helped the older to dress. He barely cast a look at Rabin as the dark man joined them.

"Can they help?" Rabin asked.

"We will return your lady to you, my friend," Jabali answered. "But it will be a day or two. First we must see to the evil that even now heads for a second village."

"Kebul is under Hag control," Kaibyn said. "Which village is next?"

"They head for the stronger of the citadels," Jabali replied. "They go now to the Panther's den."

"Evann-Sin is there already," Rabin remarked.

"It is good he is," Jabali acknowledged. "Take the Lady Tamara and join him. Set the defenses on guard before Oded's warriors and Lilit's daughters arrive."

Kaibyn turned, reaching for Rabin's arm although the dark man flinched and would have pulled away instinctively.

"Let him go on his own power, Lord Kaibyn," Jabali advised. "It will be easier on him."

"I can do this?" Rabin asked, his eyes wide.

"Will it and it will be so, my friend," Jabali replied. "Think of your destination and…" He stopped then cocked his head to one side. "How did you know where we were, Lord Kaibyn, to find us?"

Kaibyn snorted. "I smelled you, Mage."

"Much as we smell you," Tashobi suggested

"Aye, and that is not good," Jabali said. "If we can smell you, the Hell Hags will smell you, as well, and head for another citadel. They will take the harder ones first, the easier last."

"I can not help…" Kaibyn began but cut himself off as the older man handed him a vial. "What is this?"

"It will stop the odor, milord," Jabali replied.

"For good? There will be no more scent of muskiness."

"Actually, it is not muskiness," Jabali commented.

"Then what?"

"It is the scent of death, Lord Kaibyn. You must remember you are many thousands of years old. When you were buried in the tomb, your flesh became corrupted. But have no fear, the oil will erase the odor."

Kaibyn's frown would have frightened lesser men. He uncorked the vial, brought it to his nose and sniffed. A pained look spread over his handsome features. "It smells like lilies," he complained.

"The flower of resurrection," Jabali informed him.

Drawing in a long, annoyed breath, Kaibyn poured the oil in his left hand then rubbed his palms together then applied the slick substance to his cheeks.

"There," Tashobi ventured. "The smell is gone!"

Kaibyn looked to Rabin and when the dark man nodded in agreement of the Mage's pronouncement, the demon smiled. "I was worried about the stench," he confessed. "My ladies would not find it palatable."

Jabali shook his head.

"What?" Kaibyn demanded.

The Mage spread his hands. "There will be only one lady for you from now until her death, milord, and that will be the queen. Only she will be able to see you."

"Tamara sees me!" Kaibyn disagreed.

"True, but only because I willed it," Jabali told him.

"And the Lady Tamara belongs to Riel Evann-Sin," Rabin was quick to point out.

Kaibyn growled at the reminder, his eyes flashing. "It is not in my nature to be true to one woman!"

"Though you swore it," Jabali reminded. "For as long as the queen lived."

Furious, Kaibyn disappeared in a rush of hot wind.

"Such an impetuous being," Jabali said.

Rabin grinned but the happy look on his face slowly dissolved. "Will he have to spend eternity alone once Queen Lilabet leaves this world?"

Master Jabali reached out to drape a comforting arm over the dark man's shoulder. "Nay, but I would venture to say he would not have such worries about your future, my friend. Why should you be concerned with his?"

Rabin shrugged. "We're all in this together, aren't we, milord?"

"Indeed," Jabali said, exchanging a look with his assistant, Tashobi. "Indeed we are."

"My lady?" Rabin asked.

Jabali nodded. "Let us talk of her."

* * * * *

Tamara had just stretched out to rest her eyes when a gust of wind swept through the room. Without opening her eyes, she knew the demon was back. "All is well?" she asked.

"Do you really love that man?" Kaibyn snarled.

"With all my heart," Tamara answered, and slowly opened her eyes to find the demon standing over her, his hands on his hips.

"Yet you barely know him!" he accused.

"I have lain in his arms and been transported to a place I'd never been," she said. "That is all I need to know."

Kaibyn struck his chest with his fist. "I could transport you to places he could never take you!"

"Perhaps," she said, sitting up and swinging her feet off the bed. "But they would be places to which I do not wish to go."

Tamara could hear the demon's teeth grinding and though the terrible look of fury blazed from his eyes, she had no fear of the being. "Will you bring him to me?" she asked then added, "Please?"

"What am I?" he snapped. "A fucking beast of burden?"

Though the words hung on the air, the demon vanished for a moment before returning with Evann-Sin in tow, whipping the warrior to the mattress before disappearing again.

"By the Prophet!" Evann-Sin grunted, reaching up to grab the headboard of the bed to keep him anchored.

"He says we will get used to traveling in that manner," Tamara said, stretching out beside her lover. "But I don't think I'm of a mind to do it enough to find out."

"Argh," the warrior complained, and leaned over the bed to retch. Though he gagged, nothing came up.

Tamara soothed his shoulder. "Take slow, deep breaths and it will pass quicker."

"I am going to kill that bastard yet," Evann-Sin swore.

Giggling at the absurdity of the threat, Tamara pushed herself up and leaned over her man, stroking his damp hair back from his high forehead.

"The Mage says we must leave for Akkadia," Kaibyn complained as he suddenly reappeared. "The Hell Hags are on their way there next."

Easing over to his back, Evann-Sin felt the world slowly settling around him but the nausea was still thick in his throat. "Where is Rabin?" he asked.

"With the Magi," Kaibyn told him. "He'll meet us there."

"Where is my horse?" the warrior asked, using the headboard to pull himself up.

"Outside," Tamara replied. "I saw them when I went to relieve myself earlier."

"The beasts make the journeys better than you and the darkling," Kaibyn chuckled. "Although they have a tendency to shit like you can't imagine!"

"No doubt because you scare it out of them," Evann-Sin complained.

"Well, gird yourself, warrior, because you are about to travel again," Kaibyn warned.

Before Tamara and her lover could react, they were standing on wobbly knees in the room from which Evann-Sin had been extracted ten minutes before. They slumped into one another's arms to battle the vertigo. The push of hot wind against them as the demon left did not help their feelings of unease.

"I hope he's going after Rabin," the warrior muttered.

"No need for him to," the dark man spoke up from the corner of the room where he was lounging. "I am here." He struck a thumb to his chest. "On my own power this time."

"Huh," was the only comment Evann-Sin could make at the remark. He helped Tamara to his bed and the two sat down gingerly.

"When I willed myself here, I did not feel the spinning," Rabin said. "I was a bit disoriented and materialized in your father's room instead of here."

"Oh, no," Evann-Sin whined.

"He didn't see me," Rabin told him. He tapped his cheek with his index finger. "You two smell similar and that was what I was told to aim for—your smell. Master Jabali said since it worked for the demon, it would work for me."

"You're sure my father didn't see you?"

"Nay, he did not."

"You know my sisters are on the way here?" Tamara asked, returning to normal faster than her lover.

"Aye," Rabin agreed. "What do we need to do?"

"When I can walk, we will go to my father and warn him," Evann-Sin answered.

"He'll believe us?"

"When he sees you, he will," the warrior said.

"Aye, but will he see me?"

"If the Magi have made it so, he will," Tamara put in.

Chapter Nine

He kissed her awake then took her into his arms as she was overcome with a huge, unladylike yawn.

"What time is it, Kai?" the queen asked.

"Almost seven of the clock, milady," he said. "I asked the innkeeper to prepare a meal for you and the bitchlet next door. Hopefully by the time you have broken your fast and taken a long, leisurely bath, I will be back to collect you."

Lilabet pushed away from his chest. "Back from where?"

"The Akkadian palace," Kaibyn answered. "The Hell Hags will attack there next and it is up to my coalition to stop them. If luck is with us, I can prevent the plague at the Panther's lair and it will go no further. I have my people in place."

"What of *my* people?" Lilabet asked, fear in her pretty eyes.

"Your people have all been bitten by now, Lovely One. They will need to be laid to rest and your palaces cleaned before I can take you back."

A tear fell slowly down her cheek. "Then I am a queen without a kingdom to rule."

"Your people are spread out all over the world, milady. Surely there will be those who will want to return to Kebul and take up residency. There will be many fine places to live, crops to tend, businesses to run. Things will get back to normal eventually. You will make a far better ruler than your crazed husband, Oded, ever would have."

"How could he ally himself with that vermin, Lilit?" she demanded.

"She dangled the carrot of immortality before his insane eyes and he leapt for it, but she will be made to atone for such transgressions against the human race."

"And the Hell Hags will be wiped off the face of the earth!" Lilabet swore.

"The Prophet and gods willing, aye," he agreed. "Well, all but one."

The queen's narrowed eyes shot sparks of anger. "Why should we allow one of those bitches to live?"

"She is one of my coalition," he replied. "And not one of the blood-drinkers."

"What is she to you, Kaibyn?" came the regal demand.

The demon slipped his hand to his lady's breast and kneaded it roughly. "No more than any other soldier, Sweeting. She means as much to me as one more pair of eyes and ears to ferret out those who would ruin our world as we know it."

The queen relaxed as the demon's hand worked its magic. Despite her advanced pregnancy, she found she was hornier than ever. She reached for Kaibyn's staff but her lover eased her hand away.

"There is no time now, beloved, but when I return, I will make up for it."

A pout puckered Lilabet's face but she sighed. "I will hold you to it."

"As I will hold you to *it*," Kaibyn promised, wagging his brows.

With one last kiss, he vanished from the room, leaving in his wake the faint scent of lilies.

* * * * *

The Panther shot up in the bed, his heart pounding. Though his door had been locked, it was now wide open and there were strange people standing around his bed. He opened his mouth to shout for his guards, but Evann-Sin stepped up to the bed.

"It is I, Your Majesty!" the warrior said.

Though he knew the dark man standing off to one side, the king could not believe his eyes. He knew Rabin Jaspyre was dead and buried, yet here he was. Beside him stood a beautiful woman and a handsome man the Panther did not know.

"Who are they?" the king demanded.

"My lady," Evann-Sin acknowledged, reaching out to draw Tamara forward. "Tamara, this is my king."

Tamara curtseyed gracefully but remained silent.

"And this is Kaibyn Zafeyr." Evann-Sin nudged a chin toward Rabin. "I believe you know my friend."

"You," the king said, pointing at the dark man, "are dead!"

"As am I," Kaibyn chuckled.

Jerking the coverlet up to his chin, the Panther stared wide-eyed at the two men. "How can this be? How is it I see you?"

"I suspect it is the Magi's doing," Evann-Sin replied.

"I have heard that you are a wise and fair ruler," Tamara remarked, drawing the king's stare. "That you are a brave warrior whose sword has never been defeated. That you fear no man, and have the stamina of men much younger than you. That when faced with the impossible, you make it possible."

Evann-Sin hid a smile behind his fist, his lips pressed to the circle of his fingers. He knew well what his lady was doing and silently applauded her effort.

King Numair relaxed and lowered the coverlet. "You are a Daughter of the Night?" he inquired, lifting his chin.

Tamara lowered her head in agreement. "Though not of the Blood."

"Not one of those who took my son against his will?"

There was a twitch of Tamara's shapely lips. "He seemed most willing when last we trysted, Your Grace."

"Tamara!" Evann-Sin exclaimed.

"'Tis true," she said with an innocent look.

"There is no need to speak of it, though," her lover sputtered.

"As much as I enjoy watching the Akkadian squirm," Kaibyn said, bringing the king's eyes back to him. "We are here because trouble is on the way. You need to prepare for it."

The king threw back his covers. "Trouble in what form?"

Tamara looked away for the royal was as naked as the day he'd been born.

"The Daughters of the Night will be attacking at sunset," Evann-Sin answered. He stepped forward, took his king's robe from a nearby chair and held it out for him to put on. "With them will be their thralls from Kebul."

King Numair winced. "Oded is done for, then?"

"Drained as dry as a husk, though I would venture to say he'll be at the head of his column of troops," Evann-Sin remarked. "Lilit will need him."

Shivering with the thought, the Panther thrust his arms into his robe then belted it. "What suggestions have you?"

"First, you must call your council of elders together," Kaibyn spoke up. "Apprise them of the situation."

"I will go to my men and make them ready," Evann-Sin informed his king. "We will secure the gates against the invaders."

"What about those who live beyond the perimeter of the palace? How will we be protecting them?" the king asked.

"I will send men to bring them in," the warrior said. "We should be able to have everyone safely inside before the sun begins to lower."

"Rabin and I will procure what we need to fight our enemies," Tamara put in. "Evann-Sin's men need to make ready cauldrons of burning oil into which we can dip our arrows."

A pained look spread over the king's lined face. "You must burn the bodies, eh?"

"Or have them get close enough for us to take their heads," Rabin said softly.

"Give me a serviceable blade and I can scythe many a swath through their ranks," Kaibyn boasted. "Few, if any, can travel the same way I can."

"I can," Rabin allowed.

"Though not as steadily as I," Kaibyn snorted.

"How steady do you have to be to chop off heads?" Rabin snapped.

"Do we know if any other villages have been turned?" the Panther asked, looking from one face to another.

"Between here and Kebul?" Evann-Sin inquired. "Most likely each of them. The Hell Hags would want to turn as many villagers as they can to swell their invasion force."

"Perhaps we should have someone check on their route of progress," Tamara suggested.

"Consider it done," Rabin said and with that disappeared.

Kaibyn grunted. "He seems to have gotten over his dislike of astral traveling. He…"

Rabin reappeared, a wide grin on his dark face though he swayed just as little. "They took the route through Exira. Doesn't appear to be any villagers left there. I didn't see anyone at all on the road but there are a lot of bumps between Exira and Decion."

"They've burrowed underground for the remainder of the day," Kaibyn said. "Every bump is a grave."

"Could we not put some of them out of their misery while the sun is up?" the Panther inquired.

"Aye," Evann-Sin agreed, "but not nearly enough. What are talking about here, Rabin? A thousand? More?"

"At least a thousand," Rabin replied.

"I can take the two of you with me," Kaibyn told Evann-Sin and his lady, "but I don't think the darkling is up to conveying a rider."

"Well, let's see," Rabin drawled and grabbed Evann-Sin's arm.

"No!" both Tamara and the king yelled as the warrior vanished.

"He'll be useless for at least half an hour," Kaibyn complained. He held out a hand to Tamara. "Lady?"

"I want to go!" the king announced. He hurried to his armoire to extract a set of clothing.

"Then I'll come back for you," Kaibyn said.

"Can you...?" the Panther started to say but when he turned around, he found himself alone.

Tamara stumbled and would have fallen had not Kaibyn snagged her waist with a strong arm. She slumped against him, her head spinning a bit less than the other times but with enough force to elicit nausea.

"He'll be up and about in a few moments," Rabin said. "Should I go back with you and get a few others?"

Kaibyn shook his head. "And then have to transport them all back?"

"King Numair wanted to come," Tamara reminded them.

"He's fine where he is," Evann-Sin choked out. He struggled to stand and when he couldn't, dropped back to a sitting position on the ground. "I need to go back and talk to my men."

"That's something the king will do," Kaibyn stated.

"I'll do it," Rabin volunteered. Once more the dark man was gone in the blinking of an eye. It was only a moment before he was back. "He's already seeing to it."

Evann-Sin stared at his friend. "You are enjoying that shit far too much," he accused.

"What can I say? I'm good at it!" Rabin chuckled.

"Start over there," Kaibyn ordered Rabin. "You'll need to whirl the dirt out of the grave and expose the corpse to the sunlight. Some will catch fire immediately. Those are the newest

132

dead. Others, we will need to behead." From out of nowhere, he produced four scythes, the blades of which appeared razor-thin.

"I never saw him leave," Tamara whispered. Her eyes were wide. "I never *felt* him leave. Did you take me with you?"

"I will one day be that quick," Rabin said with a sniff.

Kaibyn grinned. "You're getting acclimated to the traveling, wench. The next time we make a trip, you most likely won't feel anything."

Evann-Sin struggled to his feet and grabbed one of the scythes from Kaibyn. "She won't be doing any more traveling with you, demon!"

Kaibyn shrugged, though his dark eyes took on a wicked gleam. He handed scythes to Rabin and Tamara. "Do you know how to whirl the wind, darkling?"

"Stop calling him that," Evann-Sin warned. "He has a name."

Kaibyn rolled his eyes. "All right, Rabin," he said, stressing the name, "you should…"

"Like this?" Rabin inquired and rushed across several graves. The rush of the wind at his passing partially exposed the bodies beneath.

Tamara had grown up with the Undead and had seen many of them taking to their coffins as the sun rose, but she had never seen fresh bodies squirming to get beneath the protection of the soil and it made her ill.

"We'll be doing them a favor by sending them to the Gatherer," Kaibyn told her. "Try not to think of what you are doing."

There were over a thousand raised places on the plains of Celadohr and the members of the coalition knew they would be able to lay only a few hundred—at best—to eternal rest. With Rabin and the demon whirling away the earth covering the Undead, Evann-Sin and Tamara set about beheading as many corpses as time would allow.

It was a gruesome task that brought tears to Tamara's eyes and caused Evann-Sin to grit his teeth and tamp down his human sympathy. By the time Kaibyn and Rabin were able to begin their own grisly duty, the sun was already beginning to lower toward the horizon. As the last rays of the sun began dying, those burrowed beneath the mounds began to rise. Only three hundred Undead had been delivered to the Soul Gatherer's arms.

"There are nine hundred or thereabouts rising," Rabin told them. He was staring at a hand clawing its way from the ground.

"We need to get back to the palace and make sure everything is in place. Unless I miss my guess, the battle will last most of the night," Kaibyn said.

"Longer if Queen Lilit sends replacements for those we beheaded," Tamara said. She edged away from a grave from which a rising corpse was growling its fury.

"I would if I were her," Evann-Sin told her. He held a hand out to Kaibyn. "Let's get going."

Kaibyn's teeth sparkled in the growing darkness and he winked.

"The Prophet, damn it!" the warrior shouted for his lady had been snagged up by the demon and had vanished.

"You'd better watch that one," Rabin suggested as he put a hand on his friend's shoulder.

"How, when I can't even see the son-of-a-bitch?"

Chapter Ten

Ashes floated through the dawn air and the smell of burnt flesh settled on the defenders of the Akkadian palace like a cloying, wet blanket. Those standing upon the battlements were weary—their hands blistered from pitch falling from their rag-wrapped arrowheads. Servant women went from warrior to warrior, carrying ladles of cool water, hunks of bread, wheels of cheese, apples and pears.

"Look there," Rabin said to his friend.

Evann-Sin turned where Rabin was pointing and winced. The vista for as far as he could see was rippled with raised mounds. Though the night had been lit with the rush of exploding bodies, still more corpses had appeared in what seemed a never-ending line marching across the Akkadian landscape.

"How many do you reckon are out there?" Tamara asked. Her hands were wrapped around a steaming cup of coffee, the fumes of which helped to block the stench of death.

"At least as many as we destroyed last night," Kaibyn ventured.

"With the help of my men, we can take out most of those before sunset, but will just that many appear to attack us tonight?" Evann-Sin said.

"There are hundreds of Undead on the Isle of Sanquis," Tamara replied. "I believe Lilit has brought them all here."

"We are running out of arrows," Rabin complained. He looked to Kaibyn. "Should we not go fetch some?"

Kaibyn nodded. "Aye, but I've another idea, dar..." He stopped. "Rabin."

Rabin arched a brow. "What idea is that?"

"I can time travel," the demon announced. "I don't like to go into the past, but I have been there a time or two."

"Is there something there that could help us?" Tamara asked.

"Aye, but I don't know if I have the strength to bring it here." He shrugged. "I can only try."

"You need help?" Rabin inquired.

"I'll get back to you on that," the demon remarked and was gone.

"I'll never get used to seeing that," the Panther remarked. He was sitting slumped against a barrel that was lying on its side. His face was soot-stained and his clothing peppered with holes from where burning pitch had lit upon the fabric.

Evann-Sin wrapped his arms around his lady. "I am about done in," he confessed.

"Go take a nap," the king ordered. "The both of you. Rabin and I will see to having my men start on opening those damned graves."

"I should fetch some arrows," Rabin countered, and at the king's nod, left in a rush of hot wind.

The Panther sighed and shook his head. "No, I will never get used to such things."

"I'll speak to the troops, Your Majesty," Evann-Sin said.

"You will not," the Panther denied. "You will hie yourself and that lady to your room and rest, Riel Evann-Sin." When the warrior would have argued, his king held up a staying hand. "That was not a suggestion, boy. That was an imperial command! Get yourself to bed!"

"His Majesty is right, Beloved," Tamara said gently. She was as bone-tired as her lover and barely able to keep her eyes open.

Knowing he could not disobey his king, Evann-Sin struck a tired fist to his breast. "At your command, Majesty," he replied.

It was a weary duo that sluggishly descended the steps from the battlements and entered the corridor that led to Evann-Sin's quarters. Both were hot and sweaty, uneasy with their own body odors but not willing to mention their companion's rank stench. Yet, as tired as they were, the lovers were overjoyed to find a large copper tub filled with water sitting in the middle of Evann-Sin's bedroom.

"Thank you, King Numair!" Tamara muttered, and already her fingers were tearing at the buttons to her blouse.

Discreetly leaving the warrior and his lady to themselves, two maidservants and a strapping lad of about sixteen quietly exited the room. A golden trencher piled high with fresh fruit—strawberries, figs, dates, apples, pears and bananas—sat on a low table beside the tub alongside a sweat-glistening pitcher and two goblets.

Evann-Sin was slower to undress for he was enjoying his lady's stripping. The sight of her shapely body and long limbs took away much of the fatigue that had only moments before been plaguing his aching body. His hands stilled on his shirt as she lifted a long leg and climbed into the tub for he had gotten a tantalizing glimpse of the ripples of sweetness between her legs.

Tamara plucked a bar of soap from a little wire basket fashioned like a saddlebag that was draped over the rim of the tub. One side held the soap while the other held a large sea sponge. She brought the soap to her nose and her eyes widened with delight.

"It smells of lemons, Riel!" she trilled.

The warrior could not get the sight of her most private of parts out of his mind. His staff was hardening even as he thought of that delightful, slick area. Fumbling with the buttons of his shirt, he grew impatient and finally ripped the shirt from his chest.

His lady looked up at the sound of rending material but almost immediately her gaze lowered to the swelling in his britches and her look darkened with heat. Slowly, she raised her eyes until she was looking into the lusty stare of her lover. She unconsciously stuck out her tongue and licked her upper lip, her heart skipping a beat as she saw the effect her action had upon the warrior.

Evann-Sin shrugged out of the remnants of his filthy shirt and made quick work of the belt looped at his waist. Dragging the leather from his body, he dropped the belt and stood on one foot to pull off first one boot then the other, tossing the heavy footwear away.

Tamara's attention was glued to her lover's broad chest where muscles rippled as he moved. The flex of the biceps of his brawny arms made both her mouth and her nether region water. She swallowed as she listened to the hard thump of the blood rushing through her ears. Her hands ached to touch the warrior's staff, to caress it, and the sight of that weapon as it sprang free from Evann-Sin's britches brought a groan of anticipation from her lips.

He had heard that low groan, and it caused his cock to leap with an expectancy of its own. He was at full staff, the burgeoning blood coursing through his veins as he kicked aside his britches and advanced toward the tub.

Likening her lover's approach to the fabled tales of his kingly father, the Panther, Tamara felt weak and helpless as he came toward her. He was all male—all sexual being as he hunkered down beside the tub. She could not tear her eyes from his for he held her enthralled with the mesmerizing depths of that golden, intense look. Her breathing was ragged, too fast, too shallow, and it made her giddy, caused her head to spin.

Her lover reached out and took the soap from her hand. He dipped it in the water as he knelt on his knees by the tub then lifted her arm to run the silky bar along her flesh.

Tamara closed her eyes and laid her head back along the low rim of the tub. His touch was exquisite—as soft as a feather. The slippery feel and scent of the soap was heavenly. As he laved her arm, her shoulder, her neck—her head cocked to one side to give him access—and the upper portion of her chest, she held her breath, expecting his hand to dip to her breast but it did not. Instead, she heard him stand and without opening her eyes, felt him climb into the tub with her. She drew her knees up to give him room and once he was settled, she felt his hands on her ankles, pulling her legs over his and placing them on his hard thighs. When he scooted forward in the water—his feet bumping her hips as he planted them beside her—she opened her eyes and watched him.

He took her other arm and laved it, spreading the lemony lather over her limb. He took care with her shoulder and neck, each finger of her sword hand, before lowering the soap in the water and lathering it once more.

Her legs were splayed along his thighs, her calves resting on the flanges of his hips. So large was the tub, her feet did not touch the opposite end so she rotated her ankles, grinning as each popped in turn.

Evann-Sinn laughed softly at the unladylike sound. His lady was unlike any he'd ever encountered and it was the little things—like the enjoyable cracking of an ankle joint—that endeared her to him.

Tamara opened her mouth to tease him, but his hand slid to her breast and all thought vanished from her brain. Every sensation, every emotion, every notion had settled between her legs and she felt her womb quicken as his thumb glided over a suddenly erect nipple.

"Sweet," she heard him whisper then sighed as his hand came away from her breast.

He put his hands together, lathering his palms with the soap. When his hands were alive with suds, he dropped the bar in the water and reached out to place his palms on his lady's chest.

It was a delight that sent shivers down her spine and made her quiver as her lover rubbed her flesh in lazy circles, the circuits opposite one another—one to the right, the other to the left as he massaged her heavy globes. Her nipples were in the center of his palms and being worked with a delicate, sliding friction that made her begin to pant. She could feel the sensation all the way to the core of her sex and squirmed. When he began to flex his fingers along the circumference of her breasts, she could not keep the moan of pleasure from escaping her lips.

"You like that?" he asked softly.

"Aye," she breathed.

As though he were trying to pluck her breasts from her chest, the delicate drawing of his fingers, the faint scratch of his nails upon her flesh as he drew his fingers closer to her nipples, was an exquisite torment that set her nerves to tingling. Even as she ached to have those short nails plucking at her nipples, she did not want to end the heady expectation such action brought. The intimate caress went on for what seemed an eternity to her, with each drawing coming closer to the hardened nubs of her breasts. When at last he gently pinched those turgid pebbles—working them between his thumbs and forefingers—a spasm of delight coursed through her sex and trilled over her body.

Evann-Sin felt her ankles digging into his sides as she climaxed. Her strong legs quivered and he imagined the tightening of her vaginal walls.

Before the last contraction could claim her, he snagged his hands around her slender waist and jerked her to him, his straining cock unerringly entering her deep and hard. He was well seated within her honeyed folds as another round of pleasure rippled through her and carried him along in its wake, his own climax coming strongly.

Tamara threw her arms around her lover and plastered her breasts to his hairy chest. She was sitting atop his thighs—his fleshy sword sheathed inside her. She ground against him as the second round of pleasure began, and rode him as though he were a wild mustang needing to be broken to saddle. Their body parts jammed against one another, they were satiated at the same moment and sat there straining to feel the last errant tug of completion.

"By the Prophet but I love you," Evann-Sin told her in a throaty oath. His lips were against her cheek but he pulled back and captured her lips with his hungry mouth. Stabbing his velvet tongue into the sweet cavern between her sultry lips, he claimed her once more.

Her nails were flexed into the muscles of his back, scoring his flesh lightly as she branded him her own. As his mouth left hers to plant hot kisses along her neck and shoulders, she threw back her head and pledged her love to him, as well.

"With all my heart and soul and body, do I love you Riel Evann-Sin," she swore.

Long into the morning they lay sprawled in the bed to which he had carried her, their bodies wet and smelling of lemons. He had made quick work of bathing her—and she him—then they had stretched out upon the soft bed, and he had taken her still once more. Their joining had been as frenzied as teenagers fulfilling lust for the first time, but their third joining had been slow and measured and had dropped them lazily into welcoming sleep.

* * * * *

It was a harsh, unnatural sound that thrust the lovers from sleep and to a sitting position in bed. Beneath them, the floor shook and they were off the mattress and standing at the window to gape at the monster that was pawing at the grounds beyond the palace.

Tall—at least as high as the fourth floor of the keep itself—the persimmon-colored beast roared, blowing plumes of smoke from its ass as it raised and lowered its massive head, taking huge bites out of the earth with a single wide tooth only to turn and spit the dirt away. Thick black veins ran along the creature's flexing neck and the smell from its foul body was sickening. Ugly as any beast that ever drew breath, it sat hunkered down on a bed of some kind with huge black wheels that looked as though they were padded.

"What is that thing?" Tamara whispered, her eyes bulging from her head.

"I have never seen the likes of it and Kaibyn is riding the damned thing," Evann-Sin exclaimed.

Tamara squinted against the bright glare of morning and could make out the demon sitting upon the beast's neck. Nay, she thought, her mind reeling. He was not sitting upon the beast's neck but rather inside its gullet!

"He is making it gobble the ground," the warrior marveled.

And surely, that was what the demon was doing. Like a puppet master, he seemed to be pulling strings of some sort and when he did, the beast raised and lowered its gaping jaws and took another massive bite of earth. As it did, the ground shook and the creature emitted a horrendous shriek that set the nerves on edge.

"Get dressed," Evann-Sin advised. "That thing may not remain so biddable and we might have to put it down."

"How?" Tamara questioned as her lover began throwing on his clothes. "It looks to be wearing plate mail of some sort."

"Get dressed!" Evann-Sin repeated. He was searching for one of his boots and was grumbling to himself.

Tamara reached for a pair of britches lying on a chair and as she did, scraped the edge of her palm on an exposed nail. "Shit!" she exploded and shook her hand.

"What did you do?" Evann-Sin asked as he went to her.

She held up her wounded hand. "I cut it," she murmured.

Evann-Sin carefully examined the cut then clucked his tongue. The warrior took out his kerchief and wound her hand. "It's little more than a scratch. Be more careful, will you?"

Offended by his tone, Tamara grabbed a shirt and had put it on before her lover had stomped into his missing boot. She found her own and barely had time to snatch them up before Evann-Sin took her arm and pulled her out of the room.

The lovers marveled at the mighty thump that shook the walls of the palace. All around them, people were standing well back from where the mysterious beast was devouring the ground and watching the process with eyes wide and mouths agape. Even Rabin and the king were crouched off to one side, flinching at each chomp the monster took from the earth.

"What is it doing?" Evann-Sin asked the king as he and Tamara reached him.

"Digging a pit from the looks of it," the Panther replied. "If you think that beast is ugly, look there!"

Evann-Sin turned to see another beast perched off to one side. Squat and more ugly than the one upon which the demon sat, this one was bright yellow with dark brown markings and carried a long, low shield before it. The shield reflected the early morning sun and blinded those who stared too long at it. It sat low to the ground with feet that were oblong in shape and with bones that ridged the entire circumference of its paw. It had a saddle upon its back and a pommel with what appeared to be handles sticking out from it.

"Is it dead?" Tamara asked.

"Sleeping," the king avowed. "It has yet to make a sound."

Rabin took a step or two forward but Evann-Sin put out a staying hand. "Be careful."

"He brought those creatures here," Rabin said. "He *brought* them from the past."

"He is stronger than I thought if he could lift things like that," Evann-Sin admitted. He glanced at his lady, and a wild notion took shape in his mind—if the demon could lift such beasts as this, could a warrior win in a mortal battle with him or would he lose his love to such awesome might?

Kaibyn intercepted the warrior's troubling thought and grinned. The pit was almost ready and as soon as it was, he would show that snotty boy what power truly was when he transported the machines back to their time in history.

The sun was high overhead when the mysterious monster took its last chomp out of the earth. Its roar died to a low hum then disappeared altogether as it lowered its head one last time. It sat still as death—docile and calm—as Kaibyn jumped down from its back and came striding up to the warrior and the others.

"They called it an excavator," Kaibyn remarked, glancing back over his shoulder. "The other is a bulldozer."

"These creatures came from the past?" the king queried.

"Once," Kaibyn said, "long ago, there were such things. The Burning War destroyed many of them and when they ran out of diesel..."

"Deezul?" Evann-Sin echoed. "What is deezul?"

The demon shrugged. "A byproduct of the decay of dinosaurs, which these things must have resembled."

"Die no sores," Evann-Sin repeated. "You make no sense, demon!"

"Well, no matter," Kaibyn said. "Now that the pit is deep enough, you can have your men start filling it with anything that will burn. I'll use the other beast to push the Undead into the pit and then we will have one helluva roast!"

Tamara flinched at the word. She looked at the second beast. "That will push the bodies into the pit?"

"Quicker than a thousand men could drag them there," Kaibyn bragged.

Evann-Sin shook his head. "This is more than I can contemplate."

"You don't need to," Kaibyn snorted. "Just get that pit filled with anything that will burn quickly."

Kaibyn was there one moment and the next he was prodding the second beast—the one he had called bulldozer—to shrill, thundering, blasting life. The creature farted smoke as the other had then with a shriek that made everyone cover their ears, moved forward with a horrendous clank that set nerves on edge.

Tamara stared at the beast as it lowered its shield and dug into the earth, pushing beneath the dirt to dislodge the Undead. She marveled as the thing pushed bodies this way and that— piling them upon one another close to the edge of the pit.

Evann-Sin watched the beast trundling back and forth for a moment or two then looked to his father. He shrugged and ordered one of the nearby men to begin a brigade of workers to pour whatever liquid or kindling into the pit to set it ablaze.

Rabin wandered over to the first beast and skirted it carefully, mindful of the thing coming out of its slumber. There was no movement, no sound of escaping breath and the dark man wandered if this creature from the past was as dead as those it had been brought into the future to help destroy. With more bravado than he knew he possessed, he came close enough to the beast to nudge it with his boot but the thing remained inanimate, perched on its rolling bed with head lowered, gaping mouth open but devoid of drool.

The king winced with each clank of the other beast's oblong feet. It seemed to glide along but left deep indentions in the earth as it moved. The ground shook but not as badly as when the first beast had chewed up the earth. Ordering a chair be brought for his comfort, King Numair kept a close eye on these monsters from the past. How they could be slain should they go berserk and stampede, he had no idea. He only hoped the demon could control them.

As the sun began to lower, almost all of the bodies had been pushed into the fiery pit. Flames leapt as high as the second floor of the keep and ashes formed a black cloud above. The smell of burning bodies was so intense, handkerchiefs were needed to block the stench and everywhere you looked, servants and warriors alike were covered from eyes to chin with whatever fabric could be found. When the last feeble flicker of light on the horizon died out, only a handful of mounds remained unscathed.

"Back inside!" Evann-Sin yelled for he had seen movement off to the east.

The doors to the palace locked into place just as a garrison of Daughters of the Night rode into view.

"They are all of the Blood," Tamara said from her place beside her lover on the battlements.

"How many?" the king asked. His eyesight was no longer that good in the dark.

"Forty," Evann-Sin answered. "Another fifty or so risen from the graves."

"One hundred and five," Kaibyn counted.

"They will scale the walls," Tamara warned.

"With what?" Rabin asked. "I see no ropes."

"They don't need ropes," Tamara said quietly. "They can climb the walls like spiders, like bats." She leaned out and searched those gathered. "I don't see the queen. They won't do anything until she appears and that won't be until the stroke of midnight."

"They can climb without rope?" Evann-Sin questioned. "Is that possible?"

Tamara merely nodded. "I've seen it done, warrior."

"Let them start their little crawls up the wall," Kaibyn said. He put a hand on Rabin's shoulder. "Come with me. I have a couple more things from the past that will settle this once and for all."

As often as he had seen his friend blink out of his sight, Evann-Sin was no longer amazed at it. He took it in stride as he went about to warn his men that the women warriors might attempt to scale the walls.

Chapter Eleven

Rabin was bent over throwing up and not at all happy with the demon's amused chortling. The trip back in time had been unlike the hop and skips across the countryside and materializing here and there behind locked doors. This had been a rushing river of bright lights and blaring sounds that had sent shivers of dread and fear through Rabin Jaspyre.

And the past was a place so unlike any upon which he had set foot in his forty-two years.

"I've allowed you to grow on me, darkling," Kaibyn laughed. "You aren't so bad for one of your race. I find I rather like you."

"Fuck you," Rabin mumbled. "You could have warned me this would be different."

"Oh, if you think that was bad, wait until we journey back to our time," Kaibyn chuckled.

The dark man grunted. The thought of a return trip made him wish he'd stayed in his own time. The sights and sounds around him were unnerving at best, terrifying at worst.

"We've a couple of items to pick up and then we're outta here, as they used to say in this era," Kaibyn commented.

"What year is this?" Rabin wanted to know for the strange conveyances that rolled past them on the hard black roadway were enough to stop any warrior's stalwart heart.

"I believe the year is 2004. We are well behind the start of the Burning War. That won't take place until the year 2219, if memory serves."

Rabin looked around at his companion. "You are full of shit, demon!" he sneered. "It was the Year of the Rat, 183 when we left Akkadia!"

"Aye, but after the Burning War, time began its count all over again," Kaibyn explained. He was sitting on a metal bench, his arms stretched out along the back, one knee bent, his foot upon the bench's seat. He cocked his head to one side. "Would it surprise you to learn that the world has been forced to begin its count several times and at last count, this earth is over four billion years old?"

"Ah!" Rabin scoffed, waving a dismissive hand. "You think you are fooling me but you aren't!"

"Have it your way," Kaibyn sighed.

"Where are these things you think we need to destroy the Hell Hags?" Rabin demanded. "We should be back with our people."

"In there," Kaibyn said with a nod to the building behind Rabin.

Jumping as something blared among the speeding conveyances shooting by, Rabin turned to observe the tall building behind him. He winced for the buildings here in the past were as strange as the hard black roadways and blinking lights upon tall poles.

Made of stone but encased in glass, many of the buildings had dead people standing in its windows.

"Not dead people," Kaibyn had corrected. "Dummies— mannequins."

Rabin hawked a gob of phlegm to let the demon know he thought the explanation ridiculous. He knew a dead person when he saw one and even though the corpses' eyes were wide open and staring sightlessly, they were strangely well preserved.

There was writing on the building, but Rabin could not decipher it. The letters were shaped weirdly.

"What is this place?"

"It isn't what the building is," Kaibyn responded. "It is what is hidden in the basement that we're after."

The word "basement" meant nothing to Rabin.

"Terrorists reside here," Kaibyn said as he got to his feet. "They are planning on destroying several large buildings, killing thousands of innocent people. I will see to it they do not succeed with their cowardly plan."

"Terrorists?" Rabin repeated. "What does that mean?"

"That's not important," Kaibyn answered. "When we leave, they will be leaving, too." His devilish eyes gleamed with murderous intent. "Although not in any way they ever planned."

Ten minutes later, Rabin was airborne, each hand gripping a strange weapon that was much heavier than it looked. His ears were still ringing from the gods-awful blast that had brought the building down around its inhabitant's ears—crushing them beneath tons of smoldering wood, twisted metal and crumbling blocks.

"An eye for an eye," Kaibyn said a moment before the night lit up like a bonfire.

* * * * *

"She's here," Tamara warned, pointing toward the south.

Evann-Sin's flesh crawled for even from this distance he could sense the evil bitch that had almost killed him. He thought he could feel her hands on his body and he shuddered.

"Where is the demon?" King Numair queried.

"He'll be here," Evann-Sin said quietly.

"Aye, well you have more faith in him than I," the Panther confessed.

"He won't let us down if for no other reason than to save my lady's life," the warrior said.

Tamara slipped her hand into her lover's and squeezed.

"They are beneath the walls," a soldier warned.

Ringed around the eastern wall of the palace, dead-white faces stared up at the palace's defenders. The scarlet slashes of their lips pulled back to reveal long, wicked fangs.

"By the Prophet but that is an evil sight," the king whispered.

As the defenders watched, the first wave of Undead began scaling the walls, their fingernails scraping against the stone.

"Where are you, Kaibyn?" Evann-Sin muttered. Around him, his soldiers were throwing pitch-dipped spears at the climbers and now and again, a body would burst into flames and fall, catching another body on fire as it landed among the snapping throng at the base of the wall.

"They are too fast," King Numair swore. "They scuttle up the stones like beetles! They will overrun us!"

Tamara held a heavy broadsword in her hands. She was ready to defend the walls of the palace by lopping the heads off its attackers. Already, she could smell the creeping decay that had risen up from the graves scattered across the plain and her stomach lurched at the scent.

Evann-Sin flexed his sword arm. In his strong grip, he held a wicked-looking battle-ax, the blade of which was razor-thin. His palms itched—as they did before every fight—and sweat glistened in his dark hair. His gaze was locked on Lilit, and even from the distance that separated them, could see her nasty smile.

Counting the advancing enemy was difficult at best, but the Panther was finally able to make out the remaining Undead. "Eighty-two," he told Evann-Sin. He looked around them and saw only a handful of spears left and his heart sank. "Too many. Much too many."

"The demon won't let us down," Evann-Sin asserted.

When the last spear was thrown, the defenders took up their swords and battle-axes, maces and scythes. A few had blazing torches that could be wielded as weapons but for now lit up the gathering darkness. The defense of the palace would come down to hand-to-hand combat and blood might soon run rivers on the battlements.

As full dark enveloped the night, the first five attackers popped their heads between the crenellations and were met with instant decapitation, but the second wave of the enemy managed to leap upon the stones to fling themselves at the defenders. One defender went down — the fangs of his slayer buried deep in his throat. He died screaming as both his head and that of the one who had killed him were severed by Tamara's weighty sword.

Evann-Sin had taken out six of the enemy, but he and those who stood with him were slowly being backed up to the stairs. Undead after Undead poured over the battlements and with hands bent like claws and lips skinned back from wickedly glinting teeth, hissed and threw themselves at the defenders.

"Watch your back, warrior!" Tamara yelled as she chopped the head from her opponent. Out of the corner of her eye, she saw an Undead one creeping up behind Evann-Sin.

The warrior spun around and his ax sheared an ugly head from a decaying body, but another enemy jumped on his back, wrapped its legs around his waist and went for his neck. With a bellow of outrage, Evann-Sin slammed the creature into the wall beside them hard enough to hear Undead bones break. With a hiss, the thing slid off the warrior's back and Evann-Sin made quick work of taking its head.

"Need some help?"

Evann-Sin turned around to see Kaibyn Zafeyr and Rabin standing back-to-back between him and Tamara, who was struggling with a brawny Undead warrior.

Rabin was grinning as he held two very strange weapons in his hands. He threw one to Evann-Sin and yelled for him to do as he did. He aimed the weapon at Tamara's foe and a burst of flame shot from the end of the bulky thing, instantly incinerating the Undead. He then swung the weapon in an arc toward more advancing creatures and set them ablaze as Kaibyn handed Tamara the second weapon he carried.

"Point it at the enemy and pull the trigger like so," Kaibyn instructed. He brought his weapon up and sprayed a group of Undead.

The strange weapons blazed arcs over the high walls of the palace and lit the night with bodies running in circles or else falling over the edge of the wall. Here and there a body burned like a funeral pyre to give light for the defenders.

Tamara stared at the weighty thing then followed suit, shocked by the power the thing emitted. She was careful not to aim it near one of their own and was stunned to see the Undead backing away, scrambling to retreat the same way they had come.

But Kaibyn followed suit, and he and Rabin aimed their weapons down the palace walls and turned the Undead into falling balls of fire that caught those below ablaze.

Evann-Sin could not get his weapon to work and finally resorted to using it like a club, swatting the fleeing Undead like wingless flies then jumping aside for Tamara to spray them with flame. He was grinning like a madman, and at one point laughed aloud as an enemy rushed him only to be brought up fast by a stream of fire that turned enemy to inferno.

King Numair had slain several enemies with his own broadsword, but was now bent over the wall, watching the attackers turning into crispy critters on the ground below. He lifted his head and stared at Queen Lilit, and felt the supernatural chill of her stare like a basin of cold water thrown over him.

Lilit was sitting on the back of her prancing black hell-steed, its red, glowing eyes rolling as its rider kept it under control and its mighty hooves struck sparks on the paving stones. The Queen of the Daughters of the Night stared back at the Akkadian king with such ferocity the look should have stricken the man dead. Her wrath knew no boundaries. Flanking her were her two most powerful lieutenants, Amenirdis and Hekat.

"Bring that traitorous little bitch to me!" Lilit commanded.

Shiny black leather wings unfolded from the backs of the two female creatures and spread wide. With a single mighty flap, the two were airborne and soaring over the walls of the palace.

"Riel!" the Panther screamed, the only one to see the oncoming danger.

Evann-Sin turned just the sound of flapping wings broke over the screeches of exploding, burning bodies. He looked to the king then snapped his head up just as one of the winged creatures flew overhead, obscuring the light of the moon. Instinctively he ducked, going to one knee and as he stared in horror, saw talons extending toward Tamara as a second creature dove for his lady.

"*No!*" the warrior bellowed, springing to his feet and reaching up as though he could snatch the bats from the air. The kerchief that had been wound around Tamara's bloody hand fluttered toward him and he grasped it, pulling it to his chest as though it were the most sacred of objects.

Bent over the wall, ridding the world of the last of the Undead, neither Kaibyn nor Rabin realized the danger zeroing in on Tamara. So engrossed with destroying their enemies, they did not see the winged demonesses pluck Tamara from the wall and fly away with her. Tamara's scream of denial was lost in the mindless shrieking of the Undead's destruction.

"*Kaibyn!*"

Hearing his name shouted in a tone that bespoke great anguish, the demon straightened up and turned to look behind him. He saw Evann-Sin standing alone amidst a quartet of burning bodies, behind the warrior was the horrific sight of Tamara dangling between two high-flying creatures, her legs kicking violently.

"*Kaibyn, do something!*"

The anguish in the warrior's voice bordered on hysteria, but Kaibyn could not seem to move. He stood where he was, all movement frozen, watching the diminishing trio winging beyond the limited light of the pale moon. As he watched, he saw a winged stallion sailing high overhead and the taunting sound of hateful laughter drifted down to him on a current of air that reeked of brimstone.

Rabin, alone, reacted, flinging himself through time and space after the retreating creatures but they were soon out of sight. Though he sought them with his fledgling skills, neither sight nor sound nor scent came back at him and he was soon back on the battlement walls, his apologetic eyes going to the grieving warrior.

Evann-Sin was trembling from head to toe, his heart racing so thunderously in his chest he thought the organ would soon break free. He took a few steps, then collapsed, his face stamped with hopeless agony.

"No," the warrior denied, letting his head fall back. "No!"

Chapter Twelve

Tamara was chilled to the bone with a mixture of sustained fright and frigid air that washed over her as she dangled between the two noxious creatures supporting her. Her upper arms—clamped tightly within the flexed feet of the bat-like beings—hurt with a dull ache that had spread to her shoulders and neck. So high in the atmosphere, so far beyond any source of light, the pitch-blackness of the space around her was disorienting. She had been hanging between the demonesses for what seemed like hours. The awful, interminable flapping of their wings, the ceaseless tempo of their movement, had long since dulled her mind to any chance of potential rescue. If Kaibyn followed, if he were capable of following, he would have overtaken them by now. It wasn't until she felt the downward motion dragging against her flailing legs that she knew the horrific things were lowering her to their destination.

She watched with glazed eyes as Lilit charged past them, the wash of the black-feathered wings of her hell-spawned stallion brutally buffeting. Sharp-looking hooves lashed out at the darkness and though it was impossible, Tamara could have sworn she heard the heavy tattoo of hoofbeats upon cobblestones. Blinking to rid the dryness from her eyes, she caught her first sight of the abode of the queen.

Tall, black craggy spires rose straight up from a nightmarish mountainous terrain. Like a black stone gargoyle, Lilit's fortress perched upon a good-sized plateau with the sheer face of the mountain directly behind it. The surrounding scarp had a coal-like sheen, the steep slopes appearing wet as though coated with venomous slime. There was enough sky-glow in order to see, but no lights or welcoming torches shone from the daunting arrow slits or along the jagged battlements—no beacon lit the ebon way to the keep. Only the faint glint of a faraway quarter moon upon the glistening stones broke the gloomy shadows clinging to Lilit's stronghold.

The shrill sound of a portcullis being raised screeched through the dark sky. Chains rattled like the bones of the walking dead as the vertical iron grills began to go up. Looking at the yawning gateway into the keep, Tamara was reminded of a snarling predator, opening wide its maw to swallow prey, its jagged teeth ready to crush those who would try to escape.

Gliding through the opening, the winged creatures carried their helpless captive into the inner ward and began a smooth dive that was all the more frightening for its soundlessness and ease of descent. Landing adroitly, the demonesses released their grip on Tamara then soared skyward once more, their leathery wings snapping.

There was nowhere for Tamara to run. All around were midnight-dark structures that appeared closed and shuttered. Soaring towers loomed overhead and the crenellated walls seemed thousands of feet above her head. As dark as the night was around her, she feared stumbling into a pit or falling upon the sharp pebbles beneath her feet. She was trapped in this hellish citadel with no help in sight.

The whiny of a horse startled Tamara and she looked up to see Lilit guiding her steed to the ground. The black horse's wings fluttered gracefully as it descended and when its hooves struck the stone ground, sparks lit the night.

Lilit patted the beast's neck then threw a leg over its head and slid from the saddle. The scrape of her boot heels once more sent sparks flying.

Never a coward and always a stalwart warrioress, Tamara lifted her chin and refused to be cowered by the deadly gleam in the queen's cold eyes. As the vampire ruler sauntered toward her, Tamara held her ground.

"There will be no one coming to liberate you, Traitor," Lilit told her. "You will spend your eternity here in Sheol."

"Kill me now for I will not rest until I have taken your life!" Tamara hissed.

Lilit's smile was chilling. "Kill you?" she asked, her tone soft. "My sweet child, I have no intention of killing you." She advanced to within a few feet of her captive. "I want you to live so you can suffer for what you set in motion. I want you in agony over the destruction of my shedim!"

Tamara flinched at the word for she knew it meant Lilit's demonic offspring. The Undead belonged to Lilit and those whose corpses had been incinerated would never be able to raise up to blood another innocent.

"Ah, yes," Lilit cooed, snatching Tamara's thoughts from the ether. "You speak of innocents but your handsome lover is no more innocent than my shedim. When I return to earth, his will be the first visit I will make. His enemies will jump to do my bidding."

Her blood running cold at such a vile thought, Tamara moaned in denial. She did not fear for her future or her own safety, but rather for Evann-Sin's destiny. To think the warrior would be placed into the hands of the queen sent shudders of disgust down Tamara's spine.

"Tell me," Lilit commanded. "What was it like to lie with that handsome warrior?" She came closer. "To have his strong hands on your body? His hard cock in your cunt?"

When Tamara would not answer, Lilit shrugged. "No matter. Don't answer. I will find out for myself soon enough."

With that, the queen spun around and headed for the entrance to her hellish keep. Behind her, her crimson robe billowed and her boot heels struck loudly against the stygian cobblestones.

"Until he comes, we will be alone here, Daughter," Lilit commented. "Other than Amenirdis and Hekat, I have no need for staff. Sheol runs itself."

"He?" Tamara questioned, afraid of the answer, but Lilit ignored the query. "You mean to bring Evann-Sin here?"

But Lilit was out of sight, having entered the inner bailey of the nightmarish keep.

Left with nothing to do save follow her demonic hostess, Tamara slowly entered the high archway of Sheol. Nearly unbearable, the stench there seemed to permeate the air. The copper-like scent of blood was overpowering and it made Tamara's head spin. As she rested her hand upon the soaring wall, she pulled it back, horrified to see her palm coated with a sanguine liquid.

"The walls are alive, Traitor," Lilit told her. "When you touch its rocky flesh, it bleeds." She stopped and turned to smirk at the young woman. "You will hear it moan now and again — you will hear it shriek and cry out in agony, but don't let that concern you. It is only the walls of Sheol lamenting their fate."

Slowly turning her gaze to the walls, Tamara thought she saw the layer of material expand and contract as though it breathed. She shook her head to rid herself of the notion.

"My enemies are encased within the structure of Sheol," Lilit remarked. "Just as one day you will be."

Tamara was wide-eyed as she stared at the barren bailey surrounding her. Unlike other keeps, there were no hitching posts, no doorways and no covered porticos leading to guildhalls or stores. There was no watering troughs, fountain or accoutrements that normally supplied the inner bailey of normal keeps. A deep shale into which her boot heels sank crunched beneath her feet.

"Generations upon generations of crushed bone have settled upon this sterile land," Lilit announced. "It is over the backbones of my adversaries you trod, Traitor."

Sickened by the thought, Tamara put a hand to her throat. Hot bile rose up to scald her as she tried to block out the terrible odor hovering about the place.

The huge black door to which Lilit was headed slowly opened of its own accord. Shrieking with the voice of hundreds of tortured souls, the portal swung wide and clunked into place accompanied by the grunt of many thousand more anguished entities.

Inside the keep, it was as frigid as any windless night upon the high slopes of Aymyron, the North Country at the top of Tamara's world. Cold seeped into her and she shivered, hugging her arms to keep in the dwindling body heat.

"There is no need for light at Sheol," Lilit said. "No light, no fire, no warmth ever penetrates the living walls of my bastion."

Heartsick at the thought of residing in such a desolate place, Tamara felt the last of her energy waning. It was all she could do to put one foot ahead of the other as she followed in the queen's wake.

"You won't have that long to endure the arduous travails of my home," Lilit said with a snort. "Once the bairn is delivered, I will allow you to sleep, albeit a sleep without rest."

Tamara stopped still in her tracks. "Bairn?" she questioned, her heart thudding painfully in her breast.

Lilit was at the top of the steep steps of a curving stairway. She looked down at her prisoner. "Aye," she said. "You carry his whelp."

Eyes widening, lips parting, Tamara stared up at her tormentress.

"You slew Sylviana before she could bring forth the get from the warrior's loins," Lilit reminded Tamara. "Though that whelping was denied me, this one will not be. Within that handsome fighter's body, the spores of my race are thriving. His seed is teeming with it!"

Tamara sagged against the balustrade, cringing at the feel of the slickness that slimed her hand.

"My race will once more rule the lands of the Sumer, and I will be its supreme authority!"

Slumping to the floor, Tamara had a vision of the evil that awaited the human race. She now knew why Lilit had been planning the enthrallment of the Kebullians, the Akkadians and all the other tribes—to feed the demons that would spring one day from the wombs of human mothers.

"Because of your interference, it will take longer than I had planned," Lilit allowed. "But eventually that land will know my race."

Burying her face in her hands, Tamara knew she had to find a way to end her own life. She would never breed a hellish offspring to feed upon the innocent. Somehow, she must rid herself of the thing growing inside her.

"That *thing*," Lilit sneered, "is as much a part of Riel Evann-Sin as it is a part of you. Would you deny it life?"

Tamara was shaking her head, her long hair obscuring her tearful face. "I would deny it life to keep it from your polluted hands."

Lilit came down a few steps and when she spoke, her voice was as soft as a hare's fur. "He will be as handsome as his father and as powerful. He will speak and nations will tremble at his command."

Keening lowly, Tamara was rocking back and forth in her grief.

Leaning over the balustrade, Lilit was lost in the contemplation of the child she pictured in her mind's eye. "Tall and strong, he will walk the land as its ruler and millions will bow down as he passes."

"He will be a blood-drinker," Tamara groaned. "He will be a slayer of innocents."

"He will take only what he needs to thrive," Lilit disagreed. "He will not waste one drop."

Tamara lifted her head, her face twisted with anguish. "He will be a murderer! A defiler! He will be as evil as you!"

Lilit sighed. "One can only hope," she responded.

Overcome with misery, Tamara sprang to her feet and ran for the door. She would throw herself from the rocky crags and end the burgeoning life within her.

But Lilit raised a hand and the black portal slammed shut before Tamara could reach it.

Spinning around, seeking another way to escape, the young woman could not find one. There were no other doorways, no corridors down which she could run. There were no windows through which she could crash. All avenues of escape were barred and only the stairs remained.

"I will never allow you to take the life of my progeny," Lilit warned her. "If I must, I will lash you to your bed and there you will remain for the nine months of your whelping! I will not allow you to terminate this precious life!"

Rushing up the stairs, shoving past Lilit, Tamara headed for the only doorway open to her.

There were no windows in the small room into which the young woman ran. In the strange, limited glow of light that lit the room, there was only a bed, a single chair and small table. The air was warmer here—almost pleasantly so—and the smell that saturated the rest of the keep was missing. Here, it smelled faintly of gardenia.

"I have made it as comfortable for you as I dared," Lilit said. "There is nothing with which you could harm the bairn. All the furnishings are nailed tightly to the floor. Since it is temperate enough for even one of your kind, you have no need of sheet or coverlet with which to stretch that pretty, traitorous neck."

Realizing the hopelessness of her situation, Tamara hung her head, her shoulders slumping as she stood in the middle of the room and stared blankly at the floor.

"I will leave you now to settle in. While I am gone, think of me lying in his powerful arms," Lilit purred. "I can promise you I won't be thinking of you!"

The door to Tamara's prison slammed shut and the sound of a lock being engaged was loud in the dismal room.

Chapter Thirteen

"The Undead have been destroyed," Rabin told the Panther. "There are none left lurching about."

King Numair nodded. His gaze was intent on his son, for Evann-Sin had said nothing for the last hour. Instead, he sat with his clenched hands dangling between his spread knees and stared at the floor.

Kaibyn stood at the window of the Panther's throne room and stared out into the darkness of the night. Since taking a mysterious jaunt to the fields where the Undead were being driven into the pit, the demon had been uncharacteristically quiet. His broad shoulders drooped with the weight of the guilt he obviously felt. He would not answer when spoken to, nor would he look at those who ventured close to him. He seemed locked in his own private hell.

Lilabet had been brought to the Akkadian palace by Rabin and now sat demurely off to one side, her lady-in-waiting close by. Her gaze rarely left Kaibyn though she did not try to approach the demon.

"There is no word on the lady?" the Panther inquired softly.

Evann-Sin raised his head and looked at his father. "What word of her do you need, Majesty? My lady is lost to us."

"Not necessarily," Kaibyn disagreed.

Clenching his fists to keep from attacking the demon, Evann-Sin glared at Kaibyn's back, unwilling to speak to him for fear he'd say things best not voiced.

"You do not blame me any more than I blame myself, warrior," Kaibyn said, reading Evann-Sin's black thoughts. "I could not go after her, for I would have wound up where she is and would be of no use to you."

"You are no use to us now," Evann-Sin threw at him.

Kaibyn flinched, but he made no comment to that remark. He sighed heavily then turned to Rabin. "Think you could find the Magi?"

"I think they'll find us," Rabin answered. "I saw two riders headed this way."

Kaibyn nodded. "You are probably right."

"And just what good will the Magi be to us?" Evann-Sin growled. "Can they go after my lady?"

"No, but they will find someone who can," Kaibyn answered.

"You won't," Evann-Sin accused.

"I *can't*," Kaibyn stressed. "Do you not understand she is in the Abyss, and I dare not go back there for fear of being imprisoned in that wasteland once again?"

"All I understand is that you allowed that bitch to carry my lady away from us," Evann-Sin replied.

Lilabet got up from her chair and walked to the window where Kaibyn stood. She, too, could see riders coming toward the keep. They were the only living things upon the Plains of Celadohr. Everything else had been put to the flame in the giant pit dug by one of the demon's mysterious beasts.

"Did you see Meritaten and Dakhla among the Undead?" she asked her lover.

Kaibyn nodded. "They are no more." A muscle ground in his lean cheek. "I saw to that."

The queen drew in a long breath. "I saw them as we were trying to escape." She shuddered. "They were dead, and I do not know why they were together. Dakhla should have been with her husband. Meritaten was supposed to have been well protected in the seraglio."

"Dakhla plotted my death with Oded," Kaibyn said through tightly held teeth. "She got what she deserved. Meritaten was her friend, although I doubt she knew what Dakhla plotted."

"To be the new queen?" Lilabet asked.

"Aye," Kaibyn agreed.

Rubbing her forehead where a headache throbbed, Lilabet sighed once more. "I should have known what she was about. Meritaten did not have that many friends."

"That friendship cost her her life," Kaibyn said.

"You…" Lilabet's pretty face crinkled. "You did not see her here, did you? On the battlements with the rest of the…" She waved her hand. "You know."

"No," Kaibyn lied. "She was not among those who tried to overrun us."

Laying her head on the demon's strong shoulder, Lilabet closed her eyes. "Thank the Prophetess for that."

Kaibyn put his arms around his lady, but his thoughts were on Dakhla and Meritaten. He had sprayed them both with liquid fire, taking great delight in the snarling horror that registered on Dakhla's betraying face.

"She is at rest, milady," the demon whispered. "Her soul is at rest."

Rabin had become accustomed to Kaibyn Zafeyr's moods and he knew the man was lying. He glanced over at Evann-Sin, but that warrior was still locked deep in his tortured thoughts. Once more he turned his attention to the approaching riders, and drew in a deep breath. "The Magi are here."

Kaibyn nodded. "Aye. We should go down to greet them."

"Give them my regards," Evann-Sin snapped.

Rabin started to say something but the demon shook his head. He jerked a thumb over his shoulder, looked pointedly at King Numair then departed the throne room, everyone except Evann-Sin leaving with him.

His heart breaking, his hands clenched so tightly at his side that his fingernails had dug deeply into the flesh of his palms, the warrior stared out across the plains, but did not see the vista stretched out before him. For how long he stood there in silence, he would never know, but when he felt the presence of another in the room, he turned his head and glared at the intruder.

"She is alive, milord," Jabali said quietly.

"You think so?" Evann-Sin sneered.

"No, milord," Jabali replied. "I know so. Queen Lilit will not hurt your lady before the child is born and even then, I doubt she will do harm to Tamara until the boy has reached puberty."

The warrior's eyes grew wide with shock. "Child?" he repeated. "My lady is with child?"

Jabali nodded. "Though she is as forlorn as are you, she is in good health."

"My child?" Evann-Sin whispered.

Once more the Mage nodded. "And though Lord Kaibyn can not go after her because..."

"Because he's a coward!" the warrior interrupted.

"Have you any notion of what the Abyss is like, milord?" Jabali inquired.

"I am told my lady is there and that is all I need to know!"

"Lord Kaibyn was imprisoned there for over three hundred years before Lady Dakhla summoned him. He has known only a year of freedom. Can you imagine how horrible would be his return to that evil place?"

"Do you think I care?"

The Mage's placid face turned hard. "You should, because if you are to retrieve your lady from that hellish place, you need to know everything there is to know of it!"

"And how am I to do that?" Evann-Sin shouted. He took a step toward the Mage.

Jabali was not threatened by the warrior's stance. He folded his arms, stood his ground and stared steadily back at Evann-Sin.

Unnerved by the unwavering gaze, the warrior relaxed his posture slightly. He was wound as tightly as a clock spring, aching for a fight, needing something to hit, but he instinctively knew he'd lose in a fight with the Mage. Plowing his hand through his hair, he backed off, putting distance between them. "What is it you think I can do?" he queried.

"You can become One with the Blood," Jabali declared.

The right side of the warrior's mouth lifted in a tired grin. "Is that all?" he asked.

"There is a man," the Mage said, "who lives on an island off the coast of Chale. He can help you."

"By doing what? Taking my life?"

"*Changing* your life," Jabali corrected. "Cainer Cree is a Reaper."

A deep frown formed on the warrior's handsome face. "A Reaper. What is that?"

"A Reaper is a being who must partake of blood to thrive. During certain times of the year, he Transitions and when he does, he becomes part wolf."

Evann-Sin arched an eyebrow. "A wolf?" he asked in a droll tone.

Jabali smiled. "Cainer was the second of his kind, having been changed by the treachery of a very vindictive woman long ago."

"I gather she didn't like him."

"On the contrary, she was deeply in love with him. She was obsessed with him. By all accounts, he was the most handsome man to ever walk the face of his world. He was a warrior among warriors, a powerful leader."

"How is it that I have never heard of this mighty warrior?"

The Mage spread his hands. "Because Cainer Cree is not of our world. He came from a world far from our own, from a time thousands of years in our future. He came from beyond the stars."

Evann-Sin sighed. "Well, of course, he did." When the Mage would have chastised him, he held up a hand. "So how do you know what happened in that time yet to come?"

Jabali sighed. "Much of it I learned from Cainer himself."

"Did it occur to you he might be deranged or possibly lying?"

Shaking his head, Jabali sighed again, louder. "No, milord. Such a thought never crossed my mind and besides, he has several scholarly journals from that time and place though they are all but crumbling into dust now."

"That's convenient," the warrior scoffed.

"Please put aside your flippancy, milord," Jabali snapped. "If you want your lady back, it must be through Cainer Cree. I can not help you otherwise!"

Evann-Sin lowered his eyes. "I apologize, Master. Please go on."

"Though it is our future from which he came, it was into the distant past for him. He journeyed through a portal he called a wormhole, striving to escape a woman intent upon killing him."

"He ran from a woman," Evann-Sin snorted. "And he did so crawling down a wormhole. How big is this warrior?"

Jabali waved a dismissive hand. "Stop thinking with your ego and listen to what I am trying to tell you!"

Evann-Sin looked hurt. "It was a legitimate question, Master. If he is small enough to…" He stopped. "How big was this wormhole?"

"Large enough that a fleet of ships could pass through side-by-side, he told me."

Shock registered on the warrior's face. "How big was the damned worm that made it?"

Sighing as though he were being sorely tested, the Mage covered his cheeks with his hands and shook his head.

"Never mind the worm, then. What of this woman? Am I to understand she was dangerous?"

"A very determined as well as dangerous woman. Her name was Zenia, the wife of a minor official in Cainer's government. From the first moment she saw the warrior she was obsessed with him. Wherever Cainer went, she was there waiting. Whatever he did, she was there to watch. She sent him missive after missive, asking to meet with him. She surreptitiously acquired certain belongings of his. He could go nowhere that she did not follow, even to distant worlds beyond his own. When at last she found him alone one evening, she threw herself at him, but he wanted no part of what she had to offer. He was in love with another and fully intended to take that lady to wife as soon as his Tribunal sanctioned his courtship of her."

"I bet that went over big with Zenia," Evann-Sin chuckled.

"She thought she would eventually wear him down, but she underestimated both Cainer and his ability to ignore her. Despite using every trick such women have in their seductive repertoires, Cainer did not—would not—succumb to her advances. At the end of his rope, embarrassed by her persistency, tired of her constant attempts to seduce him, he threatened to have her arrested if she did not leave him alone. By all rights, he should have killed her—or had her slain—but such was not his way."

"I can understand that. Although I entertained thoughts of killing the women who attacked me, I never would have."

Jabali did not remind the warrior that in essence he had killed those women, for they had been among the Undead that had attacked the palace walls.

"What did this Zenia do when he threatened to imprison her?"

"There is an old saying that there is nothing more lethal than a woman scorned. Enraged, she looked for a devastating way to get back at him. She tried to hire an assassin, but not even the lowest scum would dare an attempt on the life of a man such as Cainer Cree. Such was his reputation that all men feared him."

"He told you this?"

"Aye."

"He's rather full of himself, isn't he?" Evann-Sin chuckled.

The Mage ignored the comment. "In desperation, Zenia decided if the deed were to be done, she would have to be the one to accomplish it. Knowing she could never take him in any conventional way, she began scouring medical tomes in search of a poison so potent, so devastating he would die in unbelievable agony. If she could not have him, she was determined no woman ever would, and as he lay writhing in anguish she would make sure he knew who had taken his life."

"Nasty bitch."

"A very determined one," Jabali stated.

"Did she find such a poison?"

"She came across a text written by an obscure Healer that spoke of a plant that grew deep in the rainforests of Resuello, a remote region on another world. It stated that this plant, a fern called lycant, had growing upon its fronds a very deadly fungus. Upon this fungus were highly toxic spores. Inhalation of the spores caused hideous consequences to any creature that became infected with its virulent spores. The afflicted creature would convulse in torment, its bones cracking, its flesh turning to leathery consistency, its body splitting apart even as it breathed. So deadly, so dangerous was this fern, it was strongly advised that the fern be located and completely eradicated. A footnote stated that no action had been taken on the Healer's recommendation for fear anyone sent to destroy it might become contaminated with its spores."

"She somehow harvested some of the spores, though," Evann-Sin said.

Jabali nodded. "Aye, that she did."

Evann-Sin cocked his head to one side. "You said he is the second of his kind. Was she the first?"

Again, Jabali nodded. "Such was her crazed commitment to avenge his spurning of her, she journeyed to this place alone. Wearing what Cainer explained to me was a special suit of armor she thought would protect her from the spores, she ventured into the rainforest and gathered the fungus that grew on the underside of the plant. As she was scraping the fronds, some of the black spores escaped and began floating around her, sticking to her armor. She was shocked to look down and see the spores crawling about upon her armor, seemingly trying to find a way inside its protection. Terrified, she threw down the vial into which she had been scraping the spores and started to flee. But she slipped on the decaying foliage beneath her boots and lost her balance, falling into a sharp thorn bush. One of the thick thorns punctured the suit of armor to the right of her spine, near the base, and stuck into her flesh."

"Oops," Evann-Sin observed.

"As you can imagine, the spores got inside the suit of armor and when she pulled free of the thorn found their way into her bleeding wound."

"And contaminated her."

"At first, nothing happened. She was both relieved and angered. Traveling back to her home world—I believe Cainer called it Ghaoithe—she began to feel poorly. Her body temperature soared and she reported she felt as though she were encased in a giant oven. Her back hurt terribly along the wound yet when she tried to lie down, she felt as though something was lodged against her spine. She could not get comfortable for the pain kept getting worse. Within an hour of her journey home, she realized there was something alive wiggling around inside her lower back."

Evann-Sin winced. "The spores were growing?"

"*Something* was growing," Jabali replied. "Soon, she could feel whatever it was shifting, bunching up along her spine then a horrible pain lanced through her back and she fell to the floor of her airship, screaming in agony."

Evann-Sin noted the strange way the Mage labeled the woman's ship but let it pass. He was more concerned with the implication of what Jabali had said. "What was inside her?" the warrior asked, his eyes wide.

"A minute parasite that lived on the spores of the lycant plant. Cainer later learned that once the parasite enters a host body, it punctures a small artery and travels through the bloodstream until it reaches the kidneys. It is there that it feeds on the blood until it is large enough to attach itself to the host's kidney. What Zenia had felt in that terrible moment of pain was the parasite breaking free of the artery and biting into her kidney. As it grew, it produced offspring that formed a hive. Cainer likened it to a queen bee with her larvae. Once seated within the host's body, it will remain for the entirety of the host's lifespan."

The warrior looked as though he might throw up. He shifted his shoulders, squirming against the image the Mage's words conjured. "There was no way for her to rid herself of it?"

"Not once the parasite is firmly attached to the kidney. To kill the parasite is to seriously wound—if not destroy—the host. If I understood Cainer correctly, though, the chances of eliminating the entire nest are virtually impossible."

"That's a reassuring thought." Evann-Sin shuddered. "She changed to the wolf thing."

Jabali nodded. "Her skin expanded and her bones lengthened, fur sprouted all over her body, her face elongated into the snout of a wolf-creature." He held up his hands. "Her hands and feet changed into those of a beast with thick, black leathery skin. All this was accompanied by cracking, popping sounds that made her think she was about to burst apart. She snarled like a beast and salivated like one as she changed, arching her back and writhing on the floor. She found she could not speak—only growls came from behind her sharp fangs. When it was all over, the Transition complete, she stood hunkered there on all fours, amazed that she was still living. Padding over to a mirror, she rose up on her hind legs and looked into the glass, startled to see a pelt of thick white fur covering her from head to toe."

"That had to have been a horrible sight."

"Cainer said she told him she was elated to see what she had become. She grinned at herself in the mirror, threw her head back and howled! She thought she had found the way to slay Cainer and any others who might anger her. Somehow—inside that animalistic brain—she knew she would change back."

"Her main thought was still one of getting even with him."

"Aye and when the blood lust, the hunger overtook her, she thrilled to think of herself sinking her fangs into his throat, ripping him apart and draining him dry."

"Obviously that didn't happen."

"Not in the way she planned, no." Jabali noticed the warrior frowning. "What concerns you, milord?"

"If Zenia was the first of her kind…"

"The first human of her kind," Jabali corrected.

"All right, I understand that, but who discovered that evil in the first place and how did he know what it would do?"

"One day a healer was walking with his beloved pet dog in the rainforest at Reseullo. The dog was sniffing around the plant and apparently inhaled some of the spores. Once inside the animal, the spores migrated rapidly to its bloodstream and before the night was over, that once gentle, very tame dog had changed into a ravaging beast. It attacked a littermate and tore it to shreds, lapping up the blood like milk. The Healer—fearing for the safety of his wife and children—shot the animal with something Cainer called a laser weapon, yet the animal still lived."

Evann-Sin blinked. "The Healer must have been a fairly bad shot."

"The Healer shot the animal seven times at close range but he could not kill the beast. Each time, the wound would heal within a matter of moments. Stunned, the Healer finally doused the animal with fuel of some sort and set it afire. That did the trick but as the animal smoldered, something crawled out of its body and lay there slithering on the floor."

"The parasite."

"The parasite," Jabali concurred. "Now the Healer was a very intelligent man and knew there had to be a correlation between the spores his pet had inhaled and what had caused the transformation. He poured more oil on the writhing thing and burned it to a crisp. Later, he entered information about the plant in his journal, warning others not to go near it for if it did that to a dog, what might it do to a human?"

"I take it Zenia did not understand the warning."

"Or paid no heed to it in her desire to have revenge on Cainer Cree."

"Not only a vindictive woman but a stupid one."

"By the time she docked her airship at Ghaoithe, she was nearly insane with bloodlust. She realized that she would need to consume blood in order to feed the thing inside her for it was draining her own at an enormous rate. She was weak and her body aching for the taste of what Cainer referred to as Sustenance."

"A delightful thought," Evann-Sin observed, his face wrinkled with distaste.

"Once on shore, she stalked her first kill and devoured the hapless one, literally tearing the body apart in her frenzy. She found she liked the powers she now possessed—strength beyond anything she could have ever imagined and an ability to intercept the thoughts of others. She then set out to capture Cainer Cree and make him pay for spurning her."

"He must have got wind of her plans then if he ran from her."

"Aye, well, she sent word to him that she was coming after him. At first, he laughed it off, but when the mutilated remains of her victims began appearing on his very doorstep, he stopped laughing. She left mangled bodies in her wake. He would have gone after her but learned she was stalking the woman Cainer intended for his own. Knowing he had to do something, he took his own airship and fled, knowing she would follow."

"I'm beginning to like this man," Evann-Sin stated.

"He led her far out into the heavens for he wanted her well away from anyone she could harm. But a violent storm came up, and he was blown off course and into the strangeness he called the wormhole."

"And she was right behind him."

Jabali nodded. "This wormhole he likened to a mighty vortex that swallowed his ship and sucked hers in as well. It spat him out not only in the distant past but also in an entirely different heaven."

Evann-Sin sighed deeply. "Much of this is beyond my understanding, Master. It would be best if you just told me what happened next."

"His airship was fast running out of fuel, and he knew he would never be able to return home. Ahead, he saw another world and it was to this strange place he aimed his craft for he had resigned himself to die, but he had also made a sacred vow that he would take Zenia with him."

The warrior was fascinated with the tale and though he was numb inside from the loss of his lady, he had to know the rest of it. He unconsciously moved to a chair and slowly sat down.

Jabali cleared his throat and finished the tale.

"Once they had landed upon this new world, Cainer left his ship to confront his adversary. He had every intention of killing her then turning his weapon upon himself. He did not want to live without the lady he loved more than life itself."

Evann-Sin closed his eyes briefly. "I can well understand how he felt."

"As soon as she left her ship he fired upon her, cold, murderous intent guiding his aim, but he knew nothing of Zenia's new abilities. She did not go down under the assault though it staggered her. Several more times—as she calmly walked toward him, a vengeful smile on her face—he tried to put her down but it was not to be. He emptied his weapon yet still she came on."

"That had to have amazed him."

"He thought he was dealing with a demoness and—truth be told—he was. Zenia was evil incarnate. He realized he could no longer take his own life, and had no desire to allow her to put her hands upon him so he ran. She began stalking him across the green hills and valleys of Chale.

"Long into the night she toyed with him, easily keeping pace with him for her strength was much greater than his own. When at last he was winded, tired, heartsick, he came to an ancient ruin and standing at the door to that ruin was an old woman so ancient, her flesh so thin, he imagined he could see through her. She was holding up a lantern and beckoning him inside the ruin."

"She was one of the Chalean holy women?" Evann-Sin asked breathlessly.

"The most Holy of their Holies," Jabali responded.

"Who?" the warrior whispered.

"Morrigunia," Jabali told him. "The Goddess of War, Life and Death."

Evann-Sin drew in a breath. "I have heard of her!" he exclaimed. "She comes to a warrior when his life is in danger."

"Aye," the Mage agreed. "It is said she appears to a hero on the day he is to die. The old crone image is only one of her personas. She has many forms and can change her shape at will.

Most often, she comes in the form of a raven. Legend has it that in the form of that crow she will perch on a battlefield and watch men destroying men, saving those she deems worthy."

"She was there to protect him?"

"He was a warrior among warriors, was he not? And the most fine-looking of men?" At Evann-Sin's roll of his eyes, Jabali smiled. "I've seen the man, milord. I tell you now—he is an exceptionally handsome man."

"Morrigunia found him to her liking so she protected him from Zenia."

"No, for she had seen him try to kill Zenia. She was there to make sure he did not escape the woman tracking him."

"Well, hell," Evann-Sin grumbled. "I would have thought she'd keep him safe and punish the woman trying to kill *him*."

"Morrigunia knew what Zenia was. She had foreseen her coming. A human who could change her shape intrigued the Goddess. She wanted to know the secret of this ability so she could bestow it upon her favored warriors."

"I don't see it as an advantage," Evann-Sin declared. "I see it as a curse."

"And Morrigunia saw it that way, as well. Changing into an animal was a fine thing but behaving as one, drinking blood like one, was distasteful to the goddess."

"So why not destroy the woman and the evilness with her?"

"Because Morrigunia wanted Zenia to turn Cainer into one like herself. She had plans for him."

"What did he do when he saw the old woman at the ruin?"

"He ran to her and she led him deep within the ruin. The ruin had a name, by the way—it was called Speal Buanaí. Translated in ancient Chalean, it means Scythe of the Reaper. It was the home of Bás." At Evann-Sin's quizzical look, Jabali said quietly, "Death."

"She was leading him to his death."

Jabali nodded.

"Zenia, of course, came after them. She had not seen the old woman and when she finally found Cainer, he was in a small circular room, a dead end. He turned, came at her, but she threw herself on him and sank her teeth into his neck. Even as strong as he was, he could not escape her and she took him to the stone floor and tried to siphon every drop of his blood. Though he struggled, he could not dislodge her and finally stopped struggling."

"But she did not kill him as she planned."

"Before she could take all his blood and devour him as she no doubt intended, Morrigunia materialized behind her with scythe in hand and severed the mad woman's head from her body."

"Wasn't that redundant since she'd already lost her head over Cainer?" the warrior chuckled.

Jabali tried to look stern but failed. He covered his laughter with a discreet cough. "Behave, warrior," he warned.

Evann-Sin pressed his lips together—though his eyes sparkled with humor—and held up his hand to bid the Mage go on.

"Cainer was lying on the floor. He had turned over to his belly and was trying to push himself up, but he was dying and he knew it. Morrigunia stood over him—scythe in hand—and watched as the parasite wriggled free of Zenia's decapitated body. It lay there flopping on the stone floor as though its own head had been severed from its body. Bending down to push Cainer's shirt out of the evil thing's way, the Goddess of War, Life and Death lowered her scythe and cut a slit in the warrior's back."

"Over his kidney," Evann-Sin said, and then swallowed as though he were about to be sick.

"As soon as the tiny trickle of blood caught the beastess' attention, it raised its green triangular head and flicked out its forked tongue. In the space of a heartbeat, it shot forward and slithered onto the warrior's now unconscious body. Morrigunia leaned against her bloody scythe and watched the creature disappear inside Cainer Cree."

"You called the thing female," Evann-Sin remarked.

"The parasite always is. Why? I can not tell you, but that is the way of it. It slithered to Cainer Cree like a lover to its mate."

"Morrigunia knew what the thing would do," the warrior said with a shudder.

"Aye, for she had been in communication with the parasite since Cainer and Zenia entered this world. In that contact, she learned what the host was capable of doing. The possibilities intrigued Morrigunia—a warrior incapable of being killed on the battlefield, one whose strength exceeded that of ten men and whose bloodlust would be wild who could be controlled by either withholding or providing Sustenance."

"Blood," Evann-Sin mumbled.

"Aye, but the parasite whispered to the goddess that there was a brew that would keep the warrior relatively content and biddable. That brew was tenerse. Addict him to that vile brew and he would be as manageable as needed."

"I don't know which one of them was the most evil—Zenia, Morrigunia or the parasite," Evann-Sin said. He cocked his head to one side. "Does the parasite have a name?"

Jabali shrugged. "If it does, I do not know of it. Cainer calls it the queen much of the time. You will have to ask him when you meet."

The reminder that he would be taken to the Reaper and saddled with that man's curse sobered Evann-Sin completely. Though he was more than willing to do anything to rescue his lady, the thought of having to live as Cainer Cree was forced to terrified him.

"When the parasite changed Cainer Cree forever, Morrigunia hunkered there with the scythe at hand should she need it and was mesmerized by the process of the Transition. She watched him go from human to beast then back to human and realized he would pose a threat to her people if left at Speal Buanaí. He must be taken to a place from which she could take him when she needed him as the ultimate fighting machine—the indestructible warrior who could champion Chale. So before he came fully to himself, she hoisted him upon her shoulder and flew with him to an island off the rocky coast of Chale. There she lay him down and when he sat up, knowing full well he had something evil lodged inside him—having been aware of what had happened to him when that evil took over, he begged her to kill him, to put him out of his misery."

"She, of course, refused."

Jabali smiled slightly. "Did I tell you he is an extraordinarily handsome man?"

Evann-Sin groaned. "Aye, I recall you have made mention of it."

"Hearing his deep voice, looking at this striking man with his honed physique, his dark brown hair and amber eyes, and knowing she had complete control over him, Morrigunia did what any red-blooded woman would do."

"Yeah, yeah, yeah," Evann-Sin said with a pretend yawn. "She jumped his bones."

"Tried to," Jabali agreed, "but he was as repelled by her as he had been by Zenia. Thinking it was her Death persona that had caused this denial of her offer, she changed to her Life persona—a beautiful young woman with long blonde hair, a voluptuous figure, cherry red lips and eyes the color of the sea at sunset. She opened her arms to him, enticed him with suggestive body movements, but he still rejected her. Changing once more—unable to believe he would deny her a third time—she became the Warrioress persona with flowing red hair, eyes as green as a stalk of a new corn plant, and breasts that were full and bare. Yet still did he refused to accept her offer. Enraged, humiliated and stunned that he would dare show such disrespect, she imposed several Geas upon him."

"What is that?"

"Magical obligations. They can also be curses or prohibitions, or bans of some kind. The Geas is distinctive and fitting to each person. To break a Geas can cause great misfortune for those close to you and even result in the death of the recipient. Many a warrior has received his Geas from a woman, but to have been given one by Morrigunia, herself was an honor Cainer came to understand and accept—if not like."

"So what was his Geas?"

"It became his obligation to pass on a fledgling from his body in order to aid those who seek him out.

"But there were prohibitive Geas, as well," Jabali commented. "Each was designed to penalize him for rejecting her advances.

"The first was to make it impossible for Cainer to ever know sexual peace again. Since when he Transitions he takes on the form of a wolf-like creature, she made it so he would only know one mate in his lifetime. When that mate dies or leaves him, he will never have another."

"That is cruel," Evann-Sin stated. "To become celibate of your own accord is one thing, but to have it foisted upon you by a jealous, bitter woman—goddess or not—is a terrible burden. It is unnatural."

"And makes for a very lonely life. The second Geas was designed to make that life as long as possible so the loneliness would eat at the Reaper every day of his extended life. To ensure he would be as lonely as possible, she took him to the island where he resides to this day and left him there alone."

"By the Prophet, that is pitiless!"

"The third Geas placed a ban on him taking his own life. She made it so the parasite inside would not allow him to be able to get out of his punishment."

Evann-Sin shook his head. "The poor bastard."

"And to keep Cainer on the island, Morrigunia placed another Geas upon him. She made it taboo for him to swim so he could never leave the island. To this day, it is a curse of the deargs duls that they cannot swim nor can they cross running water. They cannot so much as put a foot into running water because Morrigunia willed the parasite to fear it would drown if such should happen. So the parasite will not allow the deargs duls to come into contact with running water."

"I hope that is all the shit she heaped on the warrior," Evann-Sin grunted.

"There was one last Geas. When after all attempts at seduction failed, when all punishments were silently accepted, when Cainer Cree proved to be not only an honorable man but a steadfast one, the goddess decided to take him forcefully."

"I know what that's like," the warrior said through clenched teeth.

"Morrigunia laid her hand upon his brow and he fell into a deep sleep. In that sleep, she willed his staff to rise and she impaled herself upon it. She took his seed within her in an attempt to have a girl child of the union but when it came time for her to deliver, it was a male and Morrigunia threw the babe into the fire. She did not want a male. She wanted a girl. Over the years, she tried unsuccessfully to get a bairn from the warrior but finally gave up when she realized only males would come from the loins of Cainer Cree. And so another Geas was placed on Cainer's broad shoulders—no female would ever spring from the staff of a deargs duls."

"So there will never be another female Reaper."

"Ah, but there have been several," Jabali told him. At Evann-Sin's look of surprise, the Mage nodded. "No female will ever spring from the loins of a Reaper for his seed is tainted with the spores and the spores destroy every female embryo at conception. But female Reapers can be made. Though they are rare, there have been those women who have dared to willingly embrace the parasite for personal gain and a few who have been unwilling victims of truly evil Reapers."

"That thought makes me ill," Evann-Sin admitted.

"It disturbs Cainer, as well, and in his imprisonment has made only one woman a deargs dul."

"Deargs dul. That is an evil-sounding word."

"Morrigunia called Cainer her *deargs dul* which in ancient Chalean means intense nature for he was forever brooding and ignored her whenever she came to visit him. So the Chalean term is interchangeable with Reaper."

"And she called Reaper from the ruins where she laid the trap for him?"

"Partly, I suppose. I have pondered that, myself, and think perhaps it was because she had intended for him to reap the souls of her enemies on the battlefield, but I could be wrong. She might well have had another meaning in mind."

"Does she pester him still?"

Jabali drew in a long breath then exhaled slowly. "Not as often as in the early centuries. Now, she rarely comes and then only when she needs something from him."

"How often is that?"

"I think it had been nine years since last she visited. I journeyed there about a year ago. To my knowledge we have been the only two in all that time."

Evann-Sin winced. "He must be a forlorn man."

"He is a very forlorn man, milord. The island where he is imprisoned was once called Longbhriseadh—Chalean for shipwreck—for pirates would lure unsuspecting ships to those barren shores and once the vessel broke apart on the crags, make off with the goods. Since Cainer was forced into residency there, it has become known as the Isle of Uaigneas—the Island of Loneliness—and no one goes near it."

Evann-Sin sighed deeply. "When do I meet this sad warrior, Master?"

"It would take us many weeks to reach Uaigneas by horseback and nearly a week by ship." Jabali reached down and put a hand on the warrior's shoulder. "I do not believe you want to wait that long to get your lady back."

"No, but..."

"I will have Kaibyn take you to Uaigneas. He should find Cainer Cree an interesting conversationalist."

Chapter Fourteen

Cainer Cree was dreaming.

He was dreaming of Aisling and the last time he had held his beloved lady in his arms. They had made love only the one time, and the memory of that wondrous mating would have to last him a lifetime...

Her skin was like silk and held the tawny kiss of the sun. Dewy gold to compliment the honey blonde of her waist-length tresses, her flesh carried the scent of jasmine mixed with a touch of musk and when he ran the tip of his tongue across the smooth expanse of her swan-like neck, she tasted sweet and intoxicating. She was taller than most women of his acquaintance and had the easy laugh of the self-assured. Intelligent, creative, always in search of wisdom, she exuded confidence and clearness of purpose.

With burgeoning nipples that bid a man's lips to suckle their dusky nubs, her breasts were lush, filling a warrior's hand to overflowing. The deep cleavage drew a man's eyes and beckoned exploration. To rouse those dark coral tips to arousal, to pluck at them with trembling fingers, to lave the pebbly flesh with an eager tongue – such was the way to edge Aisling toward satisfaction.

But true satisfaction had to be drawn from the juncture of her long, shapely legs – legs that could strongly – and possessively – wrap around a man's waist and anchor him to her hot, slick core. Many had been the feverish dreams he had entertained of what came after that intimate contact, but the reality of lying with Aisling Lalor far surpassed any dream he could have fashioned with his engorged member.

It had been on the cliffs of Amhantar, that windswept part of Ghaoithe that perched precariously on the shores of the Fiach Sea that they had consummated their love. The air was warm and misted with salt spray, a slight breeze plying its caressing fingers over their naked bodies. Far off to the West, the sky was darkening blue-gray with oncoming rain and now and again, a fork of lightning stabbed into the bowl of the ocean. Overhead, inquisitive seagulls soared upon the thermals and glanced down at the lover's bower where Cainer Cree had carried his beloved Aisling.

As he reclined upon the blanket he had spread for their use, she had stripped for him there on the barren cliffs where no man dwelt and no passing ship marred the glossy surface of the waters. With each piece of clothing that had reluctantly left her luscious body — for he imagined even that inanimate material was hesitant to stay its caressing of her abundant curves — Cainer had drawn in a ragged breath, licking his lips in anticipation of the meal being prepared for him.

When at last she was bare to him, as upon the day she had eased from her mother's womb, he got up and went to her, going to his knees in adoration of her grace and breathtaking beauty. He wrapped his strong arms around her and laid his cheek to the satiny indention of her concave belly. He could hear the increasing beat of her heart beneath his ear and as her fingers wound through his hair, he closed his eyes and reveled in the feel of having her in his arms.

"I am the luckiest man on the face of the earth," he whispered.

"And I am the luckiest woman," she replied.

"I have never been so happy," the warrior vowed.

"Let me add to that happiness, milord," she whispered.

She slid down to her knees and offered her breasts to him. Like a greedy infant, he pressed his mouth to her turgid nipple and suckled, drawing upon that nubbin as though it contained the very essence he needed to make it through another day.

Aisling let her head fall back and she closed her eyes to the delicious sensation his lips and tongue worked upon her body. She quivered as that wicked tongue flicked across one straining peak, and his teeth lightly closed upon the base.

"Aye, my wondrous warrior," she sighed.

His hands were now cupped on the sleek roundness of her ass, his fingers meeting there in that mysterious cleft. He eased his middle finger into that cleft and touched the opening of her anus and circled it with the pad of his digit. She lurched forward, pressing his face hard against her breast.

"Do not tease me, Cainer!" she protested.

He chuckled around the delicacy upon which he drew and eased his finger inside her.

"Ah!" his lady sighed, and quivered from head to toe.

He drew back, abandoning her swollen nipple and slid his free hand around her hip, turned it palm up and cupped her dewy sex, his thumb resting along the crease of her leg where thigh met love mound. Lightly he squeezed and felt moisture oozing on his palm.

"You are a wicked man, Cainer Cree," she accused.

"You think so?" he crooned then arched his hand so the middle finger slipped gently into her vagina.

"Oh!" she exclaimed, and quivered once more.

Impaled on both his middle fingers, she leaned against him, laying her head on his shoulder.

"'Tis no fair, Cainer. You are clothed and I am not," she pouted.

"That can easily be remedied, Aisling," he told her.

Withdrawing his fingers, grinning at her groan of objection, he moved back from her and ripped open his shirt. The black pearl buttons of his uniform scattered upon the blanket. Pulling the shirt from his britches, he shrugged out of the torn material and made quick work of his belt and the closing at his waist.

Sitting down, he pulled off his black boots and tossed them aside. In a graceful, assured move that brought a gleam of pride to Aisling's sea-colored eyes, he stood up and rid himself of his britches. As he made to kneel down, she put her hands on his muscled thighs to prevent him.

"I see something that interests me greatly, Cainer," she said. "And being the student of research I am, I would like to investigate this anomaly further."

She took his swollen staff into her hands and leaned close, studying the thick veins that pulsed beneath the thin flesh. With the tip of her tongue poking from the side of her mouth as she engaged in deep concentration, she used her other hand to cup and weigh the ridged pouches that dangled behind his fleshy weapon.

"Fascinating," she commented, as she stroked his hard rod. She gently grazed her fingernails along that firm length and ran the tip of her index finger into the tiny slit. Almost immediately, a pearly drop oozed from that opening and she caught it on the underside of her fingernail.

With her eyes locked on his, she brought her finger to her tongue and tasted his essence.

"Aisling, for the love of the gods!" he groaned. Already his cock was throbbing, aching with desire for the woman kneeling at his feet.

"For the love of Cainer," she returned, and leaned forward to draw that pulsing rod between her lips.

He had been unprepared for the immediate response of her lips sliding along his member. He had not anticipated her virginal response to be so exacting. As she took his entire rod into her mouth and she drew on his aching flesh, he grabbed her head, thrusting his fingers through her golden curls and brought her face closer to the juncture of his thighs.

He had not meant to be so unseemly. Like an untried youth, he had exploded, pulsing his juices into her eager mouth. He was lost as she suckled him, swallowed his cum as though it were the most natural thing in the world. She was laving him with her tongue, flicking it teasingly into the slit of cock and massaging his balls as though to coax from him the very last drop.

When at last she allowed him to fall to the blanket — exhausted and sated — she lay down beside him and nestled her head on his sweaty shoulder.

"Maeve instructed me quite well, wouldn't you say?" she whispered.

He should have known. Maeve was her older sister, and the woman was a professional. A Priestess in the Love Centers of Ghaoithe's capitol at Ghaoth Aduaidh, there was nothing the woman did not know about satisfying a man. That she had dared teach Aisling both angered and delighted the warrior.

"For shame, Aisling," he said. "What would your mother say?" His voice took on a strained tone. "What would your father say?"

"*Father would say I had made an informed decision to perform as best I could learn to, and Mother would want to know how big your cock is.*"

Face flaming, Cainer denied such a thing would happen. He would have chastised her for her wayward tongue, but she placed her fingers upon his lips. He groaned, inhaling the scent of his love juice on her hand.

"*Are you going to leave me wanting, warrior?*" she asked, sliding her hand down his heavily pelted chest to the equally heavily pelted realm that so delighted her. She cupped him. "*Will you let it be said General Cainer Cree cares only for his own pleasure and not that of his betrothed?*"

Aisling's eyes grew wide as she took in the wicked glint that pierced her lover's eyes. Her mouth opened into a shocked "O" only a second before he had her on her back and her legs wrapped around his neck.

"*I'm hungry,*" he said in a throaty voice.

Cainer Cree had become a legend to his people because his hand on a laser war sword could cut a swathe through the enemy like a harvester through a wheat field. Steady and sure, unbelievably brave, the warrior had gained an unblemished reputation and was feared far and wide. His word was his bond and to have his friendship was an accomplishment many warriors actively sought.

The man who lowered his face to Aisling's cunt was therefore a man of steady purpose and single-minded devotion to duty.

He was also as highly trained in the art of lovemaking as his future sister-in-law Maeve was an expert in hers.

Aisling writhed beneath the assault. She arched her hips up and wrapped her fingers around her warrior's rock-hard biceps. Reveling in the strength of those strong arms, knowing well how lethal that flesh could be, she shuddered.

"*Make me a woman, my beloved,*" she whispered, her breasts heaving in the excitement rushing through her body. "*Make me your woman.*"

The words thrilled Cainer and spurred his tongue on to quicker stabs into the velvety lips of her cunt. He lapped her juices, smacking *his lips like a man dining on food that had not been set before him for weeks.*

He was ravenous.

He was on fire with a need that had turned his cock into a rigid, pulsing, ready war engine that would soon batter down her virginal defenses.

He slid his tongue up her belly, tasted the sweat droplet that had puddled in her deep belly button, and then tasted once more the delights of her breasts as he settled his lower body between her trembling thighs.

Positioning her legs more securely over his shoulders, he bid her lock her ankles in place. Hearing only her grunt of acceptance of his request, he poised his tool at the core of her dripping box.

"Relax, my love," he instructed. He was trembling, striving to hold back the climax that was rapidly approaching.

"Relax, hell," Aisling disagreed. "Fuck me, warrior!"

Her words were like a red-hot prod against his ass, and he drove into her with far less gentleness than he had intended. Once inside, he could not stop the battering ram of his cock striking at the wall of her hymen. He broke through that flimsy barrier and thrust his weapon into the inner bailey of her dripping keep and stilled, holding that tool as deep in her as he could go.

The first ripple of her release traveled along his cock and as it moved — gripping and releasing his staff in strong little pulses — the dam burst upon the rigid hold he was striving to maintain and his cum came thick and strong into his lady's waiting receptacle.

"Aisling!" he shouted, filling her with all he had to give.

His lady dug her short fingernails into the bunched muscles of his back, scoring the tanned flesh and leaving little half moons.

"Cainer!" she returned.

When the last squeeze faded from her vaginal walls and the last pulse shot from his penis, he collapsed atop her — sweaty and spent, her arms now where her legs had been. She hugged him to her, refusing to allow him to remove the heavy weight of his body atop hers that so thrilled her. He lay with his chin braced on her soft shoulder.

"I love you," she told him, and placed her lips upon the still-throbbing hollow at the base of his throat.

"I would die for you," he vowed.

"I will die with you," she swore.

As he had for many years, Cainer woke from his wet dream to sit bolt upright upon the monkish bed he had chosen for his rest. The wetness did not come from the arousal of his staff but from the tears that had drenched his pillow.

Plowing his hand through his tousled hair, he swung his bare legs from the bed and sat there on the side, staring listlessly at the floor. His heart was hurting with the old familiar pain. His body still ached for a release he would not allow. The fragments of his dream, the sights and sounds, slowly faded—as did Aisling's dear, beautiful face—only to be replaced with awareness that he was no longer alone on his primitive prison island.

He cocked his head to one side and "listened" to the conversation coming from the two visitors headed his way. Though he had been expecting the men, knew they were coming, he had mixed emotions about their arrival.

Coming wearily to his feet, he reached for his britches and stepped into them. Since becoming trapped in his hellish jail, he had taken to sleeping in the nude. He knew it now amused Morrigunia, but for a century or two, it had only added to her frustration. As he thought of the goddess berating him for boldly displaying his wares for her to see, a slight smile tugged at the corners of the warrior's mouth.

Dressed in his black britches, he went to the door of his little hut and opened it. The night before had been a bit chilled and he had closed the portal he normally left open. Standing with his hands braced on the lintels, he waited for the two men who were making their way up the winding oyster-shell pathway to his home. When they were twenty or so feet away, he lowered his hands and went out to meet them.

As they approached the Reaper, Evann-Sin had to admit the man was as good-looking as Master Jabali had indicated. A warrior at the prime of his physical prowess with chiseled pectoral muscles, a flat belly powerfully ridged, a slender waist with not an ounce of spare flesh clinging to it and biceps that were half again as large as Evann-Sin's own. Cainer Cree was a soldier with whom he would not care to swap hits. Looking down at the Reaper's hands, he figured they were strong enough to take most any man in a fair fight.

"I don't always fight fair, Riel," the Reaper said. He stopped about five feet away from them and crossed his arms over his bare chest. "Do you?"

Evann-Sin shrugged. "Not always."

"Nor do I," Kaibyn quipped. "You do what you have to."

Cainer Cree's amber eyes slid to the demon. "Aye," he agreed. "You do."

Kaibyn surprised Evann-Sin by stepping forward and putting out a hand to the Reaper. "I am Kaibyn Zafeyr," he said.

Slapping his palm to underside of the demon's forearm in the ages-old custom of warrior to warrior, Cainer accepted the greeting then turned to Evann-Sin and repeated the gesture.

"I would invite you inside," the Reaper said, "but there is but a small cot, one rickety chair and a table large enough for a plate and cup. It is about as comfortable as a monk's cell." He released Evann-Sin's arm. "I spend ninety percent of my time outside."

Kaibyn looked toward the horizon where a storm was brewing. "Even in the rain?"

"Especially in the rain."

"Does it rain here often?" Evann-Sin inquired.

"Every day. Chale is known for its rain and fog."

Almost as though nature planned it that way, a light mist fell from the heavens and gently peppered the leaves overhead. So thick was the foliage, no moisture found its way to the men.

The Reaper led them to a greensward behind the cot where a sheltering tree rustled softly in the light breeze. Scattered around the lush green grass were several rocks that had been hollowed out to form what looked like chairs.

"They are comfortable enough," Cainer told them, sweeping a hand toward the rocks.

Evann-Sin sat down and was pleasantly surprised at the relative comfort of the rocks. "Did nature do this or was it your doing?" He wriggled around in the hollow of the rock until he was at ease.

Cainer smiled slightly. He took a seat on the ground, drew his knees up and circled them within the perimeter of his arms. "A little of both," he replied. "When I was first here, I admit I took my frustrations out on the poor rocks. I was like a man possessed — using one rock to pound another. I pretended it was Morrigunia's head I was bashing in."

"The warrior told me about that one. I can see why you'd want to beat out her brains," Kaibyn said. He shifted on the stone chair and patted it with his hand. "This isn't bad at all."

The men were quiet for a moment, their attention going to the ocean where lightning was stitching across the firmament. The breeze had become a steady wind that tousled their hair.

"How long have you been here?" Evann-Sin finally asked.

"I lost count after the first decade," Cainer admitted.

"You don't look a day over forty," Kaibyn commented.

"Nor will I," the Reaper said softly. "Such was the last Geas that damned bitch threw at me."

"You want to look older?" the demon asked in a shocked tone.

"I want to *be* older," Cainer answered. "I want to be allowed to wither and die as the gods intended it." A muscle jumped in his cheek. "I want to cease to exist."

"But she won't allow it," Evann-Sin said.

"No, she won't allow it. Along with all the other wicked things she has done to me over the years, I think keeping me alive is the worst."

"I can't imagine anything being so bad you want your life to end," Kaibyn commented. "I loathed every moment I was interred in the Abyss, but I never wanted to die. Now—for all intents and purposes—I am as dead as the rock upon which my ass is resting. Would it be the same for you, Reaper? Would you come back as I did?"

"I can't die unless someone lops off my head or burns me to a crisp, and I can't see that happening."

Kaibyn turned to Evann-Sin. "Could you take his head, warrior?"

"He could try," the Reaper answered, "but Morrigunia would prevent it."

"It must be hell for you here," Evann-Sin said.

Cainer smiled grimly. "It has its moments, but those moments are few and far between, thank the gods." He shrugged. "For the most part, I am reasonably content. I exercise, I paint, I take very long walks."

"Paint?" Kaibyn echoed.

"I'll show you sometime, demon," the Reaper promised.

"Morrigunia doesn't visit that often I take it," Evann-Sin said.

"Only when she wants to taunt me by telling me she's sending another potential candidate for Reaperhood," Cainer responded.

"How could you accept...?" Evann-Sin held his hands up. "You know—what you are?"

"What other choice did I have?" came the query. "The first time I Transitioned, I was horrified. It hurts, aye, but it is the knowing that this is going to continue, will happen every three months or so, that is the true dreadfulness of it. You can't die, you can't escape. You can simply exist."

"But the tenerse," Evann-Sin suggested. "That has to be revolting all its own, knowing you have become addicted to it."

"Aye, but without it, the situation is a thousand times worse."

"Something tells me you found that out firsthand," Kaibyn remarked.

The Reaper's handsome face turned hard. "Aye, and believe me when I tell you that is something I never care to experience ever again."

"What happened?" the warrior inquired. His forehead was creased with worry lines.

"It was the last time Morrigunia tried to seduce me," Cainer said. "She gave me a choice—mate with her or suffer the consequences." He snorted. "I told her I'd rather mate with a half-dead civet cat rather than take her loathsome body to mine."

"Ouch," Kaibyn chuckled.

"She wasn't pleased with my smart-ass comment," the Reaper stated. "So to punish me, to show me who was in charge here, she took away all the animals so there would be no food. But even worse, by taking the food out of my reach, she also denied me the Sustenance. I had been very careful to take only a little bit each day from a variety of creatures for I feared killing them and having to do without."

"Already you were in need of blood," Kaibyn said.

Cainer nodded. "But as yet, I had not been introduced to the tenerse. I went mad within a week, and by the second week was tearing at my own flesh, biting into my arm to drink the blood. She saw what I was doing and brought her Sisters to help her hold me down." He smiled slightly. "They are strong women, let me tell you, because I was a raving lunatic by then, and not many men could have restrained me. While her Sisters held me down, she poured the tenerse down my throat. Almost instantly, the madness left in a soft haze of numbness."

"She had to know what the tenerse would do to you," Evann-Sin said.

A muscle bunched in the Reaper's lean jaw. "Oh she knew, all right. She fed me that shit for a week until I was good and hooked."

"No Sustenance?" Kaibyn asked.

"Hers," Cainer replied. "One teaspoon of that potent brew lasted an entire day, but that could not go on forever. She grew tired of taking care of me and brought the animals back. One last time she tried to make me mate with her and I told her I'd rather eat dirt. I didn't see her again for almost six months."

"What of the tenerse?"

"She left me plenty and gave me the recipe to make more," the Reaper said, pointing inland. "There is wheat growing over there. I plant it and harvest it myself. It is from a type of mold on the wheat that I make the tenerse."

Kaibyn wrinkled his nose. "What does it taste like — this mold?"

"Bitter," was the reply. "But you get use to it. Without it, I don't think I could sleep and the craving for Sustenance is a hundred times worse."

"I don't know why I am being forced to do this," the warrior lamented. "Why can't I just go after Tamara and…"

"How?" Kaibyn cut him off. "You can't fly there on your own. How would you get there without the Reaper's help?"

"When a potential changeling comes to me, I always give him — or her in the case of one remarkable young lady — a choice. They must leave here before they can change, anyway. They take from here the ability to become a Reaper. If they have the courage and the desire to do it, they will. If they don't, they won't."

"What is it they take with them?" Kaibyn inquired.

"A part of the parasite that made me what I am. If they don't use it, I make them swear to me they will destroy it. They must throw it in the fire and burn it to ash. The world must not be left defenseless with those creatures breeding indiscriminately."

"Has one of the potential ones who did not use it let it live?"

"No."

"How do you know?" Evann-Sin asked.

"Because each time one of those things is cast into the fire, the queen senses it and as soon as she feels her offspring dying, she punishes me. I know when one of them meets its death."

"Punishes you how?" the demon inquired.

"By causing me such savage pain you can not begin to imagine it," was the reply. "Anytime a Reaper angers his or her parasite that is the payment to be made."

"And this is what the Mage plans for me," Evann-Sin said with a shudder.

"It has a few good sides to it, warrior," the Reaper told him.

"None that I can see."

"You will be able to read minds."

"Terrific," the warrior mumbled.

"You will have the strength of ten men."

Evann-Sin twirled his index finger in the air.

"You will be able to fly."

Kaibyn blinked. "As I do?"

Cainer shook his head. "No, in a flying ship."

"A flying ship," Evann-Sin snorted. "That I have to see."

"All right," the Reaper agreed. He got up and started walking, heading deeper into the lush foliage behind him. "Let's go see her."

Kaibyn and Evann-Sin exchanged looks then hurried to catch up with their host. Batting aside huge leaves and pushing past low-hanging vines, they were soon almost on his heels.

"This was the flying ship you came here in?" the warrior inquired, stumbling over a fallen tree trunk.

"Aye," Cainer replied.

For ten minutes, the trio traveled through the lush foliage. Ahead of them, the sound of waves crashing along the shore brought with it the smell of salt water.

"How she moved it, I don't know. I landed in a field on the mainland," Cainer explained. "I was almost out of fuel, putting her down on fumes alone."

"Fumes?"

The Reaper shook his head. "It would be too hard to explain. Let's just say that's an age-old expression for she never ran on fuel as you might know it."

Kaibyn leaned toward Evann-Sin. "Remember the machines I brought forward from the past? Those ran on what they called gasoline."

Cainer turned. "Fossil fuel, aye."

Evann-Sin shook his head. "I don't want to know what that is."

"You don't need to," the Reaper said. "You just need to know how to fly her."

"If she has no fuel, how could he?" Kaibyn inquired.

They had come to a tall bluff overlooking the heaving waves of the ocean. Mighty waves crashed against the steep cliffs and white spray leapt high into the air. Beyond the heaving waves was a smaller island.

"There," Cainer said, pointing.

Evann-Sin narrowed his eyes. What he saw amazed him. "That is your flying ship?"

"It is called a L.R.C.," the Reaper informed him. "A long-range cruiser."

Situated on a small island about a hundred yards off the coast of the Isle of Uaigneas, a large object sat perched, like a black bird of prey waiting to pounce upon its victim. The "beak" of the strange contraption pointed toward the ground as though it was in search of food. Stretched out to either side of the long neck of the object, two huge wings gleamed in the midmorning sun. Droplets of water from the earlier rain sparkled like jewels on the dark skin of the craft.

"By the gods," Kaibyn whispered. "Look at her!"

"She's a sweet machine," Cainer said in a wistful voice. "The best in the fleet, actually."

"Does she have a name?" the demon asked.

"The *Levant*," the Reaper replied as though he spoke a lover's name. "I sit here hours on end remembering what it felt to fly her, to soar into the heavens and wing my way from world to world. She is as fleet as the wind, as powerful as a vortex but as silent as a gentle breeze."

"The *Levant*," Kaibyn repeated, his tone filled with awe.

Cainer flexed his hands. "I remember well my hands on the controls." He looked down at his open palms. "I remember the feel of her instantly obeying my every command." He looked back at the ship. "I dream of flying that beauty almost as often as I dream of my lady."

"How did Morrigunia get it here?" Evann-Sin asked.

Cainer shrugged. "My guess is she used magical means to bring it here for I know damned well she couldn't fly her."

"That's how we will be traveling to the Abyss?" Evann-Sin inquired.

"How *you* will be traveling to the Abyss," Kaibyn corrected. "You know I can't accompany you, warrior."

"And you think I can fly it?" the warrior asked, his eyes wide. "You are the one who can fly, demon!"

"But he wouldn't be able to fly that baby," Cainer told him. "She was designed especially for me. Her console was built for my body and her controls operate only at my command for I programmed her."

"But..."

The Reaper held up his hand. "Once you have the fledgling inside you, you will know everything I know because it knows everything I've ever learned. My personal history will be as clear to you as it is to me. What I can do, you will be able to do."

"The f-fledgling?" Evann-Sin questioned, swallowing hard. "You mean the p-parasite?"

"Aye, warrior," Cainer Cree replied. "You must accept the fledgling as well as partake of a cup of blood. The nestling will bond to the blood as it flows through your body."

"How does he get that disgusting thing into him?" Kaibyn asked.

"One of you will need to harvest the nasty little bitch from my body, make a small incision on Riel's back and allow it to enter."

The warrior turned a pasty green color and looked as though he were inhaling a particularly noxious odor. "I think I'm going to be sick," he commented.

"But we can't do that here," Kaibyn said. "Introducing it to his body, I mean."

Cainer shook his head. "No, else he'd be trapped here just like me. You will need to take him over to the island, let the fledgling do its job then he'll be able to fly The *Levant* to the Abyss."

Evann-Sin was shaking his head. "Even if I could fly it, I have no idea where the Abyss is!"

"It's more a state of mind that an actual place," Kaibyn muttered.

"But it does exist in real time," Cainer remarked. "Once you have impregnated the warrior with the parasite, come back here and I will gather the information from your memory, give Riel the coordinates so he can program them into the navigational system and…"

"Program? Coordinates? Naviga…" The warrior threw his hands up. "This is far beyond my ability to grasp it, Reaper!"

"It won't be after you Transition."

"The Abyss is a vast place," Kaibyn reminded the Reaper. "How will we go about finding Tamara in that immensity?"

"With what is in your pocket," Cainer said.

"My pocket?" Evann-Sin questioned then remembered the bloody kerchief that had come unwound from Tamara's hand. He reached into his pocket and pulled it out.

"What is that?" Kaibyn asked.

"It is his lady's blood," Cainer replied, and before the warrior could ask, he told him it had come from her injury on the battlements during the skirmish.

Evann-Sin stared down at the blood then brought the stain to his lips and kissed it. "What good does this do?"

"Reapers can track through the DNA in that sample. I've never done it, but I know it can be done. If I can do it, you will be able to once you are Reaper. You will be able to find her from the unique smell of her blood."

"I don't know," Evann-Sin said, shaking his head. He plowed his fingers through his hair. "I just don't know that I can do this."

Cainer stared at him for a long moment. "Do you want your woman back?"

"Of course, but…"

"How much are you willing to give up in order to be with her?"

Evann-Sin lifted his chin. "I would give my life!"

"And that is exactly what you will be doing," the Reaper reminded him. "If you aren't man enough to accept that, if you are too squeamish to become One with the Blood, get the fuck off my island."

The warrior looked from the Reaper to the airship, then back again. His hands were clenched at his sides and a vein throbbed brutally in his neck. Once more, he turned to look at the black bird of prey perched upon the island.

"You think I can fly that?" he asked at last.

"You will be able to fly her as well as I ever could."

"To the Abyss?"

"To my home world if need be," Cainer agreed.

"But there is no fuel," Kaibyn reminded the Reaper.

"Ah, but there you are wrong, my friend. I have had many years to sit here on this bluff and think about what I could use to fuel her. I have spent hour after hour after hour contemplating the problem. On Ghaoithe, I was an engineer before I went to the Academy and became a pilot. I studied the properties of minerals and ores, and I knew the composition of each and every crystal, every ore that could be harvested for energy to drive that ship. A year ago—when the Mage showed up to tell me you would be coming—I told him what I needed and he procured it for me. Everything you will need to get her up and running is there on the island. You will know what to do when you come out of Transition."

Evann-Sin hunkered down on the ground and perched there with his elbows on his thighs. He was staring hard at The *Levant* and was silent for a long time.

Neither Cainer nor Kaibyn broke the other man's concentration for it was obvious he was striving to make a decision on the matter. His eyes were narrowed as he studied the ship. When at last he spoke, he didn't look at his companions.

"I have a question for you, Reaper," he said.

Cainer folded his arms over his chest. "And that is?"

"Morrigunia cast a Geas on you so you cannot cross running water."

"Aye."

"Because the parasite is afraid you will be pulled down into the water and drown."

"Aye."

"Same would hold true of crossing a bridge, I suppose. The parasite would not allow it."

"Those are statements, warrior, not a question," Kaibyn said with a grunt.

"You have the right of it. So what?"

Without taking his gaze from the ship, he got to his feet and with his hands on his hips asked if Cainer could cross running water if he was flying over it.

When Cainer did not answer, Evann-Sin craned his head around and looked up at the Reaper. The look on that man's face brought a slow smile to the warrior's.

"Am I right in thinking that if you were on The *Levant*, you could cross the water without the parasite being afraid?"

Kaibyn smacked his forehead with the palm of his hand. "By the gods, of course! He can't put even the *tip* of a toe in the water but as long as he isn't touching it, he should be able to cross it!" He drew in a quick breath. "Can we get the ship over here to this island?"

Cainer Cree turned his eyes to his ship. "She has hover capabilities and can land down on the beach. She has vertical takeoff so we have no need of a runway. I could board her unless Morrigunia stops me with another Geas."

"She's not here," Evann-Sin reminded him. "She hasn't been here in nine years."

"She's forgotten about you, Reaper," Kaibyn suggested.

"Don't count on it."

"You want off this bloody island?" Evann-Sin asked.

Cainer nodded slowly. He returned his gaze to Evann-Sin and stared long and hard at the man. "I wouldn't be *touching* the water," he said quietly. "I wouldn't be *in* the gods-be-damned water—I wouldn't be *on* the gods-be-damned water. I would be *over* the gods-be-damned water."

"That's what I'm saying," Evann-Sin agreed.

Cainer turned once more to the ship. "All that thinking," he said, unfolding his arms. "All that fucking thinking, all those fucking years, and I never thought of *that*."

"Then let's get this caravan on the road before Morrigunia thinks of it, too!" the warrior said.

Chapter Fifteen

It was the most hideous thing Evann-Sin had ever seen in his life. The wriggling creature was about two inches long, a sickly grayish-green color with a triangular head and twin rows of sharp teeth that dripped some kind of noxious slime. Whipping back and forth upon the fingers of the demon, it tried to bite Kaibyn, lashing out with a horny tail.

The Reaper sat up, the incision in his flesh over his left kidney healing as Evann-Sin watched. Within a matter of a few moment's time, only a slender trickle of blood was left to mark where the fledgling had been removed from Cainer's back.

"Another advantageous thing about being a Reaper is the almost instantaneous healing ability." He smiled. "And the long life."

"By the gods, this thing stinks as bad as the slime under the Abyss!" Kaibyn remarked. He held the parasite at arm's length.

"Put it in the jug and make sure the lid is tight else it will wriggle free," Cainer warned.

Handing Kaibyn a small stoneware jug, Evann-Sin watched as the demon dropped the wiggling creature inside and quickly plopped the lid in place.

"Once you are on The *Levant*, all you'll need to do is cut the same size incision in Riel's back as you cut into mine, and then shake the creature out of the jug. It will slither inside him of its own accord."

"Such a delightful thought," Evann-Sin whispered.

"It will hurt like hell, warrior," Cainer warned. "I won't lie to you about it, but the pain lasts only a few minutes."

"When will he Transition?" Kaibyn asked.

"Hopefully within an hour of being impregnated with the fledgling."

Evann-Sin winced. "You couldn't think of a better word than that to describe introducing it to my back?"

Cainer shrugged. "It is what it is," the Reaper told him. "And the sooner the thing is done, the sooner you can Transition. The sooner you Transition…"

"The sooner he'll be able to fly your machine," Kaibyn finished.

"And take me off this gods-be-damned island," Cainer agreed.

"Do you suppose Master Jabali knew this would happen?" Evann-Sin asked.

"The Mage?" Cainer asked. "He must have. I only wish the son-of-a-bitch had told me!"

"And run the risk of Morrigunia visiting you and finding out?" Evann-Sin inquired.

"Aye, well, I see your point."

"All right," Kaibyn said, stuffing the stoneware jug into a rucksack. "Let's get across to the island and inside the ship. Every minute Tamara remains in Lilit's hands is anathema to me."

At the mention of his lady, Evann-Sin flinched. Pain crossed his features and settled deep into his golden eyes.

"Go with the Wind, my friends," Cainer blessed them. "Now, hurry!"

The Reaper stood intrigued as the demon took hold of the warrior's arm and in the blink of an eye propelled them both off the Isle of Uaigneas. Putting up a hand to shield his eyes from the fierce glare of the setting sun, he watched as the two appeared on Achasán Isle.

"Why do they call it that?" the warrior had asked.

"Morrigunia named it," Cainer had explained. "In the Chalean High Speech, Achasán means to taunt." He had nodded toward the ship. "She put The *Levant* there to remind me of the loss of my freedom and what would never be again."

Evann-Sin and Kaibyn had reached The *Levant* and were standing there staring up at its dark hull. They appeared to be arguing about something then Kaibyn strode forward and pushed against the panel Cainer had told them would open the hatchway of the ship.

The Reaper chuckled as both men jumped back as the hatchway door shot up to grant them entry and a section of gangplank dropped into place on the ground. He shook his head as the two once more started arguing. His hardy laughter frightened a nearby flock of seagulls as he watched Kaibyn shove Evann-Sin up the metal gangplank. When both men had disappeared inside the craft, the Reaper let out a long breath.

He was not assured that he would ever leave the island upon which he was standing. The fatalist inside him warned that something would happen to prevent his leaving. It was only a matter of time before Morrigunia became aware of the plans and appeared to put a stop to his escape.

Not that it really mattered. As much as he wanted to gain his freedom again, to know the companionship of other men, he had no illusions that such would be allowed. Over the many long years he had been a captive there, he had gradually come to accept his fate and stop railing against it. He knew that everyone—most especially the lady he had loved more than his own life—for whom he had held any degree of affection had long since ceased to exist. There would no longer be anyone on his world that he would know or who would know him. He might well be found in the Ghaoithe history banks but even that would be so ancient as to have no meaning to those alive today.

"What is there for me beyond this time and place?" he asked aloud.

The wind seemed to sough the answer—only freedom.

Kaibyn appeared at the hatchway and waved his arm. It was the signal that everything was in place and he was about to insert the fledgling in the warrior.

"Hurry," Cainer whispered, his heart pounding. As much as he feared Morrigunia's appearance, a part of him hoped—nay, prayed—he would be able to bid farewell to Uaigneas.

Observing her prisoner as he paced the rocky ridge of the bluff overlooking Achasán Island, Morrigunia, the Goddess of War, Life and Death could not help but admire the sheer male beauty of Cainer Cree. With his broad shoulders and narrow hips, flat belly striated with hard muscle and his neatly turned ass, he was a specimen unlike any other with whom she had toyed over the eons. His dark hair blowing seductively in the sharpening breeze, he was—by far—the most handsome of those she had conquered.

"And yet, you insist on denying me, don't you, lover?" she whispered.

The Reaper stilled and whipped around, searching the trees. He had intercepted the emotion if not the actual thoughts and words aimed at him. His eyes were wide, full of unaccustomed fear as he sought the source of his unease.

Morrigunia cocked her head to one side and smiled. He could not see her though she was only a few feet away. If she so desired, she could reach out and caress that beautiful face, those chiseled lips. She could stroke the sleek softness of his hair, pushing it out of his eyes and run her fingers through the thickness.

She almost laughed as he stepped forward and walked right through her. Though he had not felt the contact, she had, and a shiver of pleasure ran down the goddess' spine and quickened her womb. That wide, hairy chest and those brawny arms had touched her sensitive breasts and brushed against her nipples to set them to throbbing.

"I can not let you go, my love," she said fiercely. "You belong to me!"

* * * * *

Evann-Sin was breathing deeply as he lay upon the Reaper's strange bunk. He was shivering, his heart was racing for the bunk had what appeared to be a soft glass lid that curved over the deep mattress. From the looks of it, the thing could be closed over whoever was lying upon the bunk.

"What do you suppose is the reasoning behind this?" Kaibyn asked, examining the lid.

"Like mosquito netting, perhaps?" the warrior replied, although he felt as though he would scream at the top of his lungs at any moment.

"Bugs," the demon stated and looked around. "What manner of bug would be inside this hellish thing?"

"I don't know and right now I don't care!" Evann-Sin snapped. "Just get on with it before I get up and run out of here!"

"Touchy, touchy, touchy," Kaibyn mumbled. He placed the jug containing the fledgling on a nearby shelf then took the odd-looking knife out of his pocket. "What did the Reaper call this?"

"Will you just do it?" the warrior pleaded. His teeth were chattering but it was not because he was cold. Although he had removed his shirt when he lay down on his belly on the bunk — and the mattress upon which he was reclining was a soft, leather-like material that was cool to the touch — he was sweating profusely, his nerves stretched as thin as a fine wire.

"Ready?"

"Just get on with it."

Kaibyn studied the steel knife for a moment then shrugged. He placed the tip to the warrior's back and made a two-inch incision gently through the flesh.

Evann-Sin had sucked in his breath as the stinging cut was made. He could feel blood seeping down his side and lifted his head to look around at Kaibyn. The demon had taken up the jug and was removing the lid.

"Egads, the stench is even worse now!" Kaibyn remarked.

Nothing could have prepared the warrior for the agony that invaded his system as the demon shook the fledgling out of the jug and it landed with a wet plopping sound on his back. Even as the sliminess of the feeling registered and he shuddered with disgust, the pain reached up with razor-sharp talons and drove down into his flesh.

"Shit!" Evann-Sin cried out and dug his fingers into the strange mattress. He arched his back, dug his booted toes against the bunk, feeling the acute torment burning a pathway into his body. It felt as though barbed wire was being threaded along his spine and the small of his back. Though he writhed, no position helped and he pressed his forehead into the mattress, clamped his jaw shut and rode out the brutal torture being inflicted on him.

Kaibyn was fascinated at what he was seeing. The creature had barely landed on the warrior's back before it shot down through the cut and disappeared, bunching up under the young man's flesh as it moved. It was wiggling this way and that under the skin and each time it moved, the warrior groaned in pain.

"I need to go before you Transition," the demon said. Though he did not fear the changing of man to beast, he had no desire to watch it happen. "The Reaper must glean the information about the Abyss from me."

"Go," Evann-Sin managed to say. He was shuddering violently, sweat pouring from his body, and he did not want anyone to hear him scream from the agony that was enveloping him.

"I'll return as soon as Cainer has what he needs."

"Go!" the warrior hissed, squeezing his eyes tightly shut.

Kaibyn took one last look at the young man then disappeared on a soft, cool wash of air.

The torment was increasing and Evann-Sin had begun to whimper. Tears flowed from his eyes, his breathing was harsh—ragged, and his limbs were as stiff as those of a cadaver. He was in such agony he could not imagine surviving it. Every vein in his body burned with a fiery pain that made sweat pour from him like water. Every muscle cramped and was so rigid he wanted to scream. Each of his bones felt as though it were being crushed in a vise and when the popping, cracking sounds began, he thought he was being compressed, being pulverized into dust. Even the hair on his head, his arms, his belly and legs felt as though it were growing at an alarming rate, being pulled out of his flesh with red-hot pinchers. When his jawbone began thrusting forward, elongating—his teeth became longer, sharper, decidedly pointed, he started to pant and with the panting came a salivating that snapped his eyes wide open. The first thing he saw was the thick, wiry bristle of hair protruding from the backs of his hands and he yelped with shock. So stunned was he, he leapt from the bunk and when he landed upon the floor, he was on fours, swinging his head from side-to-side for the pain had increased to such an exquisite torment that it caused him to howl from the intensity of it.

His backbone arched like that of a spitting cat then dropped back to lengthen even more, the pain so acute he thought he would pass out. Terrible pain racked his hips and he could hear the pelvic bone crunching as it contracted.

He was beyond human speech in a matter of moments and though he wanted to beg the gods to release him from this torture, the only sounds he could make were growls and snarling hisses that brought terror to his soul. The fear of remaining like this the rest of his life was an agony unto itself.

With the last waning ounce of strength, he threw back his head—now covered with a black pelt that extended from his eyes to the tips of what had once been his feet—and howled.

* * * * *

Kaibyn was looking at the Reaper when Cainer Cree shuddered and put his hands to his face. "What is it?" the demon asked.

"He is beginning Transition."

"You can feel that?"

Cainer shook his head. "I can hear his screams."

"He hurts," Kaibyn stated.

"He does."

Glancing toward the dark ship, Kaibyn took a deep breath. "You have what you need from me?"

"Aye," the Reaper answered. "You can go back to him soon. He will need you."

"Will he need...what did you call it?"

"Sustenance," Cainer replied. "And aye, he will need to feed."

Kaibyn frowned. "Ugh, that makes me sick just thinking on it."

"He'll also need the tenerse but that won't be until tomorrow. The first taking of blood will satisfy him for now."

The demon turned his gaze from the ship. "If he never starts taking that shitty stuff..."

"The parasite within him is accustomed to it, demon. It was inside me. Remember? What I crave, so too, will Riel crave."

"Oh," Kaibyn said with a sigh. "All your curses are now his."

Cainer got up from the rock upon which he had been sitting and stared across to Achasán Island. For a moment, his eyes glowed bright red and Kaibyn's mouth dropped open in shock. When the Reaper turned to look at him, the demon shot to his feet and moved back. There was cruelty in that handsome face and those scarlet eyes were fixed upon Kaibyn.

"All my curses," the Reaper said forcefully. "Aye, each and every damned one of them!"

"I didn't mean..."

"When they come here seeking to become like me, they don't realize what a vile curse it is. They hear the whispered tales of a man stronger than ten men combined. They hear they will be able to read minds and thus know what their enemies are thinking. They hear they will be nearly immortal and that disease and old age will never touch them. Wounds will heal in the blink of an eye. All those things they know will make them almost god-like and they are eager to become One with the Blood."

Kaibyn could feel the power in the hands that were clenching and unclenching into fists. He could smell the aura of savagery that had come upon his companion. More than just the brutal look snapping from those red eyes, the stare seemed as though it had a lethality of its own.

"Once, a long time ago, a woman came to me and I made her *deargs dul.*" He put the heel of his right hand to his eye and held it there as though a great pain stabbed at the orb.

"She had not wanted to come here and she did not know what it was that awaited her here. Neither did her kinsman who had sold her to me."

Despite his unease, the demon was intrigued by what he knew must be a very complex tale. Warily, he resumed his seat though kept his body rigid should he need to spring up and flee. "Her kinsman sold her to you?" he queried.

"They did not want to be burdened with her, and no decent man would take her to bride for she was considered soiled goods. It was only by chance I overheard two fishermen talking about her as they put out to sea. I knew I had to offer her a chance to have a life."

Kaibyn glanced out at the sea and knew the Reaper had gleaned that conversation from the minds of the passing fishermen. "What was she like?" he asked.

"As lovely as a spring morn, she was," Cainer remembered. "And as frightened as a doe." He smiled slightly but the smile never reached his eyes. "She had been brutalized and hated men."

"Ah," Kaibyn said. "I begin to see why you bought her."

"Do you?"

"I see a pattern emerging here. You are a do-gooder, Cainer Cree. You put things to rights." He cocked his head to one side. "Is that not so?"

"As best I can," the Reaper agreed.

"So you gave her the means to turn herself into an avenger upon the man who had raped her, but now you regret having done so because you see it as a curse."

"It is a curse," Cainer said. "Ask Riel in a few weeks if he doesn't think it is."

"And did this young woman—what was her name—think she had been cursed?"

"Kynthia," the Reaper said. "Her name was Kynthia and no, she welcomed her Transition and I imagine she still does. It set her free and she went back to her kinsmen, with the parasite confined in a jar to later be inserted into her body."

"Why did you not insert the creature here?" the warrior asked.

Cainer's smile was grim. "Because if I had, she would not have been able to ever leave the island."

"Ah," the warrior said, nodding. "I understand. If you can't leave, neither could any other Reaper. Did Kynthia leave willingly?"

"She was content with leaving for she went back the master of her own fate, never again at the mercy of any man."

"To me, that seems a blessing. So why does it bother you so badly?"

"It is no blessing, demon. It is an evil thing I help do to these people. It is a sin for which I must one day atone. Each time I feel them Transitioning and I am reminded that it is I who did this to them. I hear their screams. I sense their confusion and anger and disgust. I feel their terror by reliving my own."

"Each one who came here for you to change knew what they were doing," Kaibyn reminded him. "They came of their own free will, did they not?"

"Aye, but Kynthia didn't. They brought her here against her will."

"True, but did you browbeat her into taking the parasite?" When the Reaper remained silent, Kaibyn asked if he had forced the young woman to incise her own flesh and apply the fledgling to the wound.

Cainer closed his eyes. "No, but having given her the means to become a monster still doesn't set well with me."

"Well, you can look her up when we leave this place and you can see how she's handling being a deargs dul. For all you know, she might be avenging other women who have been hurt as she was. Would that not be a good thing?"

The Reaper chuckled mirthlessly. "Only a demon would think revenge a good thing."

Silence settled comfortably between the men, and both turned their gazes back to the airship. After a moment or two, Cainer's shoulders relaxed and he appeared calm.

"Can I join him now?" Kaibyn asked. "I am worried about the little shit."

"Surprised you are acquiring affection for a man, demon?"

"Unfortunately, he grows on you, and if I am to take his woman away from him…"

"No man will ever take a Reaper's woman away from him, demon. If you try, you will find yourself installed back in the Abyss. That, I guarantee."

"I was joking," Kaibyn said.

"Sure you were." When Kaibyn would have protested, Cainer waved him off. "Go. He is weak and he will need this."

Stunned at how quickly the Reaper moved, Kaibyn gasped. He barely had time to gain his feet before Cainer Cree was beside him, holding up a squirming rabbit.

"You must not allow him to kill the beast. Let him take only enough blood to satisfy the hunger then take it away from him and bring it back here."

"You don't kill the animals on the island?"

"I don't eat meat," the Reaper answered. "I never have. The blood sustains me, and I never take enough to do harm to the beast. If you allow Riel to kill, he will develop a bloodlust that will be unlike anything you have ever seen. It will make him even harder to live with."

Kaibyn took the animal, wrinkling his nose at the gamey smell. "When will he be strong enough to fly your airship?"

"When he has fed. The sooner, the better," Cainer replied. "I can not wait to leave this place."

Disappearing with the little animal held out in front of him as he held the fledgling, Kaibyn was barely back in the ship before the Reaper realized he was not alone on the island. He stiffened and turned slowly to find Morrigunia sitting upon the rock the demon had vacated.

"What are you up to, my love?" the goddess inquired in a soft voice.

The light died in Cainer Cree's eyes and his wide shoulders slumped. A faint groan of hopelessness pushed from his constricting throat and he looked away from his tormentress, turning his gaze longingly to The *Levant*.

"Did you really think I would allow you to leave, my deargs dul?" she asked. "Surely you knew I would not."

The Reaper hung his head. "I should have known it was too good to be true."

"Ah, my love," Morrigunia said with a sigh. "You would have left me and flown away to your world without so much as a goodbye." She made a tsking sound and waggled her finger at him. "You are a bad boy, indeed."

He looked around at her and his eyes were stricken, filled with tears. "I am a lonely man, Morrigunia."

She smiled. "And whose fault is that, Cainer? I do not count the times I offered you comfort and you threw it back in my face."

"I wanted no woman but Aisling!" he said fiercely, swiping at the tears that were falling down his cheek.

"But you couldn't have that sleeping beauty, now could you?"

"Don't remind me of her loss, you bitch!" he threw at her.

Morrigunia's smile turned nasty. "Her loss," she said, the words dropped like a heavy rock. "Did I ever tell you she was lost?"

"Stop it!" he shouted, covering his ears with his hands. He hunkered down and knelt there, rocking with the weight of his despondency.

"So pretty she is," Morrigunia said with a sigh. "That soft blonde hair and lovely blue-green eyes. She is a bit too tall for the tastes of Chalean men, but I know you admire that in her."

"Stop," he whispered, his voice breaking.

"The first time I saw her, I noticed that little scar upon her neck. How did she come by that, my love?"

"Morrigunia, please," he begged. "Stop taking her from my memory. That is all I have left of her."

The goddess lifted her head. "I have never delved into your memories, deargs dul. That is not honest!"

Cainer Cree looked up at her. "Then how would you know about the scar, you devious cunt?"

She smiled. "Because I have seen it." She tilted her head to one side. "Just this morn, as a matter of fact. I check on her regularly, hoping she will wake, but alas, she sleeps on, lovely lass that she is."

The Reaper's heart had been broken long ago but it ached anew as he took in the taunting words of his captor. "Don't," he pleaded. "That is cruel even for you."

"You doubt my words?" she asked.

"Not even you can fly beyond this galaxy and even if you could, you would not find my Aisling for she would be long…"

The word stuck in his throat so he used another, less painful one, "gone."

"You think your lady dead, my love?" she inquired then shook her head slowly. "Nay, she is very much alive yet sleeping still as she has been since the first day I found her on Zenia's ship."

Cainer's eyes flared. "What?" The question was barely a sound as he asked it.

"Lying upon this strange bed with a glass cover in place around it." She made a moue with her lips. "I tried to open the damned thing but it would not budge."

He was staring at her, his hands now covering the lower part of his face with the tips of his middle and index fingers bracketing his eyes. His breath was coming in quick, shallow pulls as he slowly came to his feet.

"You look stricken, my deargs dul," Morrigunia stated. "Did I not tell you your lady still lives and is but a few miles from your prison?" Her face held a triumphant grin. "And has been all these years?"

"How?" he managed to ask. He could feel the racing of his heart—hear the blood pounding in his ears.

Morrigunia shrugged. "I suppose Zenia brought the pretty one with her. Who knows why, perhaps to kill her in front of you? To make her watch as you Transitioned and then throw her to you for you to kill?" She shrugged again. "We will never know, will we?"

"You are lying," he accused, though a faint glimmer of hope had begun to spark in his wounded eyes.

"I never lie!" Morrigunia shrieked at him. "How dare you accuse me of such a thing!"

He went to her, falling to his knees before her, putting his hands out in entreaty. "Let me see her," he begged. "Just once. Let me be sure she is safe."

"Have I not told you she is?" Morrigunia snapped.

"She is in an extended sleep unit," he said. "You could have damaged the seal trying to open it."

"I damaged nothing," the goddess said with a dangerous narrowing of her green eyes. "Had I damaged it, would she not be so much moldering dust by now?"

Wincing at the thought, the Reaper took comfort in knowing what his tormentress said was true, but he needed to know the stasis was holding, that Aisling was, indeed, sleeping. More importantly, he needed to know she was alive.

"Why?" Morrigunia asked, reading his thoughts easily. "You are here, she is there." She pointed to the north. "You can't even see her island from here."

"Morrigunia, please," he whimpered, fresh tears starting down his cheeks. "Let me but see her just once. Bring her here, please!"

"Don't you think if I could have done that I would have long ago?" the goddess asked with a snort. "I would have liked nothing more than to see the devastated look upon your face when I took her back." She leaned toward him. "Imagine it, Reaper — your ladylove within a hairsbreadth of you being able to put your lustful hands upon here and then poof! Gone in a heartbeat!"

The anguish was almost more than he could bear and without thinking, he laid his head in the goddess' lap and sobbed. His hands were wrapped around her hips, his cheek pressed against her shimmering cloth of gold gown.

"There, there, my love," she cooed, stroking his dark hair. "Morri will make it better for you."

She crooned to him as he cried, sang an ancient Chalean lullaby to soothe him as she threaded her fingers through his thick curls and when his body convulsed with the increase in his sorrow, she bent forward to wrap him in her arms.

"Hush now, Sweeting," she said. "You will make yourself ill."

"Kill me," he said between the heartbreaking sobs. "Kill me, for I can not stand this loneliness any longer."

Morrigunia drew in a long breath and lifted her head to look out at the sea. She could see the demon standing framed in the doorway of the airship. He was waving his arm. Even as she listened, the ship came to life with a sputter of its mighty engines then began to hum in a powerful rumble that shook the ground under her feet.

"Such an impressive machine," she commented. "I look forward to flying in it."

Cainer Cree was beyond hearing. He was lost in a misery so dark, so deep he could barely move and he vowed to himself he never would again. He would lay where he was and never rise. It was a vow that communicated itself to his captor.

"That will not do, deargs dul," she declared, and pushed him away from her.

He fell upon the ground and curled into a fetal position, his palms together, hands pressed between his crooked knees.

"That will not do!" Morrigunia repeated. She stared down at him and became alarmed at the steadiness of his gaze. Though his eyes were open, she could tell they had lost their focus. "Get up!" she ordered.

The Reaper ignored her. He had willed his thoughts to The *Levant* and was listening to the warrior and demon. Riel Evann-Sin was taking command just as Cainer knew he would. What needed to be done to get the intricate ship aloft was there in the warrior's hands and he was already seated at the controls.

"Get up!" his tormentress commanded.

There was a trilling sound and Morrigunia tore her eyes from the Reaper to gaze with wonder at the airship. It was lifting from the rocky island where it had sat for centuries. Dust billowed from beneath its sleek black belly.

"Go with the Wind," she heard Cainer whisper, and looked down at him. He had closed his eyes.

"No!" Morrigunia shouted. "Get up! Get up now!"

A low hum began on Achasán Island, and she watched as the ship began to rotate, its nose coming around to face her. For a long moment, she stared at the awesome machine then slowly turned her head to look down at the Reaper. She winced for he was as still as death and she knew he would remain so.

"So be it," she said, and with a roar, vanished.

"Cainer, get up!"

It was not Morrigunia's words but Riel Evann-Sin's that opened Cainer's eyes. He stared at the ground before him and watched an ant crawling over the grass with a large leaf clutched in its mandibles.

"Cainer, get up before she comes back!"

The ground beneath his cheek was vibrating with the power from The *Levant*. He lay where he had fallen, and once more bid the warrior a safe journey to his lady.

She did not throw another Geas upon you, Reaper! Evann-Sin shouted in Cainer's mind. *You are free to leave! Do it before she realized her mistake!*

The Reaper narrowed his eyes, hearing the words, but afraid his warden would return should he attempt escape. To have freedom snatched out from under him at the last minute was something he did not think he could endure.

You have to try! came the strong suggestion.

The *Levant* was hovering just off the coast of the Isle of Uaigneas. Overhead, the leaves were whipping as though a hurricane wind thrashed at them.

Cainer straightened his legs and pushed himself up. He turned to look at his L.R.C. as it sat suspended just beyond the cliff. In the fading light, it was beautiful for the rising moon cast a shimmer of light upon its sleek, black hull.

I have her coordinates, Reaper, the warrior told him. *We can bring the E.S.U. on board.*

"Her?" Cainer questioned.

Your lady, fool! We can retrieve her but you have to hurry!

Dropping his gaze to the underbelly of his ship, the Reaper stared at the area where the tracking beams were located. They could latch on to Aisling's E.S.U. and draw her up into The *Levant* in a matter of seconds.

He took a tentative step away from the cliff and toward the well-beaten pathway that led down to the shore. Then he took another and then another until he was walking faster, then loping then running full-out as he crashed past the low hanging tree limbs. Keeping apace of him was The *Levant*, its quiet engines barely making a rumbling sound as it moved. Though he stumbled at times and had to reach out to grab a tree trunk lest he fall, he kept going, his only thought to reach the shore.

Why the hell doesn't the gods-be-damned teleporter work, Reaper? the warrior growled. *I could just transport you up here!*

Though he was barely winded as he ran, Cainer's heart was beating faster than it ever had before. His headlong rush to get to the shore took nearly all his conscious thought but he managed to convey to Evann-Sin that the unit had been damaged upon landing in Chale.

Can't I fix it?

"Later," the Reaper snapped but was overjoyed that the warrior was rapidly accustoming himself to the machine and knew the possibilities of it.

He was nearly down the cliff, holding his breath for fear Morrigunia would materialize at any moment. As his feet hit the beach, he went down, crashing heavily to his knees but was up in a flash, streaking toward the waiting ship. Already, the gangplank was lowering a foot above the lashing sand beneath it. Putting his hand up to shield his eyes from the flying sand, he raced toward The *Levant*.

Speed it up, Reaper! the warrior shouted in Cainer's mind. *We don't have all night!*

He was only a couple of yards away. He dragged in one last breath and leapt for the gangplank, propelling himself through the opening only a second or two before it came down. He rolled along the floor as the warrior banked The *Levant* steeply to starboard and the L.R.C. began climbing as it arced.

Kaibyn helped the Reaper to his feet. The men staggered for the ship was increasing speed.

"As soon as I got the ship online, I put a tracer out for your lady," Evann-Sin explained. "She is on Finscéalta na Gaoithe. Do you know that place?"

Cainer shook his head. "An island?"

"Aye. We'll be there before you can snare a rabbit," the warrior chuckled. He glanced up as the Reaper came to stand beside him. "Want to take over?"

Before Cainer could answer, Evann-Sin was out of the console chair and the ship made a sudden downward plunge.

"Shit!" the Reaper yelled, and had his hands on the controls before the vessel crashed. "Don't you *ever* do that again!"

Evann-Sin laughed, and cast Kaibyn a look but another traveler caught his eye and drew his immediate attention.

Morrigunia was sitting on the bunk of the E.S.U., her legs crossed, her arms folded over a luscious chest whose bare breasts gleamed in the overhead lighting.

Kaibyn looked around. "What is it?" he asked.

Knowing the demon could not see the goddess—nor apparently could the Reaper for he, too, looked where Evann-Sin was staring—the warrior shook his head. "I…"

"Take good care of my deargs dul and go with the Wind, warrior," Morrigunia said softly, and she winked at him. Her blessing imparted, she left.

Evann-Sin let out a shaky breath. Closing his eyes for a moment, he silently thanked the goddess.

"What are you thanking her for, warrior?" Cainer asked.

The warrior locked eyes with the Reaper. "For giving you your freedom."

"Broadcast it to the world, why don't you?" Kaibyn snarled. "You'll have that bitch on us now!"

Cainer intercepted Evann-Sin's thoughts — and his memory of a few moments past — and heaved a sigh of relief. He added a silent thank you to Morrigunia, and heard the tinkle of silver laughter in his mind. "No," he said. "I think she has moved on."

Since Evann-Sin had programmed in the coordinates to Zenia's ship, The *Levant* was soon hovering over her, the underside tracking ports opening slowly as a laser beam on the aft cut into the other ship's topside, peeling back the hull as though it were a grape. When the access hole was large enough to draw its target through the demolished hull, the Reaper lowered twin cables and locked on. There was a loud shrieking of metal against metal as the E.S.U. was pulled out of its harness. As the E.S.U. came free of the other ship — wires trailing — The *Levant* dipped slightly, but with ease and never-forgotten skill, Cainer brought the slightly swinging E.S.U. aboard and positioned it beside his own. It was a tight squeeze for The *Levant* had been built for only one occupant.

"Take over, Riel!" the Reaper ordered as soon as the E.S.U. was in place. "I have but moments to get the unit reconnected."

Evann-Sin slid into the control chair from the left side as Cainer left it on the right. "Why is there a hurry?"

"Those lines you see trailing there are receptors from a thin mesh screen situated atop Zenia's ship. The screen captures the rays of the sun and sends them down through the wires into the E.S.U, forming an artificial atmosphere in which my lady lives. The units are made so they are recharged by the power of the sun. In disconnecting the wires as I had to in order to bring the E.S.U. to The *Levant*, the life support system — that artificial atmosphere — was deactivated. My lady is in a state of stasis but that won't last long."

"Stasis?" Kaibyn repeated, his forehead crinkled.

"Inactivity resulting from a static balance between opposing forces. In this case — life and death. That means she will not be able to exist without the power generated from the sun."

And then the Reaper was standing over his lady, and for the first time in hundreds of years looked down into her beautiful face. His hands trembled as he pressed them to the glass hatch.

"She is lovely," Kaibyn whispered as he came to stand beside Cainer.

"Aye," Cainer said so softly the word was but a breath of sound.

"Will it cause her any harm to open the unit now?" Evann-Sin asked.

Cainer nodded. "I'll need to rewire this unit into my own and bring her up slowly. The artificial atmosphere must be in place before I can wake her."

As the Reaper set about doing what needed to be done to awake his lady, Evann-Sin began typing in the coordinates to the Abyss. He stopped and looked around. "You'd best go back to the island, Kai," he said.

Kaibyn tore his gaze from the beauty lying in front of him. "Why?"

"We are heading for the Abyss, demon," Cainer answered for the warrior.

"Oh," Kaibyn said. "Right."

One moment the demon was there and the next he wasn't.

"He seemed a bit dejected," Evann-Sin remarked.

"I think he wanted to wait until my lady was awake," Cainer laughed.

"Always enamored of other men's women, isn't he?" the warrior sighed.

It didn't take the Reaper long to rewire Aisling's E.S.U. As soon as he was sure the unit was working properly, he replaced Evann-Sin at the console and began typing in the data that would begin the decompression of his lady's unit.

"Have you any notion what you'll do about Lilit when we reach the Abyss?" Cainer asked.

"I intend to rid the world of the bitch. Why?"

"What about any others with her?"

Evann-Sin narrowed his eyes. "That depends. If they have harmed my lady in any way—even given her a hangnail—I will crush them."

"Good man," the Reaper said. "Best not leave anything there that can harm the human race. The Mage knew the right man to hire for this mission."

"What will you do when this is over? Will you return to your home?"

Cainer's fingers stilled on the computer's flat keyboard. "I have not had time to consider my options yet. I suppose that depends on what Aisling wants to do."

"Nice to be able to say that, isn't it?" Evann-Sin asked softly.

The Reaper turned around in his console chair and looked longingly at the E.S.U. where his lady slept. "Aye," he replied. "Life is once more worth living."

Chapter Sixteen

Kaibyn sat down on the one chair in the Reaper's hut and stared at the charcoal rendering Cainer Cree had drawn of his lady from memory. As beautiful as the sleeping woman had been aboard The *Levant*, with her eyes open and looking at the viewer, she was a veritable goddess in her own right.

"As beautiful as I, demon?"

Jumping at the sound of the voice, Kaibyn snapped his head around. His eyes went wide and his mouth dropped open.

"Morrigunia?" he breathed.

"Aye," she said and came toward him.

Lovely as Lilabet was, gorgeous as Tamara, beautiful as Aisling—none could hold a candle to the exquisite creature whose naked body glistened with dew in the moonlight cast from the single window.

"He turned *you* down?" Kaibyn asked.

"There is no accounting for tastes, eh, my demon?" the goddess laughed.

Her bare breasts were lush globes, the dark areolas around her prominent nipples like knowing eyes watching him. A flat belly, tiny waist that flared into very accommodating hips and long legs drew his gaze. The groomed patch of vibrant red hair at the juncture of her thighs was only a shade lighter than the hip-length tresses that curled possessively around her creamy shoulders. A slender tattoo banded her upper left arm, and as she drew closer Kaibyn could make out intricate knot work.

"There is a raven here," she said, lifting an elegant finger to point at the tattoo. "It is my symbol." She caressed the raven. "Do you like it?"

"Aye," the demon agreed. She was but a foot away and the sweet scent of heather filled his nostrils.

"Will you mate with me, Kaibyn Zafeyr?" she asked.

"With the greatest of pleasures," he replied.

She was on him, riding him like a crazed cat in heat and he was lying beneath her, staring up at her bucking, watching her breasts flapping deliciously. He reached up to cup those silken globes and she threw her head back and pumped even harder.

Never had a woman taken him, Kaibyn thought, as she rode him. Never had one taken charge and — well — attacked him. He decided he liked being the one used for a change and almost wished he could find out what it felt like to be...

She pried herself off him and before he could utter a sound had turned him over to his belly. Reaching beneath his hips, she yanked his ass in the air and with one swift, deft stroke prodded him with something he knew wasn't part of her body.

Yelping, but getting an erection harder than any he'd ever known, he looked back over his shoulder to see her grinning at him.

"What are y-you using?" he gasped.

"Don't worry, demon, it is quite safe. Just a little something many women find convenient when there's no man around."

She probed him deep and it was a bit painful, but as the muscles of his anus grew accustomed to the size and the deep in and out friction, he found he thoroughly enjoyed the sensation. Her fondling his balls as she thrust into him had a truly entertaining feel, too.

Kaibyn was lost in the violent sensation of being taken in such a manner. He was as hard as stone and aching, and when he was about to come, she withdrew the prod and flipped him over so quickly he knew what Rabin and Evann-Sin had experienced when he'd taken them flying.

She was on him again, pressed down to the very nub of his cock and bucking once more like a wild horse. The slap of her rump against his thighs was almost obscene. The walls of her vagina were tightening and releasing in such a way, he felt as though she milked the climax from his body. As he poured into her—his fingers pinched around her nipples—he felt her rapid succession of squeezes deep in her cunt and knew she was coming, as well.

And come she did—with a yell that shook the rafters of the little hut and rang in the demon's ears for an hour after.

"Like that, Kai?" she asked, as she slid down beside him on the floor.

"Aye," he managed to squeak. For the first time in his many thousands of years of existence, he had more than met his match.

He frowned.

"Concerned about your blood-oath to Lilabet?"

Kaibyn flinched, and his handsome face twisted. "I did not consider…"

"There is no reason to consider," she said with a grin. "I am not mortal. You are not mortal. What we do together has no effect on sweet Lilabet. Now if I were mortal, you would have been a bad, bad boy. As it is, you are simply being true to your immortal nature." She took hold of his cock. "Now, would you like to fuck me again?"

Kaibyn's leer was predatory. "Aye, I damned well do."

Chapter Seventeen

Tamara lay upon her bed and stared up at the vault of the stone ceiling above her. The palm of her right hand stroked her belly where Evann-Sin's child was growing. A gentle smile creased her lips for a moment before the first tear slid slowly down her pale cheek.

There was no moonlight in Sheol—no light, no warmth of any kind. Evil magic made it possible to see in this hellish place. The tortured sound of the walls heaving hopeless breaths had ceased to distract her, but she was aware of the lost souls encased in that hard stone. Just as Lilit had told her she would be, Tamara often heard the tormented cries and pitiful screams of the Lost Ones. She said prayers for those nameless souls when she took to her bed for sleep.

Lilit had been gone for two days now, and not even the bat-women—Amenirdis and Hekat—had shown themselves this waking period. Though one or the other brought cold, tasteless food for Tamara three times each period, the young woman's belly was growling for she'd eaten nothing in quite some time.

"Perhaps they have left me here to die, little one," she said to her unborn child.

Almost as though her words had conjured the food, it appeared on the table by the bed. For once, it was hot and smelled palatable.

Swinging her feet to the floor, Tamara attacked the food and found it was as delicious as it smelled. She gobbled it like a starving animal, mindless of the grease that dripped down her chin. A faint movement in the darkest corner of her room made Tamara start and she paused with a leg of chicken at her lips.

Amenirdis appeared from out of the darkness. Of the two fiends, she was the comelier—though no one would ever have labeled either pretty.

"We are slaves here just as you are," the bat-woman whispered. "Though Hekat doesn't mind it as much as I." She came closer to Tamara's bed. "Perhaps you will remember me when you are free of this place, milady."

Tamara dropped the de-fleshed chicken bone to the chipped platter upon which she had found it. Running the back of her hand under her messy chin, she replied she doubted she would ever be free of Lilit.

"But you will," Amenirdis said. "He comes for you."

"Evann-Sin?" Tamara asked, standing so quickly her unappeased hunger made her lightheaded.

Amenirdis came closer still and lowered her voice. "Aye, he will be with the other but it is he of whom I speak."

"Kaibyn?" Tamara prompted. "The demon?"

"Nay, he would not dare show himself in the Abyss. It is the *other*."

"What other?" Tamara questioned. "I don't know who you mean. It is Rabin?"

"I do not know his name but he has spoken to me in my thoughts. He is a powerful One with the Blood."

Tamara shrank back. "He is a blood-drinker?" Her eyes went wide. "My warrior is with a blood-drinker?"

Amenirdis nodded. "He, too, is one of us, now."

Grief drove through Tamara like a sharp quarrel and she staggered back. "No," she whispered, covering her face with her hands. "Oh, Riel, no!"

"You must not sorrow, milady. All will be well. They come to destroy Queen Lilit and take you from Sheol. Is that not what you want?"

"Who did this to my love?" Tamara asked. "Who turned my warrior to a fiend?"

Amenirdis flinched. She took a step back, hurt registering on her leathery face. "It was the only way he could save you."

Tamara stared at her companion. "He embraced the Blood for me?"

"You are his heart's desire and his life is yours."

Racked with misery, Tamara sat down on her bed and drew her knees up. "He will come to curse the day he ever laid eyes upon me," she said. Listlessly, she looked at Amenirdis. "Where is Lilit, anyway?"

"Gone to see if any Daughters remain alive. Neither Hekat nor I believe any do, but the queen would not listen. If none of her Daughters have survived, she intends to make new ones."

"I doubt King Numair will have stood idly by and not put protection out for his people. Lilit may find it harder than she imagines making new ones," Tamara said through clenched teeth.

"I think you may be right." She looked pointedly at Tamara's belly. "All the more reason you should be very careful of your son."

Tamara locked gazes with the bat-woman. "Why are you being so solicitous, Amenirdis? What do you have to gain?"

"Nothing save my freedom," the fiend answered. "I would like nothing more than to have Sheol to myself and not be at the beckoning call of the queen. Solitude suits me. When he comes, he will help your lover rid the world of the last of the Daughters. By helping you, I hope to gain pardon. I have no desire to end up like Hekat and the queen. I want to go on."

"And turn others?" Tamara accused.

Amenirdis shook her head. "Why would I want anyone else here? Everything I need is here at Sheol."

"What will you live on if there are no others?"

"Live on?" Amenirdis questioned, and then she laughed. "Milady, I am not alive as you know life. I can exist for eternities if left alone!"

"Without blood?" Tamara scoffed.

Amenirdis smiled. "Milady, look around you. There is nourishment in the very walls!"

A low keening came from the granite walls. Here and there a shriek sounded far, far off.

Tamara shuddered. She did not trust the bat-woman and she wished there were some way to set the suffering souls imprisoned within the walls free. Perhaps Evann-Sin could think of a way if—and when—he came to rescue her.

* * * * *

Lilit was infuriated. No matter where she flew, no matter where she looked, none of her offspring had survived the battle. Ashes of those she had created floated about the war-torn lands and heaps of bones were still smoldering, left in the field to join the rest of the ash. Her temple at Bandor had been demolished and garlic planted in a circle around the ruins. Adding insult to injury, the peasants now wore silver images of the Slain One or had strung garlic bulbs to wear around their enticing necks. Not one unprotected neck could be found and the Queen of the Daughters of the Night raged with helpless fury.

Back she flew to the Abyss, stopping only long enough to gather a net of moths as a treat for her remaining Daughters. Until the boy-child drew breath outside his mother's womb, there would be no one to turn except...

"Tamara," Lilit whispered, and her fangs flashed.

Thoughts of the blood of the young woman made Lilit's mouth water. She circled her lips with her pointed tongue, already tasting the salty flavor of that innocence. There would be time to go after the warrior and to bring him to heel.

"But your day will come, Evann-Sin," Lilit cackled as she swiped a tasty moth from the net, crunching its musty body between her teeth. "And you will rue the day you ever tangled with me!"

* * * * *

They were only a few leagues from their destination when Cainer Cree attempted contact. The warrior had done as the Reaper had instructed and had tasted Tamara's blood on the kerchief. Almost immediately, he sniffed the air and proclaimed he knew exactly where his lady was being kept.

"It lies in that quadrant," Evann-Sin said, reaching over Cainer's shoulder to point at a place on the star map.

The Reaper put his hand on the screen and closed his eyes. Within a matter of seconds, a slow smile stretched his expressive mouth. "It is called Sheol," he said.

"You have found her?" Evann-Sin asked anxiously.

"Nay, but I have found someone to help us."

"Who?"

"One of Lilit's underlings," the Reaper announced. "One who fancies the title of queen for herself."

"You trust her?"

"Nay, I do not, and when we leave Sheol, she will leave, too, but there is no reason to let her know that now."

"Why am I hearing screams and moans of great pain, Reaper?" Evann-Sin asked.

"Because the walls of Sheol are alive, *Reaper*," Cainer replied, stressing the last word. He took his hand off the screen.

"Don't remind me," the warrior mumbled.

"The Lost Ones call to you to help them, and that is what you are hearing. I hear it, too."

"And we will help them," Evann-Sin stated.

"Aye, that we will. Now, think of your lady and try to garner her thoughts," Cainer commanded.

Evann-Sin placed his hand where the Reaper had put his and closed his eyes, trying to blot out the anguished sounds attempting to intrude on his thoughts.

"I'm not getting anything."

"Speak her name and she will hear you," Cainer suggested.

"Tamara," Evann-Sin whispered. He was silent for a moment then removed his hand. "I am not hearing her."

"Concentrate, boy!" the Reaper ordered. "If you want it bad enough, you'll be able to contact her."

Once more Evann-Sin put his hand upon the screen. The concentration showed on his handsome face for his forehead was puckered, his eyes squeezed tightly shut, his lips pressed firmly together. His head was tilted to one side as he listened then all of a sudden his eyes snapped open—he had heard her!

Riel!

"I heard her!" he yelled. "Reaper, I heard her!"

"Tell her we are coming and to be brave. Warn her not to allow Lilit near her."

As the warrior silently communicated with his lady, the Reaper put the ship on autopilot and got up from the console chair. They were very close to Sheol and the end of their journey together, but there was a more pressing item on the agenda for Cainer Cree.

Aisling's E.S.U. readout had slowly fallen until there was only one click left on the monitoring screen. Her breathing—though very widely spaced when he had first brought her on board—was now even and smooth, natural. She was waking slowly from her enforced slumber and already her flawless complexion was returning to its natural shade of ivory instead of the stark white of cryogenic sleep. There was color to her fingertips once more and now and again her eyelids fluttered as she came up out of the REM sleep that had claimed her for so long. Soon, those beautiful eyes would open and look into his.

"Are we stationary?" Evann-Sin asked, coming over to the unit.

"Until Aisling wakes, aye," the Reaper replied.

Impatient to be reunited with his own lady, the warrior could well understand Cainer's feelings. Though he chomped at being made to wait even a second longer than necessary to rescue Tamara, he held his frustration in check.

"I'll not allow you to lose your lady, Riel," the Reaper said quietly. "Give me a moment to kiss her good morn, and you will have my sword hand at your side."

There was a pleasant ping as the last click on the monitoring screen disappeared. Closely following the sound was a light hiss of air as the seal broke on the E.S.U.

With his hands shaking, Cainer pushed the glass lid up and clicked it in place. He lowered his hands, hooked his fingers over the rim of the unit and stared unblinkingly at his lady's face, waiting for her to wake.

* * * * *

Lilit barely noticed the strange-looking bird she flew swiftly past. She had only a sense of its sleek blackness but was so enraged, even the sight of a mysterious bird in her kingdom barely registered. Her thoughts were dark, seared with a burning desire to punish Tamara for all that had been lost. Not a one of the helpless moths had survived the journey to the Abyss for the queen had reveled in crunching the little creatures and listening to their screams of agony.

Neither Amenirdis nor Hekat was waiting for her return and this slight further angered Lilit. She cursed her offspring, and shouted for them though still they were absent from her homecoming.

Her midnight steed landed with a jolt upon the ground, adding to the fury that had claimed the queen. Throwing her leg over its head, she slid to the ground then kicked the hell-steed.

Neighing its own anger, the horse leapt into the air, its wide wingspan fanning the dull, rancid air as it vanished around the side of the mountain.

"Amenirdis! Hekat!" Lilit screamed, but received no answer.

Digging her long fingernails into her palms, the queen strode heavily into her fortress. So furious was she, her shoulders were hunched, her backbone was rigid and her eyes were narrowed into thin, lethal slits.

"Amenirdis! Hekat!" she yelled once more, and became livid that no one rushed to meet her.

Tamara jumped as the door to her room was thrown open and she looked around to see Lilit framed in the doorway.

"Where are those two ungrateful cunts?" Lilit demanded, looking around Tamara's room as though expecting to find her missing servants hiding there.

"How would I know?" Tamara replied. Her hands were behind her back as she sat on her bed.

Lilit advanced into the room. "Do not dare speak to me with such disrespect, Traitor!"

There was a wild bloodlust in the queen's eyes, and as she spoke, her fangs were elongating, dripping with reddish-green saliva that sizzled as it hit the stone floor. Hands curled into claws with vermillion-tipped nails that were wickedly sharp, she came at Tamara. The rush of the queen's black silk clothing rustled like dry bones as she moved, and all around them the walls cried out in distress.

But Tamara did not appear concerned that the Queen of the Hell Hags was descending on her. She waited until Lilit was but a few feet away then removed her hands from her back. She opened her palm.

Lilit came up short, staring in horror at the object lying on the young woman's palm. Throwing up an arm to shield her face, the queen stumbled back, making an "argh" sound as she did.

Tamara got up from the bed and walked toward the queen. "Don't you want to punish me for those you lost, Your Majesty?" she cooed softly, and plucked the object from her palm to hold it up.

Another strangled cry choked from Lilit's crimson mouth, and she hissed as she moved back, away from the threat that was coming slowly toward her.

It was but a braid of her own hair, sheared away from her other tresses with a chunk of sharp rock. But it had been embedded with words that were anathema to the queen—indeed, to all evil ones—and Lilit was powerless against it.

One long braid that had been looped over at the top one inch, at the bottom five inches, and the remaining length bent to form arms then wound crisscross around the middle section to form a silken cross—the Sign of the Slain One.

"Get that thing away from me!" Lilit spat. She was backing away, hunched over like the ancient crone she was.

* * * * *

Evann-Sin knew he should not intrude upon the reunion of the Reaper and his ladylove so he quietly walked to the lone table and chair and sat down.

"They will both age before our eyes, warrior," Cainer said, gaining Evann-Sin's gaze. "They will wither and die, and we will be left alone to mourn their loss still again."

The warrior frowned. "I had not thought of that." He felt a lurch in the region of his heart and shook his head. "By the gods, I had not thought of that."

"I will ask her permission, of course," Cainer said softly, and sucked in a breath as he watched Aisling's chest rise higher than it had before and then sink slowly. "But I intend to make her One with Us."

"And if she doesn't want that?"

"I refuse to even entertain such a notion, warrior. I am a greedy man and in this, I will have my way whether she wants it or not."

"Even though you obsess about the lone woman you made a Reaperess?"

"Even so," Cainer agreed, and then was still as death as his lady opened her lovely sea-green eyes and her luscious lips smiled at him.

"Aisling," the Reaper sighed, and bent over to take her into his arms.

"I think I'll use that teleport thing we fixed and take a stroll down in Sheol," Evann-Sin remarked as he plucked an ancient weapon from the horde the Mage had left there for him. When the Reaper did not answer and seemed otherwise occupied, the warrior laughed and removed himself from The *Levant*.

* * * * *

"Get that thing away from me!" Lilit screeched again. She was almost out the door — hissing and clawing like a cat.

Beyond the Queen of the Hell Hags, Tamara could see her lover standing at the doorway but she was careful not to give away that knowledge. Though she saw the blade in his hand, watched him silently lifting it over his left shoulder, not even with a blink of her eye did she let on. And when the blade whistled through the air — gaining Lilit's attention too late — Tamara never flinched as the sharp blade bit through the queen's neck and severed her head from the rest of her.

The head rolled back into the room and came to rest against the toe of Tamara's boot. Without a thought, the young woman kicked it into the corner and smiled as she heard the sigh of pleasure come from the wall.

"Where are the others?" Evann-Sin asked. He made no move to come into the room, though his eyes betrayed his need to take her into his arms.

"I don't know but be careful, warrior. One proclaims to be our ally, but I have my doubts," she answered.

"Stay here," he ordered. "I'll be back for you."

"Oh, no!" she disagreed and ran after him. Already he was down the corridor, his sword pointed upward, both hands gripping the pommel.

"Don't you ever listen?" he asked as he felt her hand on his shoulder blade.

"Do you have a dagger?" she countered. Even as she asked, she reached for the weapon strapped to his thigh.

Hekat came at him before Evann-Sin could thrust his sword into her leathery body. Enfolding him in her wings, she snapped at his face and neck, straining to sink her long fangs into his flesh. Though Tamara struck out at the bat-woman—stabbing her repeatedly in the back—the blade seemed to make no impression and with one flick of a heavy wing, Hekat sent the young woman reeling against the wall.

It was an equal-sided fight with both combatants of like strength. Hekat was fierce as she sought to rip off the warrior's head and he was equally as brutal as he ripped first one, then the other wing from her body.

Tamara put her hands over her ears at the unearthly shriek of agony that came from the bat-woman's de-winging. The sound reverberated through the walls and down the long, dark corridors but it was accompanied by ghostly applause and sighs of contentment from the Lost Ones.

He butted the fiend with his head. Wingless—and now essentially without a way to grip her opponent—she wrapped her legs around his hips and continued to nip at his neck.

"The hell with this!" Evann-Sin snarled and broke the bat-woman's legs at the hips then tossed her body to the floor.

Even then, the fiend continued to fight. She wriggled toward her enemy on her belly and snapped at him like a rabid dog. When he kicked her in the mouth, she sank her fangs into his boot and held on.

But Riel Evann-Sin had the strength of ten men in his brawny arms and the commitment of a man who was determined to win at all costs. Angry that he could not shake the fiend loose, he set about stomping her body into a mush of blood and splintered bone.

Tamara turned her head away for the sight was not only horrifying but enough to make her lose what little food she had consumed earlier. The sounds alone were enough to make her puke. The stench was nearly unbearable and she covered her nose with the sleeve of her shirt.

At last, there was stillness and except for the whispering approval of the walls, silence fell about the corridors of Sheol. Looking around, Tamara saw her lover standing over the crushed body of his opponent and there was a deep red glow to his golden eyes.

"Warrior?" she asked softly.

He turned to look at her, and she shrank back from the savage set of his face.

"No," he said and rushed to her, but she scrambled away, no doubt afraid of what she had seen. He stopped, coming no closer to her. "Milady?" he questioned.

"There is still Amenirdis," she said. "I don't trust her."

"Neither does Cainer, but he will see to her."

"Cainer?" she questioned. "The one Amenirdis told me about?"

He nodded. "My friend. It was his ship that brought us here."

"Ship?" she echoed, her forehead crinkling.

"That is not important." Cautiously, he came to her, hunkering down before her and extending his hand. "Will you come to me, milady?"

It had been the savagery that she had witnessed that had frightened her so badly, but her love was a force much stronger than the revulsion she had felt so she took his hand and he pulled her to his chest, cradling her gently against him.

"You are well?" he asked.

"Aye," she replied. "I am now." She could hear his heart pounding beneath her ear and she was concerned with the high heat of his body.

"It will be thus from now on," he said, easily plucking her stray thought from the air. "I will explain it all later." He scooped her into his arms and stood, but before he could take the first step, she reached up for his cheek and brought his mouth to hers.

The kiss was as heady as old wine. Their tongues dueled in mimicry of the thrusting into other parts of their bodies they would much have preferred. When he broke contact, he smiled wickedly at her.

"Wait until we are soaring among the stars, Sweeting, and I will fuck you until you beg me to stop!"

She grinned back at him. "I don't think that's going to happen, warrior."

"We'll see, wench," he said as he strode down the corridor. "We'll see."

* * * * *

Cainer listened quietly to Amenirdis as the bat-woman explained why she had neither helped the queen nor attacked either him or the warrior. He stared into her eyes and heard more than her words. He delved into her miasma of savage thoughts and pulled up every vile thing she had ever done in her eons-old life. As she spoke, he blocked out her words and turned his attention to the walls to listen to the Lost Ones giving evidence of the great evil the bat-woman had thrust upon them.

"So that is why I have no desire to ever leave Sheol," Amenirdis finished. "Humankind is safe from me."

"Aye," Cainer agreed, "but the Lost Ones will continue to suffer as you feed from them."

"These old walls?" the fiend asked with a chuckle. "Who cares about such things?"

"I do," the Reaper replied, and moved so fast Amenirdis never saw the blade in his hand.

The grin was still on the bat-woman's face as her head toppled from her body. That head—eyes blinking inquisitively like those of an owl—lay wobbling back and forth on the floor as Cainer Cree pulled a laser weapon from the pocket of his tunic and fried the rest of Amenirdis to a crisp. Before he turned the white-hot point of the thing on the bat-woman's head, he shrugged.

"And so do those whose lives are trapped inside this demonic crypt," he told her.

Eyeballs popping, flesh searing off bone, hair shriveling to ash and fangs into so much dust, there was nothing left of Amenirdis when the Reaper had finished.

"Didn't buy her act, eh?" Evann-Sin asked.

Cainer turned to see his fellow traveler standing there with a very delectable woman reclining in his arms.

"She was lying through her fangs. Given time, she would have come after humankind with a vengeance," the Reaper replied.

"My thoughts, too, Lord Cree."

"Prince Cree," Cainer corrected, "but what's a title among friends?"

"Warrior," Tamara said. "Please put me down. I would like to thank your friend properly."

"I'll put you down when we are back on the ship. Until then, you are not leaving my arms, wench."

Cainer chuckled. "Horny little bastard, isn't he, Tamara?"

"Damned right," the warrior agreed.

"Well, everything we can do here on Sheol has been done. We now need to set the Lost Ones free, but I can't do that until we are back on board The *Levant*."

"How do you plan on releasing them from their torment?" Tamara asked.

"I have spoken with them and they desire light and warmth more than anything else. I intend to give them both."

So it was, that once they were back on The *Levant* and Tamara had been introduced to Aisling—and an immediate bonding between the two females had occurred — that the Reaper brought the ship around and pointed her nose toward the pile of ancient stones that was Sheol.

"Go with the Wind, Old Ones," Cainer said softly, and released a barrage of powerful missiles that turned the stone to rubble in a matter of moments. The light flared upon the jagged mountain ledge and lit the sky for hundreds of miles, the heat from the missiles melding stone to stone in a fitting sarcophagus for those who had suffered there. In the glow of the fire, the dark silhouette of a winged horse was seen heading into the far reaches of the heavens, he, too, given his freedom.

One last sigh of relief and gratitude came from the place where Sheol had once stood and then all was silent.

"Let's go home," Evann-Sin said.

Epilogue

"Rabin has been reunited with his lady-wife and is pumping away like one of those rabbits on Cainer's island," Kaibyn reported as he hugged Queen Lilabet to his side. "What are your plans, warrior?"

"We are to be Joined at the rising of the moon," Evann-Sin said with a measure of pride. "Master Jabali will perform the ceremony and the Panther will give the bride away."

"Oh, and who will be your best man?" the demon inquired casually. "Rabin?"

"Aye, if I can pull him away from Momisha long enough," he replied. "She doesn't seem to mind being dead. Have you noticed?"

Kaibyn shrugged. "I guess not."

Lilabet looked at her lover. "Why so glum, demon?"

Cainer Cree was watching Kaibyn. "He would like to be a best man one day," the Reaper said, and smiled as the demon cast him an annoyed look. "Isn't that so, Kai?"

"No," the demon lied. "That isn't so."

"Then I shouldn't ask you to be the best man at my Joining to Aisling then?"

Kaibyn blinked. "Don't jest with me, Reaper."

"I wasn't jesting, demon. It is to be a Joint Joining and I will need a man I can trust to care for my lady should the need arise."

"Nothing of his is going to rise to any lady save me," Lilabet snapped.

"It was merely a manner of speech, Your Majesty," Evann-Sin assured her.

"It had best be," Lilabet warned.

From her place sitting atop a fountain, Morrigunia giggled. Only the demon could see or hear her this time and he was looking back at her with wistful eyes. When she wagged her brows at him, he knew his days weren't as numbered as his ladylove considered them to be.

"Besides, as soon as the Joining is over, Kaibyn is going back to Nebul with me as my consort. He has vowed to help me regain my position as queen," Lilabet told them.

"You will make a far better monarch than Oded ever did," King Numair commented as he joined them.

"I intend to try," Lilabet responded.

"Where is Tamara?" Evann-Sin asked. "I thought she was with you?"

The Panther held up his hands. "She and the fair Aisling are trying on gowns. They dismissed me as though I were a mere servant in my own lair."

"I believe I will be Aisling's maid of honor," Lilabet said proudly. "Will Momisha Jaspyre be Tamara's?"

"Ah, that is what Tamara planned," Evann-Sin acknowledged.

"Prince Cree?" Lilabet asked.

"Thank you, Your Majesty," Cainer mumbled, though he doubted Aisling would be overly happy with the queen's decision. "That is most generous of you." He exchanged a look with Evann-Sin.

Morrigunia laughed and though no one save Kaibyn heard the tickling sound, all turned toward the fountain.

"I am off, demon," the goddess said. "When you are through playing consort, I'll drop by and give you a real fucking! Keep it warm for me!"

Kaibyn sighed deeply as Morrigunia vanished in a spray of multicolored lights.

"I could, of course, make you my king if you so desired it, Kai," Lilabet whispered. "We could spend eternity together."

The demon stared at her, aghast. "What?"

"I have asked Cainer if he would grant me a fledgling and he has agreed to do so. What do you think of that?"

Kaibyn turned narrowed eyes to the Reaper and when that one looked his way with a cocked eyebrow, Kaibyn mouthed, "I am going to fry you!"

Cainer smiled and mouthed back, "There is always the Abyss."

Evann-Sin hid a smile behind his hand and turned away. All he wanted was a quiet room with a soft bed and his lady in his arms. Rabin had his wife to journey through the centuries with him, the Reaper had his Aisling and Kaibyn had the woman he would be expected to satisfy.

"Serves you right, you horny little bastard," the warrior muttered.

Aye, he thought as he looked at the man who had proclaimed to the world only that morning that he was Riel Evann-Sin's father, the world had come round to rights.

"To you," the Panther said, holding up a glass of Chrystallusian brandy.

Evann-Sin nodded.

Aye, all was right with the world and his lady was walking toward him with a sultry promise in her lovely eyes.

Enjoy this excerpt from
Desire's Sirocco
© *Copyright Charlotte Boyett-Compo, 2004*

Sleep was a long time in coming for Jameela. She lay in her tiny cubicle and stared at the stygian ceiling, aching in parts of her body she had discovered for the first time this night. Turning to her side, she drew her knees up, hugged her pillow to her chest and let her mind drift back to the wondrous things that had been done to her.

Whomever the Brother was who had taken her into womanhood crossed her thoughts as she lay there. His expertise as he had copulated with her gave evidence that he was no stranger to the sexual act; he had known what he was about. The weight of his body, the feel of his smooth skin, the sleekness of his hair told her he was no more than middle age. There had been no deep lines on his face or rubbery feel to his muscles as she had held him. He did not *smell* old to her, either.

"But will you be a good master to me?" she asked aloud, sighing.

Shifting on the narrow cot, she flung the pillow atop her and clutched it tightly.

"If only it were you I held, my champion," she said.

"And what champion would that be, Wench?"

Jameela gasped, sitting up to stare into the semi-darkness. Her heart was racing for she had thought herself alone in the cubicle. "Dagan?" she asked.

"Quiet, Wench!" Dagan warned as he came to the cot. His hard hip nudged hers as he took a seat beside her. "Do you want to alert the Watch?"

Jameela tossed the pillow aside and reached for him. "What are you doing here?" she whispered. Her fingers clutched the silk of his shirt.

A rough hand smoothed her hair, the calloused flesh snagging lightly in the silken strands. "I could not sleep," he told her. "My thoughts were of you and the beauty of your body that was revealed to me this eve."

She laid her head against his shoulder as he continued to stroke her hair. "My thoughts were of you, as well," she said.

Dagan snorted. "Liar," he accused. "You were thinking of the Brother who claimed your maidenhead."

Jameela slid her arms around him. "My body might have been remembering his touch but my heart replaced his body with yours."

The warrior enclosed her in his strong embrace. "Truly?" he asked.

"You need not ask," she said in a petulant tone. "I think you know my feelings."

"All I know is what I sense in your words, Wench," he responded.

She pushed back from him and looked up, seeking his face in the darkness. "That being what?" she inquired. Jameela felt him shrug.

"That you like what you see when you look at me," he answered. "And that having me make love to you—if I could—wouldn't be so bad."

"And that's all?"

"Well that and the way you drool when you think I'm not looking," he said with a chuckle.

"You think entirely too highly of yourself," she said and would have wiggled out of his grasp but his embrace tightened.

"Do you know who claimed you this eve past?" he asked, refusing to allow her to break free.

"Someone of importance I suspect," she replied, settling down. She sighed then snuggled against his broad chest, reveling in the steady beat of his heart beneath her cheek.

"T'was the Master," he informed her.

"I thought as much," she stated flatly.

Dagan was quiet for a moment then commenced to stroke her hair once more. "And what are your feelings about it?" he asked.

Jameela cocked one shoulder. "Better than a sharp poke in the eye if what you say is true about him," she answered.

"What did I say?"

"You said that should I be lucky enough to be won by him that no other man would be allowed to touch me."

"Such is the way with the Master," Dagan agreed. "He will not share his Lady with another." He dropped a light kiss on her head. "That should please you, Wench."

"Except it doesn't," she said through clenched teeth.

Dagan flinched. "Why not?"

"Because I want you!" she said.

"Jameela," he said on a long breath. "You know…"

"I know I have fallen in love with you!" she declared. She waited for him to reply to her brash statement and when he did not, she felt like crying.

When at last he spoke, his voice was low and full of tension.

"Jameela, the Master is an exacting man. He would slice in twain any man who dared to lay hands to you now that he has claimed you as his own."

"How can you serve such monsters?" she asked.

"It was my destiny to be whom I am, where I am," he answered. "I had no choice."

"How is it you are allowed beyond the portals of this wicked place? Are all the Trainers given such freedom?"

"There is but one trainer at Lalssu Keep," he replied. "I was given permission to seek out the woman who would be the Master's Consort and that is how I came to be at Sahar Colony."

Jameela stiffened. "You were sent to fetch…"

"You ask too many questions, Wench," he interrupted her. "Let's see if I can't help you find rest this night for tomorrow will begin a more stringent instruction on how you are to satisfy your Master."

She could barely make out his silhouette in the darkness as he bid her turn over. Not daring to ask why, she obediently did as he commanded.

The cot dipped beneath his weight as he climbed upon it, straddling her body as he sat on her upturned rump. His hands were firm as he placed them on her shoulders and began to knead the tense muscles.

"Ah," she sighed on a long breath.

"You need to relax, milady," he said.

"I love having your hands on me," she told him.

Dagan grunted. "You liked his hands on you, too."

Jameela frowned. She did not want to think about the man who now owned her, the man whose right it was to touch her whenever and however he chose. "Please don't remind me," she asked.

The strong hands massaging her shoulders ceased their delightful movements. "You could have done much worse than having the Master win you," he said.

"I could have done much better if it had been the man I wanted instead," she countered.

Dagan's fingers tensed on her flesh. "And what man is that?" he snapped.

Jameela smiled, recognizing jealousy when she heard it. "The one whose hands are on me even as we speak," she replied. She felt his fingers relax and had to bite her lower lip to keep from giggling.

"You are a brazen piece of baggage, Jameela Anthus," he growled as his hands moved down her back.

She gave herself up to his firm manipulation. He was very adept at massage, knowing where to concentrate the pressure, for how long and to what depth. His fingers plied her as a sculptor his clay.

"Where did you learn to do that?" she asked.

"Does it matter?" he returned. He pushed himself up and moved to the foot of the cot, seating himself between her parted legs as his fingers plied the muscles in her rump.

"I was just…"

"Be quiet and just enjoy me while you can."

About the author:

Charlee is the author of over thirty books, the first nine of which are the WindLegend Saga which began with THE WINDKEEPER. Married 37 years to her high school sweetheart, Tom, she is the mother of two grown sons, Pete and Mike, and the proud grandmother of Preston Alexander and Victoria Ashley. She is the willing houseslave to five demanding felines who are holding her hostage in her home and only allowing her to leave in order to purchase food for them. A native of Sarasota, Florida, she grew up in Colquitt and Albany, Georgia and now lives in the Midwest.

Charlotte welcomes mail from readers. You can write to her c/o Ellora's Cave Publishing at 1056 Home Avenue, Akron OH 44310-3502.

Why an electronic book?

We live in the Information Age—an exciting time in the history of human civilization in which technology rules supreme and continues to progress in leaps and bounds every minute of every hour of every day. For a multitude of reasons, more and more avid literary fans are opting to purchase e-books instead of paperbacks. The question to those not yet initiated to the world of electronic reading is simply: *why?*

1. *Price.* An electronic title at Ellora's Cave Publishing and Cerridwen Press runs anywhere from 40-75% less than the cover price of the <u>exact same title</u> in paperback format. Why? Cold mathematics. It is less expensive to publish an e-book than it is to publish a paperback, so the savings are passed along to the consumer.

2. *Space.* Running out of room to house your paperback books? That is one worry you will never have with electronic novels. For a low one-time cost, you can purchase a handheld computer designed specifically for e-reading purposes. Many e-readers are larger than the average handheld, giving you plenty of screen room. Better yet, hundreds of titles can be stored within your new library—a single microchip. (Please note that Ellora's Cave and Cerridwen Press does not endorse any specific brands. You can check our website at www.ellorascave.com or

www.cerridwenpress.com for customer recommendations we make available to new consumers.)

3. *Mobility*. Because your new library now consists of only a microchip, your entire cache of books can be taken with you wherever you go.

4. *Personal preferences are accounted for*. Are the words you are currently reading too small? Too large? Too...**ANNOYING**? Paperback books cannot be modified according to personal preferences, but e-books can.

5. *Instant gratification*. Is it the middle of the night and all the bookstores are closed? Are you tired of waiting days—sometimes weeks—for online and offline bookstores to ship the novels you bought? Ellora's Cave Publishing sells instantaneous downloads 24 hours a day, 7 days a week, 365 days a year. Our e-book delivery system is 100% automated, meaning your order is filled as soon as you pay for it.

Those are a few of the top reasons why electronic novels are displacing paperbacks for many an avid reader. As always, Ellora's Cave and Cerridwen Press welcomes your questions and comments. We invite you to email us at service@ellorascave.com, service@cerridwenpress.com or write to us directly at: 1056 Home Ave. Akron OH 44310-3502.